# EDOGAWA RAMPO

## The Black Lizard and
## Beast in the Shadows

Translated by Ian Hughes
With an introduction by Mark Schreiber
Illustrations by Kawajiri Hiroaki

Kurodahan Press 2006

FG-JP0017A2
ISBN 978-4-902075-21-2

KURODAHAN PRESS
KURODAHAN.COM

# CONTENTS

## INTRODUCTION
## BY MARK SCHREIBER *

IN MARCH 1984, a team of criminals abducted Ezaki Katsuhisa, president of confectioner Ezaki–Glico, from his home in the Osaka suburb of Nishinomiya. After Ezaki escaped his captors unharmed, the gang embarked on a string of audacious blackmail attempts against food manufacturers in the Kansai region.

In a stream of sarcastic letters to local newspaper bureaus, the criminals taunted the police. Their typewritten notes were signed Kaijin Nijūichi Mensō (The Mystery Man of Twenty-one Faces) – an unmistakable allusion to Edogawa Rampo's fictitious criminal mastermind, Kaijin Nijū Mensō (The Mystery Man of Twenty Faces), nemesis of detective Akechi Kogorō, whose exploits first appeared in an eponymous 1936 magazine serial.

The incremental increase, from twenty faces to twenty-one, may suggest the criminals' wish to surpass the exploits of their literary namesake.† Their true motive, however, remains elusive. None of the gang was ever apprehended and the fifteen-year statute of limitations on the last of their twenty-eight crimes expired in February 2000.

Had Edogawa Rampo (*nom de plume* of Hirai Tarō, 1894–1965) still been living during the infamous "Glico–Morinaga Incident," he would no doubt have been visited by flustered detectives in hope of obtaining insights into the criminals' identity. And while

---

*Author, *Shocking Crimes of Postwar Japan, The Dark Side: Infamous Japanese Crimes and Criminals.*

†For Rampo's own character, apparently the reverse applied; Kaijin Nijū Mensō was said to have been inspired by English crime author Thomas W. Hanshew's character Hamilton Cleek, known as "Man of the Forty Faces."

this once again calls for speculation, the late author would doubtless have been secretly delighted to see his character return to the chase after a hiatus of nearly half a century.

With his reputation as the acknowledged master of Japanese crime fiction secure, Rampo certainly needed no publicity from a gang of notorious felons. In his own country, his name is intimately linked to the development of the genre from its nascent stages, and as I shall subsequently demonstrate, it is no exaggeration to state that he exerted a more influential role on mystery writing in Japan than did either Edgar Allan Poe in the United States or Sir Arthur Conan Doyle in Great Britain.

Today in Japan, a flourishing body of mystery and detective fiction entertains millions of loyal readers. It is, alas, almost entirely a domestic market. Some years back, John Apostolou, editor of the short story anthology *Murder in Japan*, made the observation that the sum total of *all* Japanese mystery titles currently available in English translation was still fewer than a single *month's* output by Japanese authors. Their monthly output may vary, but it is safe to say that since the appearance of nine stories by Rampo in *Japanese Tales of Mystery and Imagination*,* published in 1956 by Charles E. Tuttle, the number of new titles in English translation has increased by fewer than ten per decade.

In his preface, translator James B. Harris wrote that Rampo felt it was time for Western readers to know Japan boasted an extensive and growing body of mystery literature, and was eager to see his work appear in English.†

Harris' preface also gave some clues to some of the stumbling blocks Japanese-to-English translators encountered in those days.

---

*Contains "The Human Chair;" "The Psychological Test;" "The Caterpillar;" "The Cliff;" "The Hell of Mirrors;" "The Twins;" "The Red Chamber;" "Two Crippled Men;" and "The Traveler with the Pasted Rag Picture." "The

While able to read English, Rampo did not speak it well; Harris, while completely fluent in spoken Japanese, had never learned the written language. It may seem incredible in these times when personal computer software can generate approximate translations in seconds, but the two hammered out the nine stories orally, during weekly meetings conducted over a period of *five years*.

As Harris relates:

> ...for each line translated the two collaborators... were forced to overcome manifold difficulties in getting every line just right, the author reading each line in Japanese and painstakingly explaining the correct meaning and nuance, and the translator sweating over his typewriter, having to experiment with sentence after sentence until the author was fully satisfied with what had been set down in English.

Even though the language barrier no longer prevents wider dissemination of Japanese crime fiction abroad, its acceptance has been limited by other factors too diverse and complex to enumerate here. The result, however, is clear: while mystery titles on the New York Times' best-seller list invariably appear in Japanese translation within short months of their US release, the reverse, alas, is not the case. Despite the relative paucity of titles, one positive recent development was the nomination in 2004 of Kirino Natsuo's novel *Out* for an Edgar Award by the Mystery Writers

---

Psychological Test" and "The Red Chamber" were republished in the short-story anthology *Murder in Japan* (1987).

†Rampo's short novel *Ichimai no Kippu* (One Ticket) had been published in Esperanto in July 1930.

of America – the first time in that organization's history that a Japanese translation had been so honored.

This new work, containing translations of two of Rampo's best-known novelettes, will take readers back to the formative years of the genre, and for this reason some details regarding Rampo's personal background would seem appropriate.

The son of a government clerk, Hirai Tarō was born on October 21, 1894 in Nabari, Mie Prefecture, in an area once famous for *ninja*, Japan's legendary assassins for hire. His life was to coincide with the often-tempestuous reigns of three modern emperors, each of which left behind a distinctive cultural imprint. However, Rampo today stands out as a cultural icon associated with the moody times of the Taishō era (1912–1926), a *noir* period in which Japan's brief experiment with democracy and freewheeling popular culture were soon to give way, in the Shōwa era (1926–1989), to economic depression, ultranationalism, militarism and repression.

The Meiji era (1868–1912), into which Hirai was born, was notable for Japanese adaptations of cultural imports from the West. In these times, two schools of mystery and detective fiction began to develop. The first were native stories by writers such as Okamoto Kidō (岡本綺堂, 1872–1939). Okamoto was familiar with the English language and had read Sherlock Holmes stories. He was to pen some sixty-eight short stories, set in the late Edo period (1603–1868), featuring a series character named "Mikawacho no Hanshichi" who was a *meakashi*, or "paid informer" who reported to the police – as private detectives did not exist in feudal times.

Referred to as *torimonocho* ("case book" or "police blotter") Okamoto's stories nevertheless followed the structure of the modern mystery narrative in that the hero would encounter a puzzling incident and apply deduction and logic to reach a solution. The *torimonocho* never developed into a singularly Japanese mystery novel, but instead became established as period fiction, popularized by the author's ability to portray Edo period manners and customs in a realistic manner. This genre has continued to develop in parallel with contemporary stories, with works by such authors as the late Ikenami Shōtarō* enjoying a huge following.

Meanwhile young Hirai had moved with his family to Nagoya, a major commercial and industrial hub. From around the time he entered primary school his mother, Kiku, used to read him detective stories that were serialized in the Osaka *Mainichi Shinbun*. Among Mrs. Hirai's favorites were works by a writer named Kuroiwa Ruikō (黒岩涙香, 1862–1913).

Translations of stories by Poe first appeared in Japan in 1887; Conan Doyle's works made their debut in 1899. Kuroiwa took the next step in the evolution of the Japanese mystery story by adapting – "reconstructing" may be a more appropriate description – stories by such French authors as Emile Gaboriau and Fortune Du Boisgobey to fit his audience, taking liberties with the contents such as giving the main characters Japanese-sounding names.

In addition to these adaptations of mystery stories, Kuroiwa also penned his own original stories; but he is remembered mainly as a translator. Rampo was later to write an essay in defense of his works, blaming audiences for having been unprepared to appreciate Kuroiwa's original works.

While weak and sickly as a boy, young Hirai showed a fervor for the printed word, pouring his energies into producing his own magazine, from age eleven, using a mimeograph improvised from *kon'yaku*, a jellylike vegetable paste. Fascinated by the stories of Poe

---

*Two of Ikenami's books have been translated into English by Kodansha International. One, *Ninja Justice: Six Tales of Murder and Revenge*, remains in print.

and Conan Doyle, he began reading them in English and translating them during his college years. After graduating from Tokyo's Waseda University in 1916, he drifted from one job to another, at times even selling noodles from a pushcart. In the four years between 1920 and 1923, he briefly held at least six different jobs.

Hirai's big break as a writer came in September 1922, when he submitted two short stories – *Nisen Dōka* (which has been rendered as "The Two-Sen Copper Coin" and "Tuppence Coin") and *Ichimai no Kippu* (One Ticket) – to Morishita Uson, editor of *Shin Seinen*, a popular magazine that had been started two years earlier by publisher Hakubunkan. *Shin Seinen* specialized in translations of foreign crime stories and *Nisen Dōka*, which appeared in the April 1923 edition, created an immediate sensation.

For the work of a previously unpublished author, *Nisen Dōka* stands out as a remarkably polished piece. Written in a lively, contemporary style, it is credited as the first Western-style mystery in Japanese and acted to spur more writers to take up the writing of mystery stories.

Strangely, this work that launched Hirai's career has never been published in English translation. It is possible that translators have shied away because it concerns the decipherment of a cryptogram; although that part of the story, upon examination, is not especially complicated.

The story is told in the first person by an unnamed Asahi Shimbun newspaper reporter, who, together with a friend named Matsumura, attempts to earn a generous reward for recovering a stolen factory payroll of fifty thousand yen (in Taishō times a considerable sum of money).

The puzzle appears in the form of a piece of paper cunningly concealed inside a trick copper coin. The paper only bears a prayer consisting of the six characters for *namu amida butsu* (Save us, merciful Buddha). This is written out repeatedly, but with each set of six characters always incomplete. It is obviously a cipher of some kind, pointing to variations on the number six.

The story's narrator makes a brilliant deduction that establishes a connection between the six-character cipher and the copper coin in which the message was enclosed. The two, he supposes, suggest a connection with the *"Rokurensen,"* the flag hoisted in battle by a general, Sanada Yukimura, during Japan's sixteenth century civil wars. That flag was composed of two parallel rows of three coins with holes in their centers. Recalling the flag's design, the narrator aligns the six characters in the prayer, i.e., NA MU A MI DA BUTSU, into two vertical lines of three each, like the dots on a domino, thusly:

Then, he replaces the six characters with dots (or "coins," if you prefer) to give:

In a portion of the cipher with "BUTSU" missing, for example, the characters:

Would then assume the shape of:

Which, as it turns out, happens to be the Japanese Braille symbol for the syllable *te*. A blind masseur in the neighborhood is immediately enlisted to explain the Braille code, and the message is easily deciphered, revealing the location of the money (with several additional twists along the way).

The *Shin Seinen* story ran under the byline "Edogawa Rampo." Hirai deserves credit for coming up with a *nom de plume* that was both fiendishly clever and well suited for his purposes. Read aloud, it indeed sounds like a slightly mangled version of "Edgar Allan Poe," a writer whose works were already admired by many Japanese readers. But the name had an alluring visual impact as well, and it is uncertain if very many readers dwelt a great deal on the association with Rampo's literary namesake.

For reasons not entirely clear, Hirai initially originally wrote the name "Rampō" as 藍峰, using characters that mean "indigo peak" – picturesque, perhaps, but not the kind of image he was seeking to convey. This was soon discarded in favor of 乱歩, meaning "disordered steps." The character 乱 (*ran* or *midare* in its verb form) conveys the nuances of being agitated, disordered, lax, in disarray, rebellious, etc. So the ideographs in his *nom de plume* convey the connotation of something like "staggering along the Edo River." Such a name projected roguishness and perhaps a faintly unpleasant air of menace, since rivers, after all, were known to be murky places where, from ancient times, the corpses of suicides and victims of foul play were occasionally found floating.

Touches of Poe, his namesake, were certainly in evidence in some of Rampo's early works – a few were quite grotesque – but he was not loath to adapt ideas from other sources as well. To give his fictitious detective, Akechi Kogorō, the esoteric knowledge to contend with his treacherous twenty-faced nemesis, Akechi was said to have spent several years in China and India – as did Sherlock Holmes (in India), during his "missing" years.

Only four years after the publication of *Nisen Dōka*, in 1927, Akechi made his film debut in *Issunbōshi* (The Dwarf). The film, however, failed badly and cinematic adaptations of Rampo's stories did not appear again until after the Pacific War, when "The Psychological Test" was produced. To date, several dozen of Rampo's works have been adapted for TV and film, including a 1955 remake of *Issunbōshi*.

Although US air raids destroyed much of Rampo's neighborhood near Ikebukuro, his house and library, containing not only his books and writings, but a lifetime of correspondence, notes, and photographs, miraculously survived the war. He was to amass these into a voluminous 1961 memoir titled *Tantei Shōsetsu Yonjū-nen* (Forty Years of Writing Detective Stories), which provides a detailed chronology of his personal life.

At a gathering of fellow authors in 1946, Rampo proposed that they hold regular meetings and by June of the following year, the gatherings led to the formation of the Nihon Tantei Sakka Club (Japan Mystery Writers Club), for which Rampo served as the first president, from 1947 through 1952. His contributions continue to be acknowledged by the award of an annual prize bearing his name, conferred on the work judged to be the best mystery of the year. To Japanese readers, the Edogawa Rampo Prize carries the same prestige as do the Silver Dagger and the Edgar Allan Poe awards for readers in Great Britain and the US.

According to research conducted by Yamamae Yuzuru (editor of the Kōbunsha edition of Rampo's *Collected Works*), Rampo can be credited with sixty seven novels (including juvenile fiction) and seventy six short stories (counting stories within series individually). However, in his later years, Rampo increasingly channeled his remarkable energies in myriad directions, proposing new ideas to publishers, networking with fellow authors, engaging in energetic overseas correspondence and – perhaps most important – researching, translating and disseminating criticism on the genre of mystery and detective fiction.

In a rambling collection of essays titled *Gen'eijō* (The Illusory Castle), Rampo helped to classify and dissect the various elements of the mystery genre. He pointed out what he saw as deficiencies in Japan's native stories, identifying their shortcomings and comparing themes taken up by Japanese authors with their foreign counterparts.

To this end, Rampo made use of such sources as Howard Haycraft's 1941 essay "Murder for Pleasure: The Life and Times of the Detective Story," which was published in observance of the centennial year of Poe's "Murders in the Rue Morgue."

In 1946, Haycraft followed this work with *The Art of the Mystery Story*, a five hundred and sixty-page anthology that provided contributions from some of the biggest names in the genre, including *Black Mask* editor Anthony Boucher, John Dickson Carr (the acknowledged master of the locked-room mystery), Raymond Chandler, S.S. Van Dyne, Earl Stanley Gardner, Ellery Queen and Rex Stout, among others.

Criticism and analysis of the mystery genre was vital to help readers nurture an appreciation for well-crafted, original works.

Yet social mores were in flux, and books could not go against the standards of the times. When writing tales of terrible crimes, for example, how could the use of humor be justified? Yet as Haycraft astutely noted, "murder for pleasure" became socially acceptable and humorous stories about amateur detectives who are eccentric geniuses, and who inevitably outsmart klutzy policemen, came to enjoy great popularity. (Japan's master of this genre was Rampo's friend and contemporary, Yokomizo Seishi.)

We tend to forget how execrably bad many stories of mystery and detection once were, several generations ago, before critics began to lay down the rules. Such stories frequently hoodwinked readers, by giving, for example, an obvious suspect an airtight alibi, only to reveal at the end that he has an identical twin. Perplexing locked-room mysteries were resolved by disclosing the existence of secret passageways. Or detectives unmasked the killer by calling upon paranormal talents, frightening them into confessing during a séance, and so on, *ad nauseum*.

Haycraft's 1946 work provided not one, but three sets of guidelines for mysteries, all of which had been advanced during the late 1920s. First was "A Detective Story Decalogue," in which Ronald A. Knox, an English Roman Catholic priest and mystery author, laid down "Ten Commandments" of detection. Second was "The Detection Club Oath," administered to those initiated into the London Detection Club. (Sample: "RULER: Do you promise that your detectives shall well and truly detect the crimes presented to them... not placing reliance on nor making use of Divine Revelation, Feminine Intuition, Mumbo-Jumbo, Jiggery-Pokery, Coincidence or the Act of God?")

Then, in "Twenty Rules for Writing Detective Stories," S.S. Van Dyne listed devices "which no self-respecting detective-story writer will now avail himself of." A few of his examples include:

"Determining the identity of the culprit by comparing the butt of a cigarette left at the scene of the crime with the brand smoked by a suspect," "The bogus spiritualistic séance to frighten the culprit into giving himself away," "The dog that does not bark and thereby reveals the fact that the intruder is familiar," and so on. "To use them," asserted Van Dyne, "is a confession of the author's ineptitude and lack of originality."

Thus, by setting down these parameters demanding originality – and, more importantly, fair play – mystery writers, publishers and readers were able to establish a covenant that enabled the genre to take root and flourish. As a conduit for these studies taking place in English-speaking countries, Rampo deserves full credit as the "mastermind" who played the key role in transforming Japanese mystery fiction – from foreign translations, to an obscure subgenre, which eventually sprouted into a full-blown category of popular literature, over a span of less than two decades (disregarding the war years when such works were prohibited).

Despite the ravages of Parkinson's disease and increasingly frail health before his death, at age seventy, in July 1965, Rampo continued in his unflagging efforts to lay the foundations for the mystery genre in Japan, and perhaps this stands out as his most important contribution of all. Three decades after his passing, the centenary of his birth, 1994, was marked by a resurgence of Rampo-related films, articles, books and commemorative publications that attested not only to his enduring popularity as an author, but recognized his status as a cultural icon who helped to define the Taishō era.

BIBLIOGRAPHY

Apostolou, John L. and Greenberg, Martin H., eds. *Murder in Japan: Japanese Stories of Crime and Detection*. New York: Dembner Books, 1987.

Edogawa, Rampo 江戸川乱歩. "Nisen Dōka" (The Two-Sen Copper Coin) 二銭銅貨, in *Edogawa Rampo Kessaku Sen* (Edogawa Rampo Best Selection) 江戸川乱歩傑作選. Tokyo: Shinchōsha, 2005 (88th printing).

―――. *Gen'eijō* (The Illusory Castle) 幻影城. Tokyo: Kōdansha, 1979 (reprint of 1951 original).

―――. *Japanese Tales of Mystery and Imagination*. Trans. James B. Harris. Rutland, Vt. & Tokyo: Charles E. Tuttle, 1956.

―――. *Tantei Shōsetsu Yonjūnen* (Forty Years of Writing Detective Stories) 探偵小説四十年. Tokyo: Tōgensha, 1961.

Haycraft, Howard, ed. *The Art of the Mystery Story*. New York: Grosset & Dunlap, The Universal Library, 1946.

Hirosawa, Shimpo. "Parallel Lines of Japan's Master Detectives." *Japan Quarterly* 47, No. 4 (October-December 2000): 52-57.

Kawade Yume Mook KAWADE夢ムック. *Edogawa Rampo: Daremo Akogareta Shōnen Tanteidan* (Edogawa Rampo: The Boy Detectives Club That Was Everyone's Favorite) 江戸川乱歩―誰もが憧れた少年探偵団. Tokyo: Kawade Shobō Shinsha, 2003.

Ōsaka, Gō 逢坂剛 ed. *Rampo no Sekai* (Rampo's World) 乱歩の世界. Tokyo: Edogawa Rampo Jikkō Īnkai, 2003.

Queen, Ellery, ed. *Ellery Queen's Japanese Golden Dozen: The Detective Story World in Japan*. Rutland, Vt. & Tokyo: Charles E. Tuttle, 1978.

Yoshida, Kazuo. "Japanese Mystery Literature," in *Handbook of Japanese Popular Culture*. New York: Greenwood Press, 1989.

# THE BLACK LIZARD

黒
蜥
蜴

# CHAPTER 1
# QUEEN OF THE UNDERWORLD

**IT WAS CHRISTMAS EVE,** when thousands of turkeys have their necks wrung, even in this country... or so they say.

Ginza, the largest and most prosperous part of the Imperial City, where the neon lights created a rainbow of colours in the darkness and illuminated the tens of thousands of passers-by... and the streets of darkness, the underground, began only a block back from it.

Ginza, where – surprisingly to the denizens of the night, and with a propriety only reasonable for one of the most famous spots in the Imperial city – the streets empty by about eleven in the evening, while at the same time the dark district backed up against it gradually becomes more active. There, along grey streets faced by buildings with shut windows, men and women squirm and wriggle through the gloom in endless pursuit of pleasure until two or three in the morning.

It was about one in the morning on that particular Christmas Eve and in a giant building deep in the darkness that looked deserted from the outside, a wild, even insane party was reaching its climax.

Several dozen men and women occupied a floor area about the size of a nightclub: one shouted out 'Bravo!' as he hoisted his glass; another with a brightly dyed pointy party hat worn sideways on his head danced feverishly; another acted like a gorilla and chased a frantically fleeing young girl; others cried, or shouted in anger. And on top of them all fell a blizzard of multi-coloured confetti, with coloured streamers streaming down like brilliant waterfalls, while countless red and blue balloons flew aimlessly among the choking clouds of tobacco smoke.

3

'It's the Dark Angel! The Dark Angel has come!'

'The Dark Angel has come!'

'Bravo! Three cheers for the queen!'

The drunken voices were jumbled together, and suddenly a cacophony of applause broke out.

A single woman stepped lightly into the centre of the crowd as they parted to let her pass. She wore a black evening dress with a black hat, black gloves, black stockings, and black shoes. Totally framed in black, her vivacious and beautiful face was thrilled, flowering like a red rose.

'Good evening, all! I am drunk, already drunk! But let us drink together anyway! Let us dance!'

The beautiful woman fluttered her right hand above her head, and called to the crowd in a delightful voice.

'Let us drink! And dance! Three cheers for the Dark Angel!'

'Waiter! Champagne! Bring the champagne!'

Presently, tiny pistols began to make bright popping sounds and corks flew between the multicoloured balloons toward the heavens. Here, there, everywhere the sounds of glasses clinking together. And yet again a chorus of:

'Bravo, Dark Angel!'

Where did this incredible popularity of the queen of the underworld come from? Even if you knew nothing of her, her beauty, her ebullient gestures and actions, her incredible luxury, the munificent amounts of jewellery she wore… no matter which of these aspects you examined, she was every inch a queen, but she possessed an even more wonderful fascination: She was an indefatigable exhibitionist.

'Dark Angel! Show us the Jewel Dance again!'

Once one person asked, they all clamoured, and again applause erupted.

The band in the corner began to play again. An erotic saxophone tickled the ears of the listeners eerily.

She had already started the Jewel Dance, in the middle of the crowd, the Dark Angel transformed into the Angel of Light. All her beautiful and flushed body wore was a double strand of large pearls around her neck, incredible jade earrings, bracelets peppered with countless diamonds and three rings on her fingers. She wore no thread or scrap of cloth.

She had become nothing more than a lump of flesh, scintillating as she undulated her arms, kicked her feet, and skilfully danced the captivating motions of the ancient Egyptian court.

'Look! The black lizard has begun to crawl! It's wonderful!'

'You're right! That tiny lizard is moving, alive!'

The young men in their chic tuxedoes whispered and bobbed.

On the left arm of the beautiful woman a pitch black lizard was wriggling. As her arm moved, it appeared to move its suction-pad tipped feet and crawl. It seemed as if it would crawl from shoulder to neck, neck to chin, and to her red and shining lips, but somehow the creature stayed wriggling on her arm all the time. It was a black lizard tattoo, made to look incredibly real.

Her bold, incredible dance lasted only four or five minutes, and when it ended the tipsy but emotionally fired gentlemen crowded in, shouting out their excitement and emotion, lifting the naked woman off the floor and flinging her into the air, carrying her on their shoulders throughout the room with cheers and shouts.

'I'm cold, I'm cold. Carry me to the bath!'

And as she commanded, the cavalcade carried her down the hall and into a prepared bath.

Christmas Eve in the streets of darkness ended with her Jewel Dance, and the people gradually drifted off to their hotels, or their homes, in couples or groups.

After the festivities the room was left scattered with multi-coloured confetti and crêpe streamers, like a wharf after the ship has left, and those balloons still buoyant bobbed against the ceiling, sadly.

Sitting in a chair in one corner of the room, now a wasteland like the wings off the stage, one young man was left, a scrap of litter. This man, of a dandyish appearance, was wearing a red tie and a gaudy striped coat with wide shoulders, and had the flattened nose and well-muscled frame of a fighter. In spite of his appearance, he drooped despondently, and ended up looking like crumpled waste in the corner.

'*Why is she taking so long without a thought for me? I'm in a bind! Risking my life coming here! Damn detectives might bust in any time!*'

He shook himself, and ran his fingers through his frowsy hair.

A uniformed waiter wove through the streamers, carrying a glass of something that looked like whisky. The man took it, and scolded him with a 'Pretty late, aren't you?' as he downed it in one gulp, then ordered another.

'Jun-chan, sorry I kept you waiting!'

At last the person he had been waiting for had appeared. The Dark Angel.

'I finally got rid of those noisy boys and made it back here. Now what's this about the only request you'll make of me in your life?'

She sat down in the chair across from him, face serious.

'Can't talk here.'

The young man she had called Jun-chan answered quietly, his face still sour.

'Because you might be overheard?'

'Yeah.'

'A job?'

'Yeah.'

'Are you injured?'

'Nah. Wish that was all it was.'

The woman in black understood the situation and stood without any more questions.

'Right, outside. Nobody'll be in Ginza this time of night except the workers building the subway. Let's walk; I'll listen.'

'Yeah, all right then.'

The unusual couple, the young man in the ugly red necktie and the Dark Angel beautiful enough to wake anyone up, left the building side-by-side.

Outside was the boulevard at night, like a land of death where only the streetlights and asphalt were visible. The sound of their footsteps echoed.

'So? What crime have you committed now? I've never seen you look so depressed... very unlike you, Jun-chan.'

The woman in black started the conversation.

'I killed them.'

Jun-chan kept his eyes on the pavement and spoke in an eerie quiet tone.

'Who?'

The Dark Angel did not appear to be especially upset by this sudden announcement.

'My rival. That son of a bitch Kitashima and his slut, Sakiko.'

'So, it finally came to that... where?'

'In their apartment. The bodies are stuffed in the closet. They'll be discovered tomorrow morning, no question about it. Everyone knows about the three of us, and the deskman at the apartment house knows I was there tonight. If they catch me, it's all over. I want to stay on the outside!'

'Are you thinking of making a run for it?'

7

'Hmm… My lady, you always call me your benefactor.'

'Yes. You saved me from a very dangerous situation, and I've been in love with your sheer brawn since.'

'Return the favour. Lend me enough to get away, make the jump… a hundred thousand yen.'

'Well, a hundred thousand is simple, but you think you can get away? No way. They'll nab you while you're waiting on some wharf in Kobe or Yokohama. The worst thing you can do is just throw everything away and start running.'

The woman in black spoke as if she was very familiar with the situation.

'So you say I should hide here in Tokyo?'

'Yes, I think that's a much better option. Even so, it's still dangerous. We need an even better way…'

She stopped in thought, and suddenly asked an unexpected question.

'Your apartment is on the fifth floor, right?'

'Well, yeah, but so what?' he answered, irritated.

'Oh, wonderful!' The word escaped from her beautiful lips as if she was astonished. 'There's a perfect solution! Couldn't have asked for a better one! Jun-chan, I've got the perfect way to make you safe.'

'What? Hurry up and tell me!'

The Dark Angel gave a thin, mysterious smile, and powerfully uttered one word at a time as she stared into his pale face.

'You're going to die. I'm going to murder the man known as Amamiya Jun.'

'Wha–? What?'

The young man stood, with his mouth flapping open, as he stared at the queen of the underworld.

# CHAPTER 2
# SCENES OF HELL

AS AMAMIYA JUN'ICHI WAS WAITING in the appointed place in Kyōbashi for the woman in black, an automobile stopped in front of him. The young driver, dressed in a black suit and deerstalker, beckoned him from the window.

'Don't need a ride!' said Amamiya, waving the car away while thinking to himself it was pretty luxurious for a taxi.

'It's me! It's me!' called a woman's voice, laughing. 'Hurry up and get in!'

'M'lady? You can drive?'

Amamiya was astonished when he realized that the Dark Angel of the Jewel Dance had metamorphosed into a suit-attired man and driven to pick him up in only ten minutes. He'd been with her for over a year now, but even he did not know much about the real her.

'How condescending! Of course I can drive. Don't stand there with that silly look on your face; hurry up and get in! It's 2:30. If we don't hurry it'll be light soon.'

Still somewhat bewildered, Jun'ichi got into the passenger seat and the car shot down the dark empty avenue like an arrow.

'What's this huge bag for?' he asked the driver, noticing an enormous cotton bag lumped on the seat.

'That bag is going to save your life,' laughed the beautiful driver, flashing him a smile.

'Something is weird here. Where are we going, and what are you doing? This don't feel right…'

'Do I hear the hero of Ginza whining? You promised you wouldn't ask me anything, remember? Are you saying you don't trust me?'

'No, I trust you all right…'

9

No matter what he said after that, the driver kept her eyes fixed ahead and made no answer.

The car swept around the large pond in Ueno Park, and up a slope to stop in a curiously deserted spot, empty of houses, with a long, long wall running along the road.

'Jun-chan, you have gloves, right? Take off your coat and put your gloves on. Do up all your jacket buttons, and pull your hat down,' commanded the beauty dressed as a man as she turned off the headlights, running lights and cabin light.

There were no streetlamps outside and it was pitch black. In the darkness the car stood, blind, all lights off and the engine stopped.

'Right, bring your gloves and follow me,' she said.

Jun'ichi followed her directions and got out of the car. The beautiful woman in black, collar flipped up like a thief in the night, was also wearing gloves, and grasped his own gloved hand, pulling him through an open gate.

They passed under countless giant trees hiding the sky, and cut across a huge empty field. Then they went along the side of a large Western-style building. The streetlamps of the city were sometimes visible, flashing like fireflies in the distance, but ahead of them was only darkness.

'M'lady, isn't this the Tokyo University campus?'

'Shh! Quiet,' she warned, squeezing his hand. In the freezing cold, his hand felt sweaty in her warmth through the two gloves. Right now, though, the murderer Amamiya Jun'ichi did not have the time to be aware of her as a woman.

As they continued to walk through the darkness, the anger of two or three hours ago was reborn. He saw once again his former lover Sakiko as he throttled her, the tongue sticking out between her teeth and blood dripping from the corner of her mouth, as her huge, cow-like eyes looked at him piercingly. Her fingers clawed the air in her death throes, a phantom sweeping through the air in front of him, threateningly.

After a little while, they saw ahead of them a low, red brick Western-style building standing in a large open space, surrounded by a battered slat fence.

'It's inside,' said the woman in black in a low voice, fumbling for the gate lock. It seems she had a duplicate key, because suddenly the gate rattled open.

They entered and closed the gate, and then she finally turned on the flashlight she had been carrying, using it to illuminate the ground as they walked to the building. The ground was covered with dry grass, and Jun'ichi felt as if they were about to enter a deserted, haunted house.

Up three stone steps was a porch and balustrade with peeling white paint. They crunched over pieces of fallen plaster, and a few meters beyond was an old but sturdy door.

The door rattled as she opened it with another duplicate key, and then unlocked yet another similar door just inside. Beyond it spread an empty room. The powerful smell of disinfectant assaulted him, like the smell of a surgery, but mixed with a queerly sweet odour.

'We're here. Jun-chan, no matter what you see, do not raise your voice. There shouldn't be anyone inside the building, but every so often a watchman walks by the fence outside,' she whispered, almost threatening.

Fighting against an inexplicable fear, young Amamiya could do nothing but stand stock still. He wondered just where this brick building, this haunted house was. What was that bizarre smell? And what was in this huge, empty space that sounded as if it would echo his voice from all four walls?

In the darkness the terrifying death masks of the dying Ki-

'This one'll do,' the woman in black whispered...

tashima and Sakiko came again, overlaid nauseatingly on the blackness. *'Am I wandering the paths of Hell, ushered by their angry shades,'* he wondered… he felt himself in the grip of a queer illusion he had never experienced before, and his body was covered in greasy sweat.

The disk of light from the flashlight in her hand crawled across the floor, as if searching for something.

The floorboards, rough, passed under the circle of light, with no carpet to hide them. A solid desk-like object, varnish peeling, gradually crawled into the light from the legs up. It was a long, large table. Ah! a person. The legs of a person. Someone was sleeping here?

Still, they looked like the legs of an awfully old person. And why was there a little wooden tag tied to the ankle?

Hey, this old man is sleeping naked, in spite of this cold!

The circle of light moved from thighs to belly, then on to the ribs and chest, travelling on to illuminate a neck like a chicken's leg, the fallen jaw, and the gaping, black, foolish mouth with exposed teeth, and cloudy glass balls that were eyes… it was a corpse.

Jun'ichi shuddered at the eerie juxtaposition of the spectres that had been haunting him and the thing that had appeared in the circle of light. Still upset at the enormity of his crime, still unaware of where this room was located, he wondered if he had gone insane, or was trapped in a nightmare.

But when the next object came into the glow of the flashlight, he totally forgot the woman in black's warning, and let out a shout of surprise.

This was surely a scene from Hell itself! A large tub, maybe two meters on a side, was filled with a pile of naked corpses: young, old, male, female.

Could this scene, just like the ancient pictures of the damned squirming in the pools of blood in Hell, be a part of this world?

'Jun-chan, you're a scaredy cat. There's nothing to be surprised at! This is where they keep the bodies for dissection in anatomy class. All the medical schools have them.'

The woman in black gave a bold laugh that admitted no fears, no enemies.

'*Oh, is that all,*' he thought to himself. '*So we are at the university. Even so, why in the world are we here in this creepy place!?*' He may have been a criminal, but Jun'ichi could only stare in astonishment at the totally unexpected actions of his beautiful companion.

The circle of light slowly traced over the entire mountain of bodies, and finally stopped on the naked corpse of a young man.

The young man lay motionless in the darkness, his yellow flesh exposed, in a picture drawn by a spectral light.

'This one'll do,' the woman in black whispered, holding the light steady on the young man's body. 'This lad was a patient in the Kyoritsu Mental Hospital, and just died yesterday. The hospital and this medical school have an agreement. As soon as someone dies there the corpse is brought here. The person in charge of this room is a friend of mine... let's say, an underling, shall we? That's why I knew this body would be here. What do you think? About the corpse?'

'About the corpse?' he repeated, flustered. What in the world was she thinking?

'The height and musculature are about the same as yours, aren't they? Only the face is different.'

Now that she mentioned it, he noticed that it looked about the same age, the same size, as himself.

'*Of course!*' he thought to himself. '*She's going to use this corpse to take my place! Damn, she looks so refined and oh-so-beautiful, but she thinks up such bold and terrible plans!*'

'You see now, don't you? What do you think? Brilliant, isn't it?

A sorceress, aren't I? After all, we're going to make a person vanish from this world, and we'll need pretty powerful magic to accomplish that, won't we? Right, out with the bag. Sorry, it'll be a bit disgusting, but we have to stuff this guy into the bag and carry him to the car.'

Jun'ichi found his 'saviour' even more terrifying than the corpse. Who was she? Even if she was just a spoilt rich woman enjoying idle games, this plan was too detailed, too careful. She called the person in charge of the dissection bodies her 'underling,' didn't she? If she had an underling in such a place as this university, she must be a pretty big – and bad – wig indeed!

'Jun-chan, what in the world are you mooning about? Hurry up with the bag!'

Her voice prodded him from the darkness. Pressured by the voice, his mind curiously stunned and quiet, like a mouse transfixed by the gaze of a cat, he felt himself move to do her bidding.

# CHAPTER 3
# THE HOTEL GUEST

THE KEIŌ HOTEL, the ritziest in Imperial Tokyo, also hosted a grand gala for hotel guests and visitors that night, but even those who had danced through the witching hour had trundled off to bed by now, and the doormen were trying to keep their nodding heads up. At about five in the morning, before dawn, a single car pulled up in front of the swinging door.

Mme Midorikawa had returned.

The doormen all loved this beautiful woman, and when they noticed whose car it was, they competed with each other to be first to open the door.

Wrapped in furs, Mme Midorikawa stood for a moment, and then a man stepped out and joined her. An older man, maybe about forty, with a stiff, pointed moustache, dark goatee, and large horn-rimmed spectacles. His thick, heavy coat with collar did not completely hide the striped formal pants he was wearing, making him look like, perhaps, a politician.

'This is a friend of mine,' announced Mme Midorikawa to the hotel manager, who was waiting at the front desk. 'The room next to mine was free, I believe? Please arrange for him to stay there.'

'Yes, it is still open. Of course!' he replied, delighted to help, and ordered one of the clerks to take care of it.

The bearded man signed his name in the guest book, without speaking, and followed Mme Midorikawa into the front hallway. His signature read Yamakawa Kensaku.

Now that the booking was settled, they bathed in their separate rooms, and then rejoined each other in her bedroom.

Kensaku wore his trousers and shirt only, not having donned

the jacket again. As he rubbed his hands together, he spoke in an almost childish voice that seemed at odds with his stern expression.

'Ah, I can't stand it! That smell is still on my hands! M'lady, that was the first time I have ever done anything so, so, horrible!'

'My, melodramatic, aren't we? And after murdering two people!' she chuckled.

'Please! Don't just say things like that! Someone might hear it in the hall!'

'Don't worry. Who could hear so low a voice?'

'Ahh, it almost makes me sick just to think of it,' shuddered Kensaku. 'I felt terrible when we smashed the face of that corpse just now at my apartment. And when we dumped the body into the elevator shaft... and that terrible spattering noise... ugh! I can't stand it!'

'Weakling. Don't think about things that are over. You died there! I'm talking to Yamakawa Kensaku, a fine and upstanding scholar. Snap out of it!'

'But will it really work? Nobody will notice that a body has vanished from the university?'

'What in the world?! You think I wouldn't notice something that important? I said the person in charge was my underling, remember? You think one of my people would commit such a gross error? The school is on holiday now; no students or faculty are there at all. All my person has to do is just fiddle the books a little. Nobody remembers the face of a corpse, and nobody would ever notice one less cadaver in that pile... except my man, of course.'

'So you'll have to tell him about what happened tonight, then.'

'Yes. All I have to do is make a phone call a bit later this morning... To change the subject, Jun-chan, there's something I want to talk to you about. Come sit here.'

17

She was wearing a brilliantly coloured *yuzenzome* kimono with long, hanging sleeves. Sitting on the bed, she pointed at the sheet next to her, and invited him over.

'This beard and spectacles are obnoxious! Is it all right if I take them off?'

'Of course. The door's locked, so it will be safe.'

And so, like young lovers, they sat together on the edge of the bed, talking.

'Jun-chan, you're dead. Do you understand what that really means? This brand-new person sitting next to me is just like my baby, someone I have given birth to. You cannot refuse any command of mine, ever again.'

'And if I should?'

'I'll kill you. You know I'm a sorceress, and a terrible one at that. Yamakawa Kensaku is my doll. And since you have no records, no registry in this world, there's nobody to complain should you suddenly vanish. The police can't do anything, and won't. I got a new doll today: you, with your oh-so-strong arms. Rather than a doll, you could say a slave. My slave.'

Jun'ichi was totally under her enchantment, and did not feel the slightest bit upset about what she said. In fact, he felt a curiously familiar and sweet emotion.

'Yes, I will become the queen's slave,' he said. 'I'll do whatever you command. I'll kiss the soles of your shoes. All I ask is that you do not discard this child you have birthed. Don't throw me away!'

He placed his hands on her lap, covered with beautiful *yuzen* patterns, and pleaded, almost crying. The Dark Angel smiled gently, wrapped her arms around Jun'ichi's broad shoulders, and gently patted him on the back, as if reassuring a child. She felt the hot droplets on her lap, through the fabric.

'Ha, ha, ha! Look at us! Getting so sentimental! That's enough, don't you think? We've something important to discuss.'

She unwrapped her arms.

'Who do you think I am? You don't have the faintest idea, do you?'

'It doesn't matter. I don't care if you're a thief, or even a murderer. I'm just your slave.'

'Oh, my, right on the button, aren't we?' she laughed. 'That's right. I'm a thief. And I may have murdered a few people, too.'

'Huh? You?!'

She laughed again.

'Just as I thought. I figured that'd surprise you! You have nothing to worry about, though, because you've entrusted me with your life. I'm sure you wouldn't try to run away. Would you?'

'I am your slave,' he said, as his fingers dug powerfully into her lap.

'Oh, you say the cutest things. From today, you're one of my underlings. You'll have plenty to do.

'Do you have any idea why I'm staying at this hotel? I've been using this room for the past four or five days, under the name of Mme Midorikawa. The reason is that my mark is staying at the same hotel. It's a big, big job, and just as I was feeling a little underpowered to take it on, just look! You come along, with perfect timing!'

'Someone rich?'

'Yes, rich, but I'm not after the money. I collect the most beautiful things in the world: jewels, art, beautiful people...'

'Excuse me? People?'

'That's right. Beautiful people are ever so much more beautiful than art. My mark is a beautiful girl from Osaka, here together with her father.'

'And you plan to steal his daughter?'

He was, once again, bewildered by the unpredictable things the Dark Angel said.

'That's right. It's not just kidnapping a girl, though. I plan to use her as bait to get hold of the largest diamond in Japan, which her father happens to possess. He's a leading jewel merchant in Osaka.'

'That would be Iwase Trading?'

'Oh, very good! And President Iwase Shōbei is staying at this hotel. The minor problem is that he is accompanied by that private detective, Akechi Kogorō.'

'Um. Akechi, huh?'

'Not someone you take on lightly. Fortunately he knows nothing about me, but Akechi just drives me crazy!'

'Wonder why he hired a private eye? Maybe he noticed something?'

'I gave him a few things to notice. You see, Jun-chan, I dislike attacking when people are unprepared. I've never stolen anything without giving notice. I warn them, wait for them to arrange protection, and then fight on an equal basis, otherwise it's not interesting. Rather than the spoils, it's the thrill of the fight that makes it worthwhile.'

'So you gave him warning, then?'

'Yes, in Osaka. Oh, I'm so excited! Akechi Kogorō is an opponent worthy of me! When I think of taking him on in single combat like this, I'm so happy! Jun-chan, don't you agree how wonderful it is?'

Growing intoxicated by herself and her words, she took Jun'ichi's hands, squeezing them and swinging them in her fevered excitement.

## CHAPTER 4
## THE MAGICIAN

IN THE SPACE OF AN EVENING, Jun'ichi completely immersed himself in the role of Yamakawa Kensaku and when he had finished dressing the following morning he looked just like a physician – an impression aided by his horn-rimmed spectacles and false beard.

And he was faultless both in word and gesture as he took his porridge opposite Mme Midorikawa in the hotel dining room.

After finishing his meal, he returned to the room to find a hotel clerk waiting.

'Sir, some luggage has just arrived for you. Would you like me to bring it here?'

This was the first time in his life Jun'ichi had been addressed with such respect, but he did his best to remain calm and answered with gravitas, 'Yes, bring it would you.'

As part of the plans drawn up the previous evening, they had arranged for a large trunk to be delivered in his name the following morning.

A little while later, the clerk and a porter brought a large wood-ribbed trunk into the room.

'Your performance is improving all the time. I'm sure you'll be fine now. Not even Akechi Kogorō could see through you.'

After confirming that the pair had left, Mme Midorikawa had entered from the adjoining room.

'Hah! I guess I wasn't too bad, was I? But what's inside this huge trunk?'

He hadn't been told its purpose yet.

'Here's the key. Why don't you open it?'

*That peculiar malady was upon her.*

Taking the key, the magnificently bearded underling put his head to one side quizzically.

'My attire by any chance? It would be strange if such a personage as Mr Yamakawa had no change of clothes...'

'Ha, ha. Maybe you're right.'

He turned the key and lifted the lid. Inside were many layers of tightly packed objects thickly wrapped in rags.

'Hah!? What's this?'

He whispered, realizing his guess had been wide of the mark as he gingerly unwrapped one of the objects.

'Hey, this is a rock, isn't it? Are all these other carefully bound objects rocks too?'

'That's right. No change of clothes for you I'm afraid. They're all rocks. The trunk had to have a little weight.'

'Weight, you say?...'

'Mmm, exactly the weight of one person. Stuffing the trunk full of rocks might seem pointless, but think about it. We can easily dispose of this stuff. The stones we can throw out of the window onto the ground and if we put the rags between the bed base and the mattress the trunk will be empty with nothing left over. Just a little magic trick.'

'Oh, I see. But once you've emptied the trunk, what will you put inside it?'

'Ha, ha, ha! It's pretty clear what is usually put in trunks, isn't it? Anyway, come on, help me get rid of these pebbles.'

Located in the recesses of the hotel on the ground floor, his room had a window that gave onto a small secluded inner garden covered with coarse gravel. The perfect place for them to throw the rocks. They ditched the stones quickly and disposed of the rags.

'Right, now it's completely empty. Next I'll show you how magicians use trunks, shall I?'

Looking laughingly at the surprised Jun-chan, Mme Midori-kawa quickly locked the door, pulled down the window blind to prevent any prying, and suddenly began to remove her black dress.

'This is a little strange isn't it, m'lady? You're not about to perform that dance, are you?'

'Ha, ha, ha. You're frightened!'

As she laughed, her hands removed each layer of clothing without pause. That peculiar malady was upon her. The exhibitionism was starting.

Even the most delinquent of youths would blush and fidget in the face of this beautiful stark naked woman. Next, the bright, beautiful lump of peach-coloured and pleasingly curved flesh stood before him in a shockingly frank pose.

Try not to look as he might, his gaze went toward her. And when his eyes met hers, he blushed even more. Whatever the pose she struck in front of her slave, the queen remained composed and without a trace of embarrassment. Unable to endure the stimulation and sweating nervously, it is always the slave who cries out.

'My! What a fluster you are in! Is the sight of a naked person such a rarity for you?'

Unabashedly revealing to him various curves and deep shadows, she straddled the trunk's edge, then pulled up her arms and legs so that her whole body fitted inside, just like a baby in the womb.

'This is it, my lad – the way my magic trick works. What do you think, sweet? How do I look?'

Curled up in the trunk, the flesh-mound spoke in a mish-mash of mannish and girlish words.

The knees of her bent legs pressed so tightly as to appear stuck to her breasts, while the skin near her hips was drawn tight and her rump jutted out oddly. Her hands were crossed behind her head, ruffling her hair and leaving her armpits completely exposed. An unusually shaped being, rounded, peach-coloured, and a very beautiful colour indeed.

Growing bolder, Jun-chan/Yamakawa leaned over the trunk and looked down at the body lasciviously.

'So it's a beauty stuffed into a trunk then, is it, m'lady?'

'Ha, ha, ha. Indeed it is. Here and there, the trunk has little ventilation holes that cannot be seen from outside. So there's no need to worry about suffocation if the lid is closed.'

No sooner had she said this than she slammed the lid shut, sending up into the excited young man's face a billow of warm air filled with the scent of her body. Once the lid had been closed, all that could be seen was a plain, black rectangular trunk. No one would have imagined that hidden inside was a mound of sexy, amply rounded peach-coloured flesh. This stark contrast explains why, from ancient times, conjurors have used an unattractive trunk and a beautiful woman's body.

'What do you think? No one would suspect that a person might be inside.'

Having slightly opened the trunk's lid, she sought his agreement with a smile, looking much like Venus appearing from within the shell.

'Oh! So you... I mean, you intend to put that jeweller's daughter in this trunk and kidnap her?'

'Yes. Of course. You've finally worked it out, have you? I was only providing you with a little simulation.'

After she had put her clothes back on, she filled him in on the details of her daring kidnap plan.

'Putting that girl into the trunk as I've just shown you is my job and I've got everything prepared, including the knock-out drops. Getting the trunk away from here is your job – that'll be your first big test.

'You make it appear that you are catching the 9:20 train leaving Tokyo tonight and have the hotel purchase a ticket beforehand and then leave the hotel with the trunk. The hotel porter checks it in as hand luggage and sees you board the train. So, everyone will think you have gone to Nagoya, but you actually get off the train at Shinagawa Station, the first stop. Are you getting this? You disembark at Shinagawa – of course you have the trunk offloaded too – tell the guard you've remembered some urgent business or something. It might be somewhat arduous work, but I'm sure you won't make any mistakes. Next, you return by taxi to Tokyo with the trunk and you go to the Meiji Hotel. Make them think you're a rich man – act confident, choose the best room and check in. I'll check out of here tomorrow and meet you at the Meiji. What do you think of my plan?'

'Well, it's certainly interesting. But I'm not entirely sure about fooling everyone. I'll probably feel pretty insecure all by myself.'

'Ha, ha, ha. You've killed people and yet you're behaving like some nervous rich kid. Don't worry! The safest way to carry out something bad is to do it confidently and in full view – and not secretly and quietly. If you're found out, you can just get rid of the luggage and run for it! It's a breeze compared to murdering someone.'

'But couldn't you come with me?'

'I have to take on Akechi Kogorō. Who knows what might happen if I don't keep a watch on him until you make it through!? My task is to hold back that interfering detective. And that will probably be much harder than transporting the trunk.'

'Oh, I see. Yes, that will make me feel safer. But... you'll be sure to come to the Meiji Hotel tomorrow morning won't you? If the girl wakes up before and starts kicking up a fuss inside the trunk I'll be in a real fix!'

'You do worry about the small stuff, don't you? Well, I suppose that's where slip-ups can happen. We'll gag the girl and tie her arms and legs very tightly. When the knock-out drops wear off, she won't be able to speak or even to move.'

'Oh, my head doesn't seem to be working normally today. It's because you put on that display. In future, please spare me that at least would you? I'm just a young man you know. I'm still all excited! Ha, ha, ha! Anyway, what happens after we meet up at the Meiji?'

'What happens then is top secret. That's not something underlings need to ask about. You just keep quiet and follow orders.'

And thus was the kidnapping of the young lady organized right down to the last detail.

# CHAPTER 5
## THE LADY-THIEF AND THE MASTER DETECTIVE

THAT NIGHT, there was a lively atmosphere in the hotel's spacious lounge as guests chatted or smoked for a while after dinner. A radio in the corner of the room murmured out the evening news. Here and there, gentlemen leaned back into soft cushions with evening editions of the newspapers spread wide before their faces. The high-pitched voice of an American lady could be heard from a group of foreigners around one table.

Among the guests were Iwase Shōbei and his daughter Sanae. Large for her age, she stood out in the lounge because she was one of the few wearing Japanese clothing – a kimono with bright yellow stripes, a sash shot with shiny silver thread, and an orange *haori* shawl. It was not only her clothes. The calm and composed young lady also caught the eye for the frameless spectacles, apparently prescribed for myopia, that she wore in front of her white, almost translucent, face.

Stout, clean-shaven and with a greyish bald pate, her father had the appearance of a merchant of some importance. He followed her every movement very closely, as though guarding her.

Business was not the only purpose of this trip; he also intended to finalize marriage negotiations for his daughter with a well-known family in the capital and Sanae was accompanying him so that she could be presented to the family. Now, it just so happened that Iwase had been receiving persistent letters predicting a crime nearly every day for about two weeks before their departure.

'Watch carefully over your daughter. A fearsome demon is plotting her kidnap.'

Each time the frightening message was couched in different

phrases and handwriting. The letters piled up and it seemed to him that the hour of her kidnap was drawing nearer with every day.

At first, he was not particularly worried, thinking it just a prank, but as time passed he became more concerned and finally contacted the police. However, not even the might of the constabulary was sufficient to determine the source of these strange missives. Of course, the letters did not bear a sender's name, while the postmark – whether from within Osaka, or Kyoto, or Tokyo – differed each time.

Given the situation, Iwase considered cancelling the appointment with the family into which his daughter was to marry, but thinking that a move away from the house to which the unpleasant letters were directed might be better for her he decided to make the journey.

Nevertheless, determined to take every precaution, Iwase requested protection for his daughter from a private detective who had shown his ability in the past when the jeweller had hired him to investigate a break-in at the store. Akechi Kogorō was less than enthusiastic, but giving in to Iwase's pleas he undertook to prevent the strange 'theft' indicating that he would stay in an adjacent room while they were travelling.

Wearing a black suit over his slender frame, the famous detective was now sitting on a sofa in a different corner of the same lounge. Much as expected, he was with a beautiful lady in a black dress and they were talking about something in low voices.

'May I ask why you are so interested in this case?'

The detective looked steadily at her eyes as he put the question.

'I'm a devotee of detective novels. When I heard about this business from Iwase-san's daughter, it seemed exactly like something that would happen in such a novel and I was completely captivated. Then, getting to know the famous detective Akechi Kogorō on a familiar basis made me feel, well, as though I too had become a character in one of those books,' answered the woman in black.

Doubtless the reader will have divined that this dark-garbed woman was none other than our heroine, the Black Lizard.

Through her mania for jewels, she had become acquainted with Iwase as one of his customers. When they happened to bump into each other at the hotel, the relationship became closer. Using her amazing social skills, she quickly mesmerized Sanae and they became so intimate that the girl revealed her innermost secrets.

'But the real world is not like a novel, you know. I think this business is probably just a prank being played by some delinquent.'

The detective seemed very low-key about it all.

'But I think that you carry out your investigations with the utmost earnestness. I'm well aware that you walk the hotel corridors at night and that you question the hotel clerks about everything.'

'You must be very interested indeed if you know about that. I can't hide anything from you can I?'

He spoke with irony, looking intently at her beautiful face.

'I don't think this has anything to do with a prank at all. I just feel it – sixth sense maybe. And I think you should be very careful yourself,' she countered significantly, returning the detective's look unwaveringly.

'Thank you very much. But don't worry. I am looking after the young lady, so she is safe. Not even the most dastardly of villains can go unnoticed by me.'

'Yes, I am well aware of your capabilities. Still, I can't help but feel that it might be different this time… that you face a terrifying opponent who possesses tremendous magical powers.'

Ah! How audacious she was, praising herself before the most famous detective of the age.

'It seems that you very much favour this hypothetical criminal. Perhaps we should make a wager?'

Akechi made the strange proposal with a laugh.

'A wager, you say? What fun! To gamble with Akechi. Well, let me bet this – my most precious necklace.'

'It seems you are serious. All right, what should I forfeit if I lose and the young lady is kidnapped?'

'Why don't you stake your occupation as a detective? In that case, I would wager all of the jewels I possess.'

It was the sort of outlandish, fanciful thing one could imagine a lady of leisure might say. But could the famous detective sense behind the words the lady-thief's burning desire to engage him in combat?

'Interesting. So, you are suggesting that if I lose, I give up my profession? You throw down all your jewels – next to life itself in importance for a woman – while for a man like me work is no great thing.' Akechi was holding his own.

'Well, the bet is on! I shall see if I can't cause Akechi Kogorō to give up his profession.'

'All right, I accept the bet. I'm looking forward to seeing your splendid jewels come tumbling down! Ha, ha, ha.'

Thus, the joke had all of a sudden become something serious. Just as the incredible exchange ended, Sanae approached all un-witting and spoke genially.

'Now what are the two of you talking about so secretly? Can I join in?'

She spoke in an improvised blithe tone, but her face could not hide a slight trace of uneasiness.

'Oh, it's you my dear. Come, sit down here. Why, just this min-ute Akechi-san was complaining that he was bored because this business was just some sort of a prank.'

31

Mme Midorikawa spoke to Sanae with a kindness that belied her heart.

Then Iwase came over and the group of four began to make small talk, tacitly avoiding any reference to the case. Through a natural momentum, two separate conversations developed – one between the two men and another between the two women.

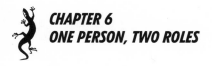

## CHAPTER 6
## ONE PERSON, TWO ROLES

AFTER A WHILE, the pair of women stood up and leaving the men deep in conversation began to walk slowly shoulder-to-shoulder between the lounge seats as though taking a stroll. Apart from the sharp contrast between the pitch black silk dress and the orange shawl, from behind the two looked almost the same in respect of hair style and age. They say that beauty is ageless and indeed Mme Midorikawa, though past thirty, looked youthful and innocent as a maid. Without either woman making any specific suggestion, the pair at length glided out of the lounge and walked along the corridor toward the stairs.

'My dear, would you come to my room for a little while? I would like to show you the doll that we spoke about yesterday.'

'Oh you have it here with you? I should like to see it.'

'Oh, I keep it with me always. Why, it's my sweet slave.'

Aha! And who could this be, this 'doll' of whom Mme Midorikawa spoke? Sanae had not the slightest idea, but perhaps a more apt adjective for the 'sweet' slave would have been 'weird.' The reader will have guessed straight away that the slave was actually Jun-chan/Yamakawa Kensaku.

Mme Midorikawa's room was on the ground floor, while Sanae and her father were staying on the second floor. The pair hesitated for a moment at the base of the stairs, but finally they moved on down the corridor to the older woman's room.

'After you,' said Mme Midorikawa opening the door to her room and inviting Sanae to enter.

'Oh, isn't this the wrong room? I thought yours was number twenty-three?'

33

And indeed it was. The number above this door was twenty-four. This was actually Yamakawa Kensaku's room, which was adjacent to Mme Midorikawa's room.

Having finished dinner early and returned half-fleeing to his room, the man-slaying pugilist would now be awaiting the arrival of the fateful moment with bated breath. Also awaiting the victim would be a strip of gauze soaked in knock-out drops and a trunk exactly like a coffin.

Sanae had every reason to hesitate. Somehow she seemed to sense something was afoot. Her sensitive subconscious had perceived the hellish scene that was to unfold momentarily.

But Mme Midorikawa kept her poker face.

'No, this is it. This is my room. Please hurry on in, now!'

And saying this she put her arm around Sanae's shoulders and passed together with her through the door.

When they had disappeared, the door slammed shut behind them. Strangely, immediately after the door closed, a key was heard to turn in the lock. The door had been locked from inside.

At the same time, there came from inside a faint sound like a smothered cry of pain.

For a short space of time the interior of the room fell silent again as if completely empty. Then came sounds – a tapping, whispering voices, footfalls moving around quickly, and something bumping into an object. This continued for about five minutes, and then subsided. Then a key could be heard turning in the lock again, after which the door opened slightly and a white face with spectacles peeped out into the corridor.

After establishing that there was no-one around, the full figure emerged – and strangely enough it was not Mme Midorikawa, but Sanae. The same Sanae one would have supposed had just now been stuffed inside the trunk.

But, no, it was not. The hairstyle, the spectacles, the kimono, and shawl were just like Sanae, but there was something different. Her breast was just a little too prominent. She was a shade too tall. And more than that, the face... Though the make-up was truly masterful – and made all the more plausible by the hairstyle and spectacles – a person's face does not change no matter how much it is made up. This was only Mme Midorikawa disguised as Sanae. Nevertheless, to have effected such a transformation in just five minutes was indeed a feat worthy of this self-styled magician.

What, then, had happened to poor Sanae? There can be no room for doubt. The lady-thief's kidnap plan was progressing smoothly. Sanae had been forced into the trunk. Given that Mme Midorikawa now wore all her clothes, it seemed certain that Sanae had been stripped naked – as in Mme Midorikawa's 'simulation' that morning – then bound and gagged and cruelly squeezed into the trunk.

'Right, I'm counting on you!' whispered Mme Midorikawa, now transformed into 'Sanae', while closing the door.

From within came a deep male voice in answer, 'Yeah, it'll be all right.'

It was Jun-chan/Yamakawa Kensaku.

She had a bulky cloth bundle under her arm. Carrying this and trying to avoid being spotted, she climbed the stairs. When she came to Iwase's room and peeped quietly in, she found that as expected the jeweller had not yet returned. He was still deep in conversation with Akechi Kogorō in the large lounge downstairs.

The suite comprised three rooms, one leading on to the other: a living room – with a sofa, armchairs, and writing table – a bedroom, and a bathroom. Entering the living room, she opened the drawer of the writing table and took out a small box containing Iwase's Calmotin sedatives. She removed the pills, replaced them with some that she had brought with her, and then returned the box to the drawer as it had been.

Next she entered the bedroom, turned off the bright light on the wall, and after switching on a small stand-lamp she pressed the room-service bell.

Soon there was a knock on the door and a bell-boy came into the living room.

'May I be of any service?'

'Yes, my father is in the main lounge downstairs and I wonder if you would let him know it's time for bed.'

Opening the bedroom door a crack so that her face was in shadow and the living room light fell only on the kimono, she mimicked Sanae's voice skilfully. A little while after the bell-hop had left on his errand, there was a loud sound of footsteps and Iwase came in:

'What, you're all alone? I thought you were with Mme Midori-kawa,' he said as if scolding her.

The only thing visible in the dark bedroom was the kimono and Mme Midorikawa cleverly copied Sanae's voice as she murmured, 'Yes, I felt a little ill so I parted with her at the stairs and returned alone. I'm going to sleep. Are you going to bed?'

'You shouldn't do that! I've told you over and over that you are not to be by yourself. What if this business happens?!'

Sitting in the armchair, Iwase spoke quietly, evidently believing that the voice from the bedroom belonged to his daughter.

'You're right. And that's why I sent for you,' came the innocent voice from the bedroom.

Akechi Kogorō had come in following Iwase.

'Is your daughter going to bed?'

'Yes, she's just changing her clothes now. She says she's feeling a bit off colour.'

'I see. Well, then, I'd better leave. Good night.'

After the detective had left for the adjacent room, Iwase locked the door. He wrote some letters for a short while, then, as usual, he took out the Calmotin from the drawer, drank some with water from a bottle on the table and went to bed.

'Sanae? How do you feel?'

As he asked this he moved around her toward the bed in the corner. She pulled the blanket up to her chin, turned her face into the shadow, and with her back to him answered somewhat grumpily, 'I'm fine! I'm a bit sleepy.'

'Oh dear, you're a bit strange tonight. You seem a little angry.'

But he was not particularly suspicious and being careful not to upset his out-of-sorts daughter he sang softly to himself while putting on his nightclothes and slipping into bed.

The powerful sleeping pills – with which Mme Midorikawa had secretly replaced the jeweller's night-draught – proved effective. As soon as Iwase laid his head on the pillow he was overcome by drowsiness and, without any time for thinking, he soon fell into a deep sleep.

Just over an hour later, around ten o'clock, Akechi Kogorō was reading in his room when he was startled by a loud knocking at what seemed to be the adjacent room. Stepping out in the corridor to investigate, he saw a hotel clerk holding a telegram in his hand anxiously trying to rouse the jeweller.

'It's strange that he isn't replying even though you've tried so many times.'

A little anxious, Akechi joined the clerk in knocking loudly at the door, regardless of any disturbance to the other guests.

The repeated knocking seemed to counteract the powerful sleeping draught, for Iwase's drowsy voice came from within the room.

'What is it? What's all this racket?'

'Could you just open the door a minute. There's a telegram for you.'

After Akechi had shouted this, a key scraped in the lock and the door opened.

In his nightclothes and looking very sleepy, Iwase rubbed his eyes as he opened the telegram, and looked at it in a daze.

'Oh hell! More pranks! And you want to wake a man from his sleep for this!' he said, tutting disapprovingly as he passed the paper to Akechi.

'TONIGHT – STOP – BE CAREFUL AT TWELVE – STOP'

A simple note, but the meaning was clear. This was one of the threatening messages and its meaning was 'Sanae's kidnapping will take place tonight at midnight.'

'Is your daughter all right?'

The tone of the private eye's question showed he was somewhat concerned.

Approaching the door of the bedroom a little unsteadily, Iwase looked at the bed in the corner and said in a reassured voice, 'She's fine. Don't worry. She's sleeping right next to me.'

Akechi also went behind and peeped in to see Sanae sleeping peacefully with her back turned to them.

'Recently Sanae has been taking Calmotin every night just like me so she sleeps soundly. And tonight the poor thing said that she wasn't feeling particularly well so please don't wake her up.'

'Is the window closed?'

'Yes, don't worry. It's been latched shut all day.'

Iwase then climbed into bed.

'Akechi-san, would you mind locking the door and looking after the key.'

The jeweller was so sleepy that even locking the door seemed a bother.

'Actually, instead of that, I'll stay in the suite for a while. Please leave the bedroom door open. If we do that, I'll soon realise if anyone breaks the window and tries to get in while you're asleep because I can see the window from here. We only need to watch the window – there's no other way in or out.'

Once Akechi had taken on a case, he discharged his duty faithfully. He sat down in a seat in the lounge, lit up a cigarette, and steadily monitored the bedroom.

Some thirty minutes passed without anything happening at all. Occasionally the private eye got up to go and peep into the bedroom, but Sanae remained asleep in the same position. Iwase was snoring loudly.

'What! Are you still up? I came because the hotel clerk told me just now that a strange telegram had arrived and I was a little worried.'

Surprised by the voice, Akechi turned to see Mme Midorikawa standing just outside the half opened door.

'Is that you, Mme Midorikawa? There was a telegram, but I'm here, so everything will be all right. I'll stand guard, even though it's pointless.'

'So, did a threatening telegram arrive at the hotel, then?'

As she said this, the lady in black opened the door and came into the room.

Now perhaps readers will think that the author has committed a major bungle here. They might object that because Mme Midorikawa had disguised herself as Sanae and was sleeping in the bed beside Iwase, it would make absolutely no sense for the same Mme Midorikawa to be coming into the room from the corridor.

But the author has not made a mistake. Both are correct. And this is the only Mme Midorikawa in existence. What this all means will become clear as our story unfolds.

*...the lady in black opened the door
and came into the room.*

## CHAPTER 7
## TWILIGHT KNIGHT

'IS SANAE SLEEPING QUIETLY?' asked Mme Midorikawa as she closed the door and sat down in front of Akechi. Her voice was low and she was looking toward the bedroom.

'Um,' responded Akechi absently-mindedly, obviously deep in thought.

'With her father?'

'Hmm... yes.'

As mentioned in the previous chapter, Iwase Shōbei was still in a drugged sleep in the bed adjoining Sanae's bed, after having asked Akechi to guard them.

'Not very informative answers, are they?' smiled Mme Midorikawa. 'So what are you so deep in thought about? Surely you're not worried now that you're on guard here?'

'Oh, you're still talking about that silly wager,' said Akechi, finally lifting his head to look at her as he took up the challenge of the beautiful woman. 'You're hoping I'll lose, and that poor girl will be kidnapped, right?'

'Oh, how could you say such a thing? That I would wish such a terrible tragedy on Mr Iwase! I'm just worried about her. So tell me, what did the telegram say?'

'Just to be careful at midnight,' he explained, as if he found it humorous.

He glanced at the clock on the mantle. It read 10:50.

'There's still a little over an hour. And I'm sure you'll sit here the whole time. Won't you be bored?'

'No, not at all. I'm enjoying myself. If I weren't a detective, how many times in my life would I be able to enjoy such dramatic moments? But you must be tired, Mme Midorikawa. Please, take your rest.'

'My, selfish, aren't we? I'm enjoying myself perhaps even more than you! Women just love wagers. May I stay here with you, although I'm sure I'm a bother to you?'

'Still talking about that wager? As you wish.'

The unlikely couple sat silently for a while facing each other, and then Mme Midorikawa noticed a pack of playing cards on the desk. She proposed a game to fight off sleepiness, and when Akechi agreed they began a strange game of cards while waiting for the midnight caller.

It was a very long hour indeed, precisely because it was so threatening, but thanks to the cards it seemed to pass fairly quickly. Of course, throughout their gaming Akechi never failed to look into the bedroom through the open door, noting that the window remained perfectly normal – and if the kidnapper was to enter the bedroom, the window was the only route left open.

'Let's stop, shall we? It's five to twelve now,' suggested Mme Midorikawa, with an irritated expression showing she could play cards no longer.

'Still five minutes. We have time for another hand. And if we keep playing, I've no doubt that midnight will pass with nothing untoward happening,' drawled Akechi, inviting her as he shuffled.

'Oh, stop that! You mustn't slight the kidnapper. As I said before, I don't think this person will break that promise. I'm sure... even now...'

Her face was tense, taut.

'Mme Midorikawa, you mustn't get so nervous,' laughed Akechi. 'Where in the world is this mysterious kidnapper going to enter from?'

At his words, she lifted her hand, and pointed at the room entrance.

'Ah, the front door. Well then, to set you at ease, why don't I just lock it?'

He rose, and walked over to lock it securely with the key he had received from Iwase.

'There. Unless they break down the door, no-one will be able to approach Sanae's bedroom. As you know, there is no way in except through this room.'

Mme Midorikawa, like a child terrified by a ghost story, raised her hand again to point at the window, shadowed in the gloomy bedroom.

'Ah, the window. So you suggest the kidnapper could enter the courtyard and use a ladder? But the window is securely locked from the inside. And even assuming the criminal should break the glass and enter, I can see the window quite well from here – and in that event you would be able to witness my ability at shooting a pistol.'

As he spoke, he tapped his right-hand pocket meaningfully. A small pistol was hidden there.

'Sanae is sleeping so peacefully, unaware of what's happening,' said Mme Midorikawa, peering quietly into the bedroom. 'But why doesn't Mr Iwase wake up? He's far too unconcerned for my taste!'

'He mentioned that they both take sleeping draughts every night before retiring. They must be worn out by the fear of that terrible note.'

'My goodness! There's only one minute left! Akechi-san, are you sure everything's all right?'

She stood, voice quavering.

'Yes, everything's just fine. Absolutely nothing will happen.'

Akechi had also stood, quite unconsciously, and was peering bemusedly at Mme Midorikawa's face, which was so unusually agitated.

'But there are still thirty seconds,' she argued, returning his gaze with fire in her eyes. The woman thief was drunk with the thrill of victory. At last, the time had come to surpass Akechi Kogorō, the famous detective, and scream in triumph.

'Mme Midorikawa, are you so certain of the kidnapper's skill?'

His eyes, as well, were smouldering: he was trying valiantly to decipher the bizarre expression on her face. What was it? What in the world was this beautiful woman thinking, to be so excited?

'Yes, I am. Although it could just be my imagination running off with me. But when I think that even now the twilight knight could be sneaking closer, ready to snatch this beautiful child from our midst, I can see it happening right in front of my eyes!'

'Ha, ha, ha!' Akechi finally burst into laughter. 'Please, Mme Midorikawa, take a look! While you've been enjoying your medieval storytelling, the clock has already passed midnight! Looks like I've won the wager after all. Shall I claim your jewels now? Ha, ha, ha!'

'Akechi-san, do you truly believe that you have won the wager?'

Her red lips were twisted now, speaking oh-so-slowly. As she savoured the ecstasy of victory, she had even forgotten her assumed role as a lady of class.

'What..? You mean, you are...?'

Akechi discerned the meaning of her comment instantly, and his face drained of colour as a terrifying and unknown fear swept through him.

'You haven't yet checked to be sure that Sanae is still safe or not,' she prodded, crowing in victory.

'But, but... Sanae-san is still...'

The famous detective was foundering fast. His broad forehead was suddenly shiny with greasy sweat.

'You will tell me she is quietly asleep in bed, I'm sure. But I wonder if that is really Sanae-san, sleeping there... I wonder if it couldn't be a totally different girl?'

'That's... impossible!' he asserted powerfully, but it was clear he recognized the threat in her words as he ran into the bedroom and roused Iwase.

'Wha...? What is it? What's happened?' asked Iwase, sitting bolt upright as he finally defeated the last traces of sleepiness and woke up fully.

'Please, look at your daughter. Is that truly your daughter sleeping there?'

A most absurd question, one hardly worthy of the famous Akechi.

'What in the world are you talking about? Of course it is. If it isn't my daughter, who could it possibly...'

He broke off suddenly. As if suddenly noticing something, he stared at the back of Sanae's head as she lay sleeping with her face turned away from him.

'Sanae! Sanae!'

Although breaking into coughs, Iwase continued to call her name. There was no answer. He left his bed, and approached hers, wavering unsteadily, then placed a hand on her shoulder to awaken her.

'Akechi-san! She's gone!' the old man shouted, furiously.

'Who is it? The person sleeping there, it's not Sanae?'

'Look! This isn't a person at all! We've been duped like fools!'

Akechi and Mme Midorikawa ran to her bed... it wasn't a person. What they had been so sure was Sanae was actually just the head of a doll. The head of a storefront mannequin had been decorated with a pair of eyeglasses and a Western-style wig to look just like her. The quilt had been bunched up to simulate her body, and a blanket thrown on top.

## CHAPTER 8
## THE DETECTIVE LAUGHS

THE HEAD OF A DOLL. What a trite device; what an out-standing scam. A trick played by children. But, exactly because it was the sort of trick you would expect from a child, the adults fell for it completely. Even Akechi Kogorō had never thought the kidnapper might do this sort of thing.

Even so, who in the world was the 'twilight knight' that Mme Midorikawa had mentioned? Who in the world could have kidnapped Sanae and left that silly doll's head in her place? The reader already knows: the twilight knight was, of course, none other than Mme Midorikawa herself. As mentioned in the previous chapter, she disguised herself as Sanae and climbed into bed, fooling her father. After he had drugged himself asleep, she set up the doll's head and returned to her own room. Readers will recall that when she visited Iwase's room she was carrying a bulky bag with her. That was the core of the trick, the doll's head.

In all his years learning to be a detective, Akechi Kogorō had never felt so miserable. There was nothing he could say in response to Iwase's betrayed trust, or to Mme Midorikawa, either. And for the root of the failure to be this doll's head, this child's prank, was so embarrassing as to be unbearable!

'Akechi-san, my daughter, whom I begged you to protect, has been stolen! You have to get her back! Hurry and get started! And if you can't handle it by yourself, call the police... yes, I'll have to rely on the police now! Call the police! Or shall I?'

Iwase Shōbei was furious, so furious that he had forgotten to be a gentleman, spitting out words to savage Akechi.

'Please, wait. If you start a ruckus now, we won't be able to capture the criminal. The kidnapping has happened within the last two hours.'

Through incredible effort, Akechi had recaptured his composure, and was thinking keenly again.

'I can say with confidence that nothing happened while I was on guard here. The only conclusion is that the crime was carried out before that telegram was delivered. The intent of that telegram, in other words, was not to warn us that the girl would be kidnapped, but rather to make it look as if the crime was to be committed at midnight, and keep all our attention focused on this room until then. The criminals planned to make good use of that time to flee to a place of safety.'

Mme Midorikawa chuckled.

'Oh, excuse me. I laughed when I shouldn't have. But when I think of the famous detective Akechi Kogorō spending two hours faithfully guarding a doll's head…'

Ignoring where she was entirely, Mme Midorikawa was belittling Akechi. She had won a complete victory, and could not restrain the fierce joy bubbling up.

Akechi ground his teeth together and withstood her derisive laughter. He had lost, he admitted it. But he could not accept that his defeat was total. Deep in his heart, he felt that there was still a chance, a hope. And until he found out for sure, he could not accept defeat.

'Even so, my daughter will not come back to us if we just stand here and wait,' interjected Iwase, growing more irritated by the unsympathetic words of Mme Midorikawa, and turning to attack Akechi. 'Akechi-san, I'm calling the police. Surely you have no objections?'

Without waiting for a reply he staggered off toward the living room, and reached for the telephone. And at exactly that instant, as if it had been carefully planned in advance, the bell began to ring.

Although Iwase tutted in irritation, he was left with no choice but to lift the receiver. He began ranting and shouting at the poor operator, but then called in anger for Akechi instead.

'Akechi-san! It's for you!'

Hearing this, Akechi snapped alert and leaped for the phone as if he had suddenly remembered something.

He conversed with the other party attentively, and then closed the conversation mysteriously, saying 'Twenty minutes? It doesn't take that long! Fifteen? No, that's too long, too. Ten minutes. Come running in ten minutes. I can only last for ten minutes. Got it?'

'If you've done, would you kindly have the operator telephone the police?' asked Iwase sarcastically, confronting Akechi.

'Don't be in such a hurry to phone the police. Let me think for a moment. I've made a terrible error.'

Not wasting another word on Iwase, Akechi stood there, deep in thought and seemingly unaware of the room around him.

'Akechi-san, perhaps you could be bothered to think of my daughter? You accepted the work with confidence, and now...'

It was only reasonable that Iwase's anger would be further inflamed by Akechi's unfathomable attitude.

Another laugh was heard.

'Iwase-san, poor Akechi-san doesn't have the leeway to think of your poor daughter right now,' came Mme Midorikawa's boastful voice. She had moved from the bedroom back to the living room.

'Wha–? What?'

Iwase was astonished.

'Shall I guess what Akechi-san is thinking of right now? He's thinking of our wager – aren't you, Akechi-san?'

The lady thief's enmity for the detective was unmistakable; her attitude bold and indomitable.

'Iwase-san, Akechi-san made a little wager with me. He wagered his profession as an amateur detective. And since his defeat is now unmistakable, he's just lost in thought, head drooping. Isn't that right, Akechi-san?'

'No, it's not, madam. I was hanging my head because I was thinking how I pitied your position,' he replied, returning her volley full-force. What in the world was he thinking, ignoring the kidnapped girl like this? Iwase was totally lost by developments, and stood looking at their faces.

'Me? You pitied *my* position? Why, I wonder?' she asked, pressing. Even the master thief was unable to fathom the smile lurking, hidden, behind Akechi's eyes.

'Well, madam,' drawled Akechi, obviously enjoying his own words as he spoke, 'that's because the loser of our wager is not me, but you!'

'Whatever are you talking about. Are you so unable to admit defeat?'

'Is that what it is?' he rebutted, obviously enjoying himself.

'Yes, clearly. How can you say otherwise, with the kidnapper at large?'

'Ah, so you think I've allowed the kidnapper to escape, do you? Not by a long shot! I've got the perpetrator right under my thumb!'

When she heard that, even the lady thief couldn't restrain her reaction. This man had been in the pits of despair a moment ago; what had he suddenly started saying?

'Ha, ha, ha! You're a delightful man! So good at making jokes!'

'So you think it a joke?'

'Well, naturally! What else could it be?'

'In that case, let me show you some evidence, shall I? Let me see... Suppose I can tell you where your acquaintance Mr Yamakawa Kensaku went after leaving this hotel? What would you think then?'

Mme Midorikawa blanched, and staggered.

'Why did Mr Yamakawa purchase a ticket to Nagoya, and then get off before the train arrived there? And why did he take a room at the Meiji Hotel here in Tokyo? And what was in his oh-so-large trunk? Suppose I know the answers to those questions? What would you say then?'

'Lies! It's all lies!'

She no longer seemed to have the energy to speak properly, merely muttering denials.

'Lies, are they? Ah, so you haven't noticed where that phone call was from, then. Shall I explain? It was from an assistant of mine. I was merely waiting for his phone call, while I endured your insults. If Sanae was carried out of this hotel, one of my five assistants surrounding the hotel would be sure to see. You see, I told them that if anyone suspicious, no matter who, came from the hotel, they were to follow him.

'Ah, I waited so long for that call. And now it seems that I have won, doesn't it? You made a mistake when you assumed that I was here all alone. You decided that I had no assistants helping me. And now shall I take all of your jewellery, Mme Midorikawa? Ha, ha, ha!'

He laughed, long and loud. Their positions were reversed now, the victor and the vanquished. And the delight of victory tickled Akechi's heart as much as it had pleased Mme Midorikawa until now, or even more. Even if he had tried to stop laughing, he would have been unable to control it. Yet Mme Midorikawa had the force of will Akechi had shown moments ago to endure the derisive laughter.

'So you have already recovered Sanae, then? Congratulations. And what have you done with Yamakawa-san?' she asked in a frigid tone, struggling to hold her voice steady.

'Unfortunately, he seems to have slipped away,' admitted Akechi honestly.

'You let the criminal escape! Oh, my...'

She was unable to hide her relief.

Iwase spoke up, good humour regained at the unexpected positive news. 'Thank you, Akechi-san, thank you. I must apologize for becoming so excited without knowing that! Please forgive me. I had thought I heard you to say that you had captured the criminal, but now it seems you have let him escape after all.'

'No, not at all. Yamakawa is not the mastermind behind this little plot. I was not lying when I said that I have captured the criminal.'

His words were enough to bring a purple flush to Mme Midorikawa's face. Like a cornered animal, her face grew fearsome, and her eyes searched round and round the room.

But even were she to try to escape, the door was locked!

'Then where is he?' asked Iwase, unaware of what was happening.

'Here. Right in front of us,' said Akechi with satisfaction.

'Right in front of us? But there's nobody here but you, and me, and Mme Midorikawa...'

'Mme Midorikawa is a terrible thief. She is the one who kidnapped Sanae!'

The deathly silence held for several seconds. The three of them stared at each other, each with a different expression.

It was Mme Midorikawa who finally broke the silence.

'Surely you're kidding. I would hardly have any idea of what Yamakawa-san might be doing. I merely introduced the hotel to him because we had an acquaintance in common! It's too much, really! To accuse me!...'

But that was the enchantress's last piece of acting.

Even as she finished speaking, a loud knock was heard at the door.

As if he had been awaiting this, Akechi quickly approached the door, and unlocked it with the key he held.

'Mme Midorikawa, no matter how much you try to deny it, here is living evidence. And will you repeat that dreadful lie in front of Sanae-san?'

Akechi drove home the blade with his words.

There in the doorway appeared one of Akechi's young assistants; the pale Sanae, leaning heavily on his shoulder; and a uniformed policeman guarding them.

The Black Lizard was in mortal danger! On this side, there was only a woman, and opposing her were four men (excluding Sanae)... she couldn't possibly escape!

But what stubbornness! She yet looked as if she refused to admit defeat!

More than that, astonishing as it was, her pale cheeks were suddenly shot through with colour, and she gave a hideous smile that rapidly grew and grew.

Here, brought to bay at last, the audacious woman thief burst into bizarre and incomprehensible laughter!

'Hah! So this is the climax of tonight's entertainment, is it? Well, you certainly showed yourself to be worthy of your name as a famous detective, didn't you! It seems I have lost tonight. Let us call it a defeat. And what of it? Do you honestly think you can take me prisoner? I think you're expecting a little too much, Mr Detective. Don't you remember? Are you sure you haven't forgotten something? Are you sure you haven't lost something while you were so busy? Ha, ha, ha!'

What could she be thinking of to speak such words in her situation?

What could Akechi have forgotten?

## CHAPTER 9
## THE MASTER DETECTIVE'S DEFEAT

**AN ORDINARY PERSON** cannot imagine the delight a detective feels at capturing a formidable criminal. That Akechi had become a little careless due to his extreme delight, then, was perhaps understandable. Though pushed toward defeat, the Black Lizard wracked her sharp brain to come up with a way out of the tight corner in which she now found herself. Then, in an instant, she hit on a daring idea.

The drawn expression on her face softened and she was able to laugh back at the detective.

'So, what do you think you are going to do? You don't suppose you can capture me, do you? That would be just a little too easy now wouldn't it?'

What audacity! For here she was, a mere woman on her own going up against four dour males (excluding Sanae who to all intents and purposes was incapacitated), one of whom was a stern-looking policeman in uniform.

The only escape route was the door to the corridor. But standing in front of the door barring the way were the policeman and the detective's assistant, who had just now come back. There was the window, but the room was high above the ground and the inner garden below was surrounded on all sides by buildings. So how in the world did she plan to get out of this tight spot?

Ignoring the Black Lizard's challenge, Akechi spoke to the policeman at the door.

'Don't try to bluff your way out! Officer, I am putting this woman in your charge. Please arrest her without delay. She is the mastermind of the kidnapping plot.'

Not knowing the details of the situation, the officer seemed taken aback when told that this beautiful lady was a criminal, but because Akechi was held in high regard by the police investigation unit and the policeman knew the detective by sight, he did as he was told and moved toward Mme Midorikawa.

'Akechi-san, please feel your right pocket. Ha, ha. Empty isn't it?'

Staring balefully at the approaching policeman, the Black Lizard spoke in a high voice.

Surprised, the detective put his hand to the pocket without thinking. It wasn't there! The Browning that he was sure he had put in his pocket wasn't there! The lady thief's magical powers extended to her fingertips. During the confusion in the bedroom shortly before, she had taken the precaution of removing the pistol from Akechi's pocket.

'Akechi-san, you really ought to include pocket picking in your research. Your precious pistol is here!'

With a cheery laugh, the lady thief reached to the clothing at her breast and drew out the compact weapon, which she then levelled at them.

'Now then everybody, please do me the favour of putting your hands up. And if you don't – well I'll just let you know that I'm as sharp a shot as Akechi. And I'll also add that human life doesn't mean much to me.'

The policeman, who had taken a step toward her, retreated.

Unfortunately only the officer was armed and he would not have enough time to reach the pistol at his hip.

'Right then, I told you to put 'em up!'

Licking her red lips, the Black Lizard fixed her eyes on the four men, pointing the muzzle of the gun at each in turn. The white finger holding the trigger quivered slightly as if about to apply pressure at any second.

They put up their hands when they saw the expression on her face, which was more manic than murderous. The policeman, the detective's assistant, Iwase, and even the master detective – found themselves in an embarrassing position for grown men – their arms up in the air as if frozen half way through a gesture of 'hurrah!'.

Mme Midorikawa rushed to the door with an alacrity befitting her reptilian nickname.

'Akechi-san, this is your second slip up. Look...'

Saying this, she put her empty left hand behind her, took the key from the lock where it had been left by the detective just a little while ago, and waved the shiny object in front of her face.

Not imagining for a moment that this would happen, the detective had in the bustle of the moment unthinkingly left the key in the lock. Such was the lady thief's acuity that she had quickly thought of a way to use this.

'As for you, my little lady!'

Opening the door and with one foot in the corridor – but not forgetting to keep the pistol aimed – she called to Sanae.

'I really feel very sorry for you, but today just resign yourself to regretting having been born a jeweller's daughter. Another thing – you are too beautiful! Obsessed though I am with jewels, I've come to desire your body even more. And I won't give up. Do you hear that Akechi-san? I won't give up! I'll be back to claim the little lady again. Well, I'm off!'

The door slammed shut and the key could be heard turning in the lock outside. Sanae and the four men were now locked in the room. And there was only one key. With that taken away, their only way out was to break down the door or to climb down from the window, which was high above the ground.

Still, they had an alternative – the telephone.

Akechi sprang to the handset on the table and rang the switchboard operator.

'Hello? Hello? This is Akechi, the detective! It's very urgent! I want you to make sure the hotel exits are guarded. It's Mme Midorikawa, Mme Midorikawa. She's going to leave the hotel now and she has to be captured. She's a major criminal. Whatever happens, she mustn't escape. Quick now, tell the manager and everyone else. Got it? Oh, wait! Send someone up to Iwase-san's room with a duplicate key. That's also very urgent.'

After putting the phone down, Akechi stamped back and forth in the room before again snatching up the receiver.

'Hello? Hello? Have you done it yet? Did you tell the manager what I said? Oh, good, good. Thanks. Right, now tell them to hurry up with that duplicate key.' Then he turned to Iwase and said, 'The switchboard operator seems to be on the ball. She did everything very quickly. All the exits are being watched. No matter how fast that woman runs, there's still a fair distance from here to the stairs and it would take a while to descend them and then reach an exit so I think it should be all right – perhaps. The famous Mme Midorikawa wouldn't happen to have somebody in her employ that we don't know about, now would she?'

But in making these prompt arrangements Akechi had slipped up again.

For, while the Black Lizard had swiftly descended the stairs, she had gone not toward an exit but to her own room.

Three minutes passed, exactly three minutes.

And lo and behold, when the door to her room opened again, a young gentleman stepped out. Sporting a felt hat, a brightly patterned suit, aristocratic spectacles, and a thick moustache, he carried a snake-wood cane in his right hand and an overcoat on his left arm.

Only the Black Lizard – in keeping with her description of herself as a magician – could perform the astounding feat of putting on a disguise in just three minutes. (She always carried clothes for changing her guise in the bottom of her travel bag.) Avoiding even the slightest oversight, she had also put every last one of the jewels from the trunk into her coat pockets.

When the young 'gentleman' came to the corner, he hesitated slightly. Should he exit from the front or the rear?

Meanwhile, the duplicate key had arrived in time and Akechi and his companions had descended the stairs. However, supposing that Mme Midorikawa would not try to escape by the front entrance they had left this for the manager and split up to guard the rear exits. The Black Lizard, though, had apparently got wind of this, for in a show of daring she went out the main entrance holding her head high, and swinging the cane as her shoes clacked loudly on the floor.

The manager and three doormen were guarding the main entrance in a very nervous state. However, considering that there were nearly a hundred guests staying in the hotel, each with visitors from outside, the manager and his assistants could not recognise each guest by sight. Moreover as they were looking for Mme Midorikawa they focused their attention on the female guests. Accordingly, it never occurred to them that the young man who smiled and bowed as he passed out could be Mme Midorikawa and they actually bowed politely as they saw him out and wished him a good evening.

The young gentleman's shoes clacked on the stone stairs as he descended. Then, whistling as he went, he strolled leisurely out through the hotel gates.

Walking along the shadowy pavement beside the hotel's boundary fence, the young gentleman came across a man in a suit who for some reason was standing there smoking a cigarette.

Surprisingly, the young gentleman suddenly slapped the man on the shoulder and spoke to him with an air of bonhomie.

'I expect you're one of Master Detective Akechi's men aren't you? What are you doing loafing around here? There's a great commotion going on in the hotel at the moment because they've just caught a thief. You'd better get a move on and see.'

And indeed it appeared the man was one of Akechi's assistants for though he replied with extreme caution, 'I'm afraid you're mistaken. I've never heard of a "Detective Akechi",' the young gentleman had not taken more than one or two steps before the man, belying his own words and gestures, scurried off toward the hotel.

The Black Lizard turned around to watch him run off. Overcome for a moment by the comicality of it, she forgot herself and let out an eerie laugh.

## CHAPTER 10
## THE STRANGE OLD MAN

**ALTHOUGH AKECHI HAD BEEN BEATEN,** we can at least say in his defence that he had fulfilled the task he had undertaken – protecting Sanae.

Iwase was simply grateful that his daughter had been saved, considering the fact that the lady-thief had escaped to be of secondary importance. He did not praise the private eye's abilities. But then it would seem that the majority of the blame for the way things had turned out rested with the jeweller, for it was he who had slipped up by being taken in by the Black Lizard's disguise and falling asleep in the adjoining bed rather than seeing through the thief's ruse.

However, this was no consolation to Akechi. The frustration he felt at having been defeated by a mere woman was too much for words. And when he learned that thanks to a quick change of disguise his opponent had escaped right under the nose of his lookout, the detective involuntarily shouted angrily at his assistant 'Fool!'

'Iwase-san, she beat me. I can't understand why such a formidable opponent wasn't on my black list. I shouldn't have underestimated her. But I won't make the same mistake again. Iwase-san, I swear on my honour that if she should make another attempt on your daughter I will not be beaten again. While I am alive your daughter is safe. This much I promise.'

The passion in the pale-faced detective's pledge was almost frightening. Having set himself against this unusual and powerful foe, his fighting spirit welled up.

Dear readers, please record the private-eye's words somewhere in your memory. Will he be able to keep his promise? Or will he fail yet again? And if he should fail, he would have no other choice but to give up his profession...

The following day, Iwase and his daughter changed their schedule and returned in haste to their home in Osaka. They were very uneasy on the way, but rather than stay on in the hotel they preferred to return quickly to their home where they could relax among family.

Akechi Kogorō also advised this course and undertook to guard them en route. As there was no telling where the criminal might intervene, he was extremely careful when they went by taxi from the hotel to the station, when they were on the train, and in the taxi that met them when they arrived at Osaka.

In the end, Sanae's party returned home without incident. Akechi then became a guest of the Iwase family, never straying far from Sanae's vicinity. Some days passed with nothing untoward taking place.

Now dear readers, it is time for the author to change the scene and relate the strange experience of a lady who has not yet appeared in our tale. Perhaps this will seem something completely unrelated to the Black Lizard, Sanae, and Akechi Kogorō. However, without a doubt astute readers will easily discern the close relationship between our case and the woman's strange experience.

It took place one evening shortly after Sanae had returned to Osaka. A young lady was strolling along a street in the bustling district of Shinchi with no particular purpose, looking at the show windows on either hand.

Her coat was fringed with fur at the collar and the cuffs, and it became her well, while her high-heeled legs moved lightly. However, her beautiful face conveyed a somewhat dispirited air. She had about her a rather desperate look as if to say 'I'm beyond caring,' and for that reason, she could perhaps have been mistaken for a streetwalker.

Indeed someone had been surreptitiously following her for some time as if she was that type of woman. This vaguely disturbing personage was an old gentleman who wore a brown felt hat and a thick brown coat and carried a stout rattan cane. A large pair of horn-rimmed spectacles sat on his shiny ruddy face and his moustache and hair were completely white.

Although it seemed the young woman knew she was being followed, she made no effort to flee. In fact, using the show window as a mirror, she even looked at the old man with what seemed to be some sort of interest.

Now, in a slightly crooked dark alley just off the well-lit avenue running through Shinchi, there is a café that is famous for its delicious coffee. As if on impulse, the woman glanced back at the gentleman who was tailing her and entered this café. After taking a seat in a booth in the corner hidden from view by a potted palm, what should the brazen miss do but order two cups of coffee! Naturally, one of these was for the old gentleman she presumed would come in after her.

As expected, he entered the café. After peering about in the dark interior, he spied the young woman and with even greater audacity than she had shown he approached her booth.

'Excuse me, all alone are we?'

So saying, he sat down opposite her.

'I felt sure you would come so I ordered a coffee for you.'

She outdid him for cheek.

Even the old gentleman seemed to be somewhat taken aback by this, but soon regained his aplomb and looking the beautiful young woman straight in the face asked her a peculiar question.

'So, what does it feel like to be out of work?'

*'I wouldn't do anything so uncouth as to offer advice.
I'm going to save you from your predicament.'*

Now it was the woman's turn to look shocked. Blushing, she stuttered out, 'You know about that? Who are you?'

'I'm an old buffer you know nothing about. But I know a little about you. Shall I show you? Your name is Sakurayama Yōko and you were a typist for Kansai Trading. However, you had an argument with your boss and he fired you today. Well, what do you think? Am I on the mark?'

'Yes, you are. You're just like a private eye.'

The desperate look had quickly come back to Yōko's face and she shrugged off what he had said as though it was not in the least surprising.

'Wait, I haven't finished yet. You left the company around three o'clock, but you still haven't gone home. Neither have you visited any friends. You've just been wandering aimlessly around the city. What on earth do you intend to do?'

The old man seemed to know everything. He must have been tailing Yōko constantly since three in the afternoon until the early evening. But why would he undertake such a tiring and foolish task?

'What do you expect me to do? What if I decide to change my profession and become a streetwalker from tonight?'

A weak couldn't-care-less smile appeared on her face.

'Ha, ha. So I look like that sort of a delinquent old man, do I? No, you're mistaken. And what's more, you're not the type that could do such a thing. Do you think I don't know that you went into a pharmacy about two hours ago to make a purchase?'

He looked at her eyes intently, confident of his impact.

'Do you mean these? They're sleeping pills.'

Yōko produced two boxes of Adalin tablets from her handbag.

'I doubt a young person like you would be suffering from insomnia. No, I'm sure it wouldn't be that. And why would you need two boxes of Adalin…?'

'Are you suggesting that I intend to kill myself?'

'That's right. You see my dear, I'm not completely unacquainted with the feelings of a young lady. Ah, the heart of youth is beyond the fathoming of adult imagination. Death appears so beautiful, no? The pure-hearted virgin wishes to die with her body unsullied. But alongside this there's a masochism that seeks to throw self and body into the slimy swamp. And only a hair's breadth between them. Hah! It's a trick of youth that makes you babble the words "street walker" and buy your Adalin.'

'All right then, does this mean you are going to favour me with some advice?'

Yōko spoke coldly and looked at him icily.

'Oh goodness, no! I wouldn't do anything so uncouth as to offer advice. I'm going to save you from your predicament.'

'I thought it would be something like that. Thank you, lovely to be "saved" by you I'm sure.'

Her cynical reply suggested that she still misunderstood his intentions.

'Don't be so tasteless. I'm seriously trying to help you. I'm not trying to turn you into a kept woman – there's no strange meaning intended at all. But will you agree to be my employee?'

'I'm sorry. Do you really mean it?'

Yōko was finally beginning to perceive the old man's real intentions.

'Yes, really. Now, forgive me for asking but what was your salary at Kansai Trading?'

'Just 45,000 yen…'

'All right then, let's agree that I pay you a salary of 90,000 yen a month. In addition, I'll bear your costs for lodging, food, and clothes. As for the job, all you need to do is enjoy yourself.'

'Ha, ha, ha. Now wouldn't that be fantastic!'

'Listen, this isn't a joke. Actually there are some special circumstances here – so much so that the employer thinks these benefits might be insufficient. Anyway, what about your parents?'

'I don't have any. If they were still alive I probably wouldn't have had to endure this unpleasant experience...'

'So now you...'

'I live all by myself in a small rented place.'

'Good, good, that's perfect. Now, will you come along with me just as you are? I'll sort things out for you at your lodgings later.'

It was a very strange proposal and under normal circumstances, she would certainly not have felt like accepting. But such was Sakurayama Yōko's state at this time that she was thinking of selling her virtue or committing suicide. This desperation it was that made her nod in agreement.

Outside the café, the old man hailed a taxi and took the woman to the second floor of a ramshackle tobacconist's located in an area she had never visited near the outskirts of the city. The small, plain room was floored with six discoloured *tatami* mats and the only objects it contained were a little mirror-stand in the corner and a trunk.

Although the old man's behaviour was becoming increasingly strange, Yōko was not at all uneasy because he had let her in a little on the secret behind her employment contract while they were in the car en route to the room. Actually, she was beginning to feel considerable interest in her unusual role.

'All right now, I'll have to ask you to put some things on. This is one of the conditions of the job.'

From the trunk, he took out a full set of attire, including a brightly patterned kimono exactly suitable for a woman of Yōko's age, an obi-belt, a long undergarment for the kimono, a black coat with a fur collar, and a pair of *zōri* sandals.

Before going downstairs he said, 'It's only a small mirror stand, but please dress yourself very nicely.'

Yōko changed clothes as she had been instructed, and she was not entirely displeased to be thus wrapped up in luxurious Japanese apparel.

'Very nice. That's good – it really suits you.'

The old gentleman had come back upstairs and was standing behind looking at her.

Peering at the mirror Yōko spoke slightly under her breath,

'But this hair style doesn't look quite right for a kimono.'

'I've arranged that too. Here you go. You'll have to put this on.'

The old man pulled out something wrapped in a white cloth from the same trunk. He undid the bundle to reveal a weird lump of hair. It was a high-quality Western-style wig.

Stepping around in front of her, he carefully arranged the hairpiece. The face in the mirror was transformed completely.

'All right, now this might seem to be going too far, but just put up with it.'

So saying, he produced a pair of rimless spectacles for shortsightedness. Without demur, Yōko took the glasses and put them on.

'We don't have much time. We've got to be there at ten on the dot, so we have to leave now.'

Chivvied by the old man, Yōko hurriedly bundled up the Western clothes she had taken off, pushed them into the trunk and went downstairs.

Leaving the tobacconist's, they walked to a major road nearby where an automobile was waiting. It was not the taxi they had used earlier. Though past its prime, the car was chauffeured by an imposing man who appeared to know the old gentleman.

Once they had got in, he started to drive without waiting for any directions. After making several turns on big avenues with street lamps, they eventually came out into a dark suburb.

Then the driver turned and said, 'We have arrived. How is the time sir?'

'Just right. It's exactly ten o'clock. Now turn off the lights would you.'

The driver turned a switch, dousing the head and tail lights as well as the lamp in the passenger cabin. With all lights extinguished, the dark vehicle moved along in the pitch black.

Presently the automobile was moving slowly along beside the concrete wall of a large mansion. It could just be made out by the glimmer from the safety lamps standing at half-block intervals.

'Right, Yōko-san, get ready. Quickly now.'

The old man spoke as if urging an athlete.

'Yes. Understood!'

Yōko was all aflutter with the mysterious adventure, but she answered firmly.

Suddenly the car stopped in front of what appeared to be the service entrance to the mansion. At the same time, someone outside jerked open the car door and whispered only 'Quickly.'

Without saying a word, Yōko dashed out of the car. Then, as she had been previously instructed, she rapidly scuttled in through the small doorway.

At the same time, somebody came bundling out in the other direction like a rubber ball, bumping into Yōko's shoulder before bouncing into the car seat she had just vacated.

For the space of an instant, Yōko caught a glimpse of the person by the wan light of a distant electric light. She could not suppress an involuntary shudder.

Had she seen a ghost perhaps? Or had everything up to now been a frightful nightmare?

Yōko had seen another Yōko. In the past, she had heard tell of *doppelgängers*. Was she, then, perhaps seeing one now?

There were now two Sakurayama Yōkos. One had gone in through the side-door – and another had come out and entered the car. And the two people were almost identical in hairstyle as well as clothing. Nor was that all. What scared Yōko to her core was that the other woman's face appeared to be exactly identical to her own.

However, like a black wind, the car containing this other woman had now disappeared down the road from whence it came, leaving Yōko and her bottomless fears behind.

'Right, come this way.'

In the pitch black, she suddenly became aware that the face of the shadowy male figure, who had opened the car door a moment before, was now near her ear.

## CHAPTER 11
## THE SPIDER AND THE BUTTERFLY

THE HOME OF JEWEL MERCHANT Iwase Shōbei was located in Himematsu, on the Nankai Railway Line south of Osaka. Just recently, the top of the concrete wall surrounding his property had been planted with glass shards.

The local people were suspicious, commenting that Mr Iwase had never acted like that sort of unfriendly person before.

But that was not the only thing strange about the Iwase house recently. First of all, the tenants of the old-style *nagaya* house at the gate had changed. Although the family of a long-standing employee had lived there until recently, they had suddenly been replaced by the family of a certain local police inspector, said to be a master of *kendo* swordsmanship.

Poles had been erected here and there throughout the garden, with bright outdoor lanterns hanging from them, and the windows had all been fitted with sturdy steel bars. And in addition to the usual hired help, two well-muscled young men now roomed in the building as bodyguards. The Iwase house was now a small fortress.

And what was he so frightened of, that he felt he had to take such precautions? He was, of course, expecting another attack by the Black Lizard, that woman thief often called the 'female Arsène Lupin.' For a terrible danger was drawing close to Iwase's beloved daughter.

The Black Lizard's kidnapping plans had been foiled by Akechi Kogorō at the Keiō Hotel in Tokyo, but that hadn't been enough to make her give up. She had vowed to capture Sanae. No doubt she had already come to Osaka, incognito. It would not be surprising if she was already in Himematsu, close to Iwase's house.

Akechi was determined never to forget just how tricky she was, what magic she could utilize, as so amply demonstrated at the Keiō Hotel. After that, anyone would have taken these precautions, not just Iwase Shōbei.

And poor Sanae was trapped all alone in an inside room, surrounded by steel bars, and essentially being watched all day long. One adjacent room was occupied by her favourite maid-in-waiting, while Akechi Kogorō slept in the room in front, Akechi having come from Tokyo for that purpose. On both sides of the front hall were the three houseboys and various other maids and helpers. They were all determined to be the first to run to Sanae's aid, if it should come to that, and were waiting eagerly.

Sanae stayed hidden away in her room, not taking a single step outside the walls. And on those rare occasions when she walked in the garden, Akechi or the servants were right with her.

Even that sorceress, the Black Lizard, would not be able to find a loophole here! Demonstrating, perhaps, that it was impossible, Sanae had returned here over two weeks ago and there had not been a single sign of the lady thief.

'Perhaps I was too scared,' thought Iwase, increasingly often. 'Maybe I shouldn't have taken her threats so seriously. Or maybe she has seen our preparations, and given up, recognizing she doesn't have a chance.'

Even as his worries about the kidnapper faded, however, his worries about Sanae grew.

'I wonder if I've been too strict with Sanae. Maybe I shouldn't have imprisoned her in the living room like I have. She was nervous to begin with, and I've only made it worse. It's like she's become a different person: silent and still, with a pale face. If I speak to her, she answers as if she hates talking to me, looking elsewhere. I wish I could improve her mood somehow.'

And as he was thinking, he suddenly recalled the Western-style furniture in the drawing room, which had been delivered just today.

'Of course! She'll be delighted if she sees that!'

The luxurious set of chairs had been ordered over a month ago, and Sanae herself had chosen the fabric to be used.

Iwase felt much better himself for having thought of it, and promptly went to Sanae's room in the depths of the house.

'Sanae, those chairs you liked so much were delivered today. I've already had them placed in the drawing room. Come and see them! They look much finer than I had expected!'

He opened the *fusuma* sliding panel as he spoke, and though Sanae jumped and looked at him, she quickly turned back and slumped down over the table again.

'Ah... but not right now...'

Her voice revealed she had little interest.

'What a cold response! Anyway, get up and come see!' In spite of her unwillingness to go, he led her from the room, calling out to the maid next door, 'I'm going to take Sanae for a few minutes.'

The adjacent room, where Akechi Kogorō slept, was open and empty. He had left earlier that morning to take care of some business. Naturally, before he left he had carefully checked the house, and warned the servants to keep their eyes on Sanae.

Sanae finally arrived at the drawing room, following in the wake of her father.

'How do you like them? Maybe even a bit too pretty, eh?'

He sat down on one of the new chairs as he spoke.

It was an elegant seven-piece set, with sofa, armchairs, backless chairs for the ladies, and a small chair with a wooden back arranged elegantly about a round table.

'Oh, they're beautiful!'

The silent Sanae at last opened her mouth; obviously, she loved the new chairs. She at once sat down on the sofa to test it.

'It's a little too firm,' she said. It felt somewhat different to most sofas.

'It's a little stiff when it's brand new. It'll soften up as we break it in.'

The sofa felt so unusual that if Iwase had only sat down next to Sanae, he would have been suspicious. But he sat there in one of the armchairs, and made no move to try any of the other pieces of furniture.

As they sat there, a houseboy suddenly stuck his head around the corner to say there was a telephone call; someone from the office in Osaka, it seemed. Iwase hurried off to the desktop telephone in the other room, but even so he did not forget to call into the houseboys' room and order them to watch out for Sanae, who was in the drawing room.

When he called, two servants at once stepped into the hall and took up watch. At the end of the hall was the drawing room, and no-one could enter that room except by passing the servants.

Of course, the drawing room had a number of windows opening on to the garden, but they were all fitted with those stern steel bars. Every path to Sanae, whether from the hall or the garden, was blocked. And had they not been, Iwase would never have left Sanae alone in that room even for an urgent telephone call.

The telephone call made it necessary for Mr Iwase to travel to Osaka immediately. He changed quickly, and left the house, seen off by his wife and the servants.

'Watch after Sanae. She's in the drawing room right now. I asked the servants to keep an eye on her, but please go watch her yourself, too,' he begged of his wife as the servant tied his shoelaces.

She waited for him to climb into the motorcar, and then went toward the drawing room to see how her daughter was doing when suddenly she heard the sound of the piano.

'Sanae's playing the piano! She hasn't played for quite some time now. I'm so glad she's feeling better! I'll just leave her to herself for a bit longer.'

Feeling much happier now about her daughter, she warned the servants not to let down their guard, and returned to the living room.

After her father had left, Sanae sat in each chair in turn, comparing their softness, or stood looking out the window. Finally, she opened the piano and began to tap keys at random. She gradually became interested in what she was playing and began a child's song, then changing to a selection from an opera.

She remained fascinated by the piano for some time, but at last even that palled, and she stood to return to the living room. As she turned, she was transfixed with horror at the totally unexpected sight that met her eyes.

But how could it happen? All paths to this room were locked, whether from the garden or the hallway! There were no spaces behind the piano or any of the furniture that a person could hide in, and these modern chairs were so low nobody could possibly hide under one. Until just a moment ago there had been no other living thing in this room, even a cat, other than Sanae.

In spite of which, a bizarre figure now stood in front of Sanae. Hair stuck out in all directions, scraggly whiskers covered its face and constantly glittering, terrifying eyes watched, above a suit torn and filthy... Without even stopping to think of who this demonic man might be or how he had gotten here, she had no doubt that he was one of the Black Lizard's minions!

It had started exactly as the Black Lizard had promised. Just as people had begun to let down their guard, the kidnapper slipped

*It had started exactly as
the Black Lizard had promised.*

through their defences like a magician, sneaking through the door like a ghost.

'Ah, ah, ah! Mustn't make a sound, dear. I'll not hurt you, never fear. After all, you're a precious daughter to us, too.'

His threatening voice was pitched low.

Even without his warning, though, poor Sanae was so terrified that she could not move a muscle or even think of screaming for help.

Smiling eerily, the kidnapper stepped smartly around behind Sanae, and pulled something like a balled-up handkerchief from his pocket. He suddenly swooped down on her, covering her mouth with the handkerchief.

Sanae felt a disgusting pressure along her shoulders and chest, as if she was being smothered by a giant snake. With the handkerchief pressed against her mouth, it was difficult to breathe. She could not remain still an instant longer! She gathered all the strength she had, and struggled to escape from her tormentor's grasp. Like a beautiful butterfly caught in a spider's web, she fluttered hopelessly.

But her furious hands and feet gradually lost their power, and she finally fell still. The anæsthetic had done its job.

When the butterfly's wings stopped fluttering, the kidnapper laid her down gently on the carpet, rearranging her clothing primly and looking down into her gentle, sleeping face with a malicious smile.

## CHAPTER 12
## TRANSFORMATION OF A YOUNG LADY

ALTHOUGH THE SOUND of the piano had stopped over thirty minutes earlier, there was still no sign of Sanae leaving the drawing room. Until just a few minutes ago random noises had issued from the room, but now there was only silence, and the room behind the door was quiet as the grave.

'She's been in there pretty long now... 'bout time she came back, isn't it?'

'It's so quiet... Too quiet! Something funny's going on here!'

The two houseboys on guard, unable to stand it any longer, began to whisper to each other, and just then the maid-in-waiting came from the back, worried about her charge.

'Is the young miss in the drawing room? And the master is with her, of course?'

She was unaware that Mr Iwase had left suddenly on business.

'No, the master had a call from the company, and has gone to Osaka,' they informed her. She looked unhappy at the news.

'That's why we're on guard here, but quite some time has passed and she still hasn't come out. It's been so quiet we were beginning to get worried.'

'Well, then, I'll just go and have a look myself!' said the maid-in-waiting, walking briskly to the door and pulling it open. She took a glance inside, then abruptly slammed it shut and ran back to where the houseboys were waiting. Her face was white as a sheet.

'This is terrible! Go look for yourselves! A strange person is sleeping on the sofa! And I can't see the young miss at all! Seize him, quickly! Oh, it's so frightening!'

The houseboys did not believe her, of course. They wondered if she might be crazy. However, they had no choice but to go and look for themselves. They swung the door open and rushed into the drawing room.

Astonishing at it was, the maid-in-waiting had not been lying. As she had said, there was someone lying on the sofa, slumping as if dead. A man who looked like a beggar, with a torn suit and bewhiskered face.

'Get up! Who are you!' shouted one of the houseboys, a well-built man with a first *dan* judo belt, as he shook the man's shoulder.

'Ugh! He's drunk as a skunk! And the cheek of him scattering his junk on the sofa!'

The houseboy jumped back, almost comically, holding his nose.

And as evidence of his drunken state, the man's face was unnaturally pale; and large – and empty – whiskey bottles rolled on the floor under the sofa. If he had indeed been drinking in this room he was perhaps a little too drunk for the short time he must have been there, but the houseboys were too shocked at events to notice.

They shook him awake. He opened his eyes to slits, then shakily raised his upper torso as he moistened his disgustingly dirty lips with a red tongue.

'Ah, very sorry chaps. I'm done for. Can' drink 'nother drop.'

As if mistaking the stately drawing room for a bar, he babbled incomprehensibly at the houseboys.

'Idiot! Where do you think you are!? Wake up and tell us how you got in here!'

'Wha...? How I got in? Heh, heh, takes a thief to catch a thief, right? I know where the best liquor's hidden, easy enough...'

'Enough of that. Where's the young lady? I can't see her anywhere! He must have done something!' broke in the other houseboy, suddenly noticing her absence.

They searched every corner of the room, and strange as it was, there was no sign of anyone except for the totally unknown drunkard. What in the world could it mean? Had Sanae, in some feat of magical art, been transformed into this disgusting drunkard in a matter of only 30 minutes or so? When they thought about what had happened before they took up watch, and what they saw now, they could think of no other answer...

'Hey, when did you enter this room? There should have been a beautiful young girl in here; you didn't see her? Answer me properly!'

No matter how they shook his shoulder, the man showed no sign of feeling it.

'Ooo... a beautiful young girl, huh? That'd be nice, huh? Well, bring her in! ...to see the face of a beautiful girl again, after all this time... Lemme see! Hurry up, come on! Bring on the gals! Yee-haw!'

It was inconsequential drivel.

'We're just wasting time asking this fool questions. Let's just call the police and let them take care of him. Leave him here any longer and he'll cover the whole room with his disgusting filth!'

Mrs Iwase, alerted by the maid-in-waiting, came running in, but when the fastidious woman heard that a drunkard who looked like a beggar was vomiting in the drawing room, she was unable to force herself to enter the room at all. Surrounded by a bevy of maids, she timidly peered into the room from the doorway, but when she heard the houseboy's comment she immediately agreed.

'Yes, do so at once! Call the policeman right now! Someone! Call the police!'

And so the vagabond was thrown into the jail at the local police station, but after the two policemen had frog-marched him off, feet dragging, the room was left with a thick miasma of vomit, which emanated from the disgusting pool on the sofa.

'And that was such a beautiful sofa, just delivered today!' said the maid-in-waiting, looking in the door with a frown on her face. 'Oh, dear! It's more than just dirty. Look! It's ripped, too! My goodness! He must have been carrying a knife! The upholstery is ruined!'

'Oh, and it was just finished! What a shame! We can't leave that here in the drawing room. Somebody call the furniture store and have them come pick it up at once! It'll have to be reupholstered.'

The fastidious Mrs Iwase demanded that the filthy sofa be removed from her home as soon as possible.

Once the uproar about the drunk died down, people once again noticed that Sanae had vanished. Of course, Mr Iwase was notified at once. Akechi, who had told them where he would be, was also notified by telephone to return at once.

A manhunt was started through every corner of the house... three policemen and all of the houseboys and other servants began the search in the drawing room, moving to Sanae's room, then upstairs, downstairs and even under the garden patio.

However, the beautiful girl had vanished like the mist in the morning sunlight. Strange as it was, there was not a single trace of her anywhere in the house.

## CHAPTER 13
## THE MAGICIAN'S STRANGE TRICK

HAVING BEEN INFORMED promptly about the commotion with the drunk, Iwase and Akechi arrived back from Osaka a couple of hours later. In Iwase's lounge the pair were talking animatedly about the baffling event. Mrs Iwase and the nanny looked on from the side. The two servants on duty at the time had been summoned and were waiting self-effacingly.

'What a mistake on my part. Really, it seems I let my guard slip.'

Akechi appeared to feel he was very much to blame.

'No, no, it wasn't your mistake. I'm the one to blame. My daughter seemed extremely downcast and I let her go into the drawing room because I felt sorry for her, but that was wrong of me. If anyone let his guard slip, it was me.'

Mrs Iwase spoke in a similar vein to her husband.

Putting an end to something that was now in the past, Akechi said, 'But it doesn't help to say these things now. Rather, we need to find out when your daughter left the drawing room and where she was taken to.'

'You're right. And that's just what I can't understand. You, Kurata, you lot didn't keep your eyes open, did you? Didn't you see my daughter leave the room?'

The servant named Kurata replied to Iwase with a somewhat disgruntled expression, 'No, I am sure she didn't! We guarded the door carefully. And if Miss Sanae left the drawing room to go to another room, she would have to use the corridor where we were standing. There is absolutely no way that we would not see her passing in front of our eyes.'

'Hrrmph! You're very cocky aren't you! So how did my daughter disappear then? Are you saying that she broke through those thick steel bars on the window and jumped out or something? Well, what do you say? Perhaps the grille wasn't on properly, mmh?'

When Iwase's emotions got the better of him, he tended to become sarcastic.

The servant instantly assumed a respectful demeanour and, while scratching his head, provided straight answers regarding what he actually knew.

'There is no sign that the grille – or for that matter the window glass and the latch – had been tampered with.'

'There you have it then! She must have slipped past you, right?'

'Let's hold on shall we. I don't think they overlooked anything. They would have had to have missed not only your daughter but the drunk coming into the drawing room... and, no matter how inattentive they might have been, I think it unlikely that they would not have noticed the entrance and exit of two people.'

Akechi was lost in thought.

'Well it might appear unlikely but that is what happened!'

Iwase spoke with increasing vitriol, but Akechi continued unheedingly.

'The steel bars have not been broken. And if the servants let nothing slip there is only one conclusion. No-one came into the room or left the room.'

'Hah! So are you saying that Sanae transformed into that drunk? You've got to be kidding. My daughter isn't a hermaphrodite!'

'Mr Iwase, you showed your daughter some newly built chairs, didn't you? Were those chairs delivered today?'

'That's right. They were delivered just after you went out.'

'Somewhat peculiar, don't you think? Doesn't it strike you that there might be a link between the delivery of the chairs and the abduction of your daughter? It does me...'

The detective narrowed his eyes and seemed to sink into deep thought for a while. Then with a start he lifted his head and uttered something that seemed without meaning.

'"The Human Chair." Could that novelist's fiction become reality?'

Then Akechi stood up and with a very preoccupied look suddenly went out of the room without saying anything to anyone.

Surprised by the famous detective's outlandish behaviour, they all just stood there dumbstruck looking at each other. Then they heard Akechi run back and shout from the corridor.

'Where has the sofa been put? I can't see it in the drawing room!'

'Mr Akechi, calm down please. At the moment we are concerned about my daughter.'

After Iwase spoke, Akechi finally came back into the room. But standing fixedly in front of them he asked, 'No, I want to know where the sofa is. Where has it gone?'

One of the servants answered, 'Well, I said so before, but ... The man from the furniture shop came to pick it up and I handed it over. He had been told by Mrs Iwase to replace the torn section.'

'Is that right Mrs Iwase?'

'Yes. That drunk left it in such a state – all ripped up and filthy – I told them to come and pick it up quickly.'

'Ah... is that so. You've gone and done something unwise. And it's probably too late now... But, then maybe... yes, just maybe I was wrong. May I use your phone?'

Muttering softly in a somewhat distracted way, the detective snatched up the receiver from the phone set on the table.

'You there, tell me phone number of the furniture shop.'

Akechi repeated the number loudly to the operator as he heard it from the servant.

'Hello, is that the Nakano Furniture Shop? This is the Iwase residence. Your people just came to pick up a sofa. Has it arrived at your end yet?'

From the other end of the line came a confusing response, 'Eh? A sofa? Oh, yes, I understand. Er, sorry about taking so long. Actually, I was just about to send one of my men to pick it up.'

Akechi shouted back impatiently, 'What did you say? You are going to send someone to pick it up now? Are you certain? We have already handed it over at this end.'

'I'm afraid that can't be. No-one has gone from here yet.'

'Are you the boss? Look I want you to make sure. Is it possible that someone came here without you knowing?'

'No, they couldn't have. I haven't yet told anyone from the shop to visit the mansion, so there's no reason why any of our people would go there.'

Once he had heard this, Akechi slammed down the receiver. Still standing, he looked as though he was about to run off somewhere again, but he seemed to change his mind. Instead, he rang the local police and asked for the officer in charge of investigations. On the first day that he had become a guest of the Iwase household, Akechi had made sure to establish himself on friendly terms with this officer. In the present situation, this stood him in good stead.

'This is Akechi, the detective, at the Iwase house. It's about the sofa that was damaged by that drunk. Someone pretending to be from the furniture shop has taken it from the mansion, stuck it on a truck and made off. I don't know where they went, but could you put out an all-points-bulletin and have the criminal arrested? That's right. Yes, the sofa... "The Human Chair," see? "The Human Chair." No, I'm not kidding. Huh? I think so. There's no other possibility is there? Thank you officer. I am sure that my guess is accurate. I'll telephone you later to give you the details.'

Just as he was about to end the call, he received some important information from the officer.

'What's that? Escaped? He was a vital link! They didn't pay enough attention because they thought he was drunk? Mmh, well it wouldn't hurt, but he's extremely deceptive. I'm sure he's in league with the Black Lizard. And we actually had him! Can't you lay hands on him again? Please do all you can. Lives depend on it... two. Both the sofa and that drunken villain... All right, speak to you later.'

The receiver clattered down. Akechi remained stooped over with a disappointed expression. Everyone had been listening to the phone conversation very anxiously. With each phrase, they had come to understand why the detective had behaved so outlandishly.

'Akechi-san, thanks to that phone conversation I more or less understand what happened. And I'm amazed at your insight. Still, I can't get over the daring, unparalleled trickery of that criminal. So the man who passed himself off as a drunk hid inside a specially prepared sofa that had been switched at some point with the real sofa made by the furniture shop. Then the sofa containing a human being was placed in the drawing room. Next Sanae enters... the man sneaks out from the sofa and my daughter... Akechi-san, was my daughter... did the villain murder...'

Alarmed, Iwase broke off in mid sentence.

Seeking to set Iwase's mind at rest, Akechi replied, 'No, there's been no killing. As you will remember from the Keiō Hotel, she wants your daughter alive.'

'Well, I think so too but... So next, he put my unconscious daughter in the hollow inside of the sofa where he had previously hidden. Then he lay on top and began to feign that he was in a drunken stupor. Ah, that filthy villain.'

86

'Excellent, Mr Iwase. You are as imaginative as the Black Lizard. I believe things happened as you say... The frightening thing about her is that alongside such an extraordinary way of thinking she has the audacity to calmly implement such silly tricks. This idea is exactly like something you would read in a fairy story. There is a certain novelist whose works include a story called "The Human Chair."* The story is about a villain who hides inside a chair and gets up to mischief. The Black Lizard has artfully enacted this novelist's nonsensical imaginings. The soiled man can be found in a story too. The liquid didn't come from his mouth onto the sofa – it was prepared beforehand and then poured on top of the sofa from a bottle. That's right, a bottle. I'm sure that if you checked the liquid remaining inside that large whisky bottle, you would find it is vomit. This actually comes from a story in a very old Western fairy tale. In that story, it isn't vomit but something more disgusting.'

*The reader will find this story, by a certain Mr Edogawa Rampo, in the collection *Japanese Tales of Mystery and Imagination* (Tokyo: Charles E. Tuttle, 1956).

'So what about the drunk escaping from the lock-up?'

'Yes, it seems he got away. Both the drunk and the sofa disappeared just like in a fairy tale.'

Without thinking, Akechi let out a bitter laugh, but he resumed his serious expression and added,

'However, Mr Iwase, I haven't forgotten the pledge I made in the Keiō Hotel. Please rest assured that I will guard your daughter with my life. I have no intention of doing anything foolish. Please have faith in me... Look at my face. Do I seem pale? Do I look worried? Not at all! I am calm! See how calm I am.'

Akechi laughed cheerfully. It did not appear to be bravado. He was grinning in all earnestness. They all looked at the master detective's bright cheerful countenance.

## CHAPTER 14
## THE STAR OF EGYPT

THE NEXT DAY, the story of the abduction of the jeweller's daughter was carried in the national dailies. The local police and the Osaka district constabulary applied all their might to the search for Sanae. Sofas in department store displays, the show windows of furniture stores, and railway station freight storehouses were all the subject of suspicious scrutiny. Some nervous citizens would not sit on their drawing room sofas without first checking the condition of the base.

A full day passed without any news as to the whereabouts of the sofa into which a person had been crammed. Was the beautiful Sanae still alive or had she died? It was as if she had completely vanished from the face of the earth.

Naturally, Mr and Mrs Iwase were very distressed. And given that it was entirely their fault that Sanae had been led into a perilous situation and that the kidnapper had been overlooked, they could not hate anyone. Still, overwhelming sadness and rage caused them to lose perspective and they felt like blaming Akechi for his imprudence in leaving the house.

Of course, Akechi was aware of this feeling. Moreover, in light of his reputation as a master detective, he felt a heavy sense of responsibility regarding the abduction as well as frustration that mistakes could not be undone. Nevertheless, he was not in the least disconcerted, like an ever-victorious army chief who always retains hope in his breast.

'Iwase-san, please believe me when I tell you that your daughter is safe. I promise that I will get her back. Even though she is in the kidnappers' hands, she will definitely come to no harm. They will treat her as carefully as a treasure. There are reasons why they must do so. You should not be concerned in the slightest.'

Rephrasing the same message several ways, Akechi sought to assuage Mr and Mrs Iwase.

'You say you can get our daughter back Akechi-san, but where is she now? Are you suggesting that you know her whereabouts?'

Iwase's question was full of sarcasm.

'Yes, I do. Or as good as.'

Akechi was unmoved.

'Hah! Then would you be so kind as to go and bring her back? Since yesterday, you seem to have just folded your arms and left everything up to the police. If you know as much as you say, please take the appropriate action quickly.'

'Well, actually I'm waiting.'

'What do you mean waiting?'

'For a message from the Black Lizard.'

'For a message? That's silly. Do you mean to say that the criminal will send a message saying "Please come and collect your daughter"?' Iwase's question was laced with loathing, and he snorted derisively.

'That's right!'

The master detective answered like an innocent child.

'I think the criminal might send a message asking us to come and collect your daughter.'

'Hah?! Are you in your right mind? The criminal would never do such a thing... Akechi-san, I'm offended that you make jokes in this situation.'

The jeweller spoke bitterly.

'It's no joke. You're certain to find out at any moment...Aha! Perhaps there'll be a message among these.'

They were sitting facing one another in the drawing room where

Sanae had been kidnapped and just then one of the servants brought in a bundle of letters that had arrived in the afternoon post.

'Among these, you say? A message from the kidnappers?'

Iwase replied absently with a look suggesting this was nonsense. At the same time he took the letters from the servant and checked the sender's name on each. All of a sudden, he let out a sound of surprise and then asked in a panic,

'What's this? What on earth can this be?'

The letter was enclosed in a high-quality Western-style envelope, whose reverse side contained no sender's name. In the lower left corner, however, there was a skilfully-drawn image of a pitch-black lizard.

'It's the Black Lizard.'

Akechi was not in the least surprised. His expression seemed to say 'I told you so!'

'The Black Lizard! It's an Osaka city postmark.'

Iwase's attentive merchant's eye had quickly discerned the seal.

'Akechi-san, how did you know about this beforehand? It is indeed a message from the criminal. Well, I must say...'

He looked at the master detective in admiration. Cantankerous the old fellow might be, but he also regained his composure quickly.

'Please open it. There will be some sort of demand from the Black Lizard.'

Following Akechi's prompting, Iwase opened the envelope carefully and unfolded the letter contained within. Written on the sheet of white paper within, with a clumsiness that somehow looked studied, was the following:

*Dear Mr Iwase,*
*Please excuse yesterday's commotion. Your daughter is in our*

*safekeeping. She is hidden in a place that the police can never find.*

*Would you like to buy your daughter back from me? If you would, you must meet the following conditions for the deal.*

*Payment: The 'Star of Egypt' (which is in your holding)*

*Time: 5:00 p.m. on the seventh (tomorrow)*

*Place: The observation deck at the top of Tsutenkaku Tower in Tennoji Park*

*Method: Iwase Shōbei will bring the item at the above time to the top of Tsutenkaku. He will come alone.*

*If any of the above conditions are not fully met, or this is reported to the police, or there is any capture attempt after the item has been handed over – your daughter will be killed.*

*The above conditions having been carefully adhered to, your daughter will be delivered to her home in the evening of that day. You must comply with the above. Do not reply to this letter. Unless you come to the designated place at the designated time tomorrow, the transaction will be considered incomplete and I will then immediately proceed to the prescribed action.*

*The Black Lizard*

When Iwase had finished reading the letter, an expression of great perplexity came onto his face and he appeared to fall into deep thought.

'Is it the Star of Egypt?'

Akechi had realized what was on the jeweller's mind.

'Yes, I don't know what to do. It's my personal property, but it would be more correct to classify it as a national treasure. And I don't want to turn it over to a vile thief.'

'I understand it is extremely valuable.'

'The market value is a hundred and fifty million yen, but it is too valuable a treasure to exchange for that sum. Do you know the history of the piece?'

'Yes, I have heard.'

The most precious diamond in Japan, The 'Star of Egypt' had originated in South Africa, and as the name suggests, this thirty-carat brilliant cut gem was once kept in the treasure vaults of Egyptian royalty. Later, the stone passed into the hands of various European nobles, before certain circumstances resulted in it being purchased by a jewellery merchant at the time of the Great War. Having changed hands several times thereafter, the diamond had been acquired by the Paris branch of Iwase Co. just a few years ago. Now it was in the keeping of the Osaka head office.

'This stone's got a long history, you know. For me, it's just about as valuable as my own life. I've taken every precaution to make sure that it is not stolen. Apart from me, no-one else knows where the jewel is kept. That includes all the staff at the store and also my wife.'

'So, for the thief, it was easier to steal a living person than a single jewel.'

Akechi was intently nodding to himself.

'Yes. There have been several attempts to steal the Star of Egypt. Each time, I got a little wiser. Finally, I decided to make the hiding place a secret that only I knew. Even the smartest thief can't steal the secret from inside my head... But that trouble is all to no avail now. It didn't occur to me that someone might get their hands on the jewel by demanding it as ransom for my daughter... Akechi-san, it may be a priceless treasure, but it isn't as important as a person's life. I'm afraid I give up. Let's hand over the jewel.'

Iwase's pale face bespoke the firmness of his resolution.

'There's no need to hand over such a valuable piece. You can just ignore that blackmail letter. Nothing will happen to threaten your daughter's life.'

Akechi sought to reassure Iwase, but the stubborn man was not convinced.

'No, there's no knowing what that fearful fiend might do. No matter how valuable the jewel is, it's still just a stone. I couldn't bear it if something should happen to my daughter just because I was reluctant to let go of a stone. I want to go along with the thief's proposal.'

'Well, if you have made up your mind, I can't stop you. Indeed, one stratagem would be to let the enemy think we have fallen into her trap and hand over the jewel. And from my experience as a detective, I think that might even work to our advantage. But please do not worry at all. I make you a firm promise that I will get back both your daughter and the jewel. We will let the thief rejoice, but only for a short while.'

Akechi's confidence and forceful tone suggested that he might have something up his sleeve.

*Thinking she would take out a pistol,*
*he watched as she strode sharply over to the shop,*
*and brought back a pair of rental binoculars.*

## CHAPTER 15
## BLACK LIZARD ON THE TOWER

THE FOLLOWING DAY, just a little before the designated five o'clock in the afternoon, Iwase Shōbei followed the instructions of his enemy to the letter, arriving under the steel tower that scraped the sky, at the entrance to Tennoji Park, without telling anyone other than Akechi Kogorō.

Tennoji Park was the largest amusement district in the Osaka region, its enormous space thronged with pleasure-seekers every day. The interwoven streets were packed with theatres, movie houses, restaurants, and bars of all types, while a veritable symphony was created by street vendors hawking their wares, the sound of record players, crying children, and tens of thousands of shoes and wooden sandals, all shrouded in the dust of their passage. And there in the middle of it all was the Tsutenkaku steel tower, modelled after the Eiffel Tower of Paris, soaring into the clouds and looking down over the streets of Osaka.

How bold! How daring! The Black Lizard had designated the top of a popular sightseeing tower in a bustling amusement zone as the place to pay the ransom. No-one but she would have had the audacity to dare such a drama, such an adventure.

Iwase was a merchant, with fairly steady nerves, but when he realized he would soon be face-to-face with the kidnapper his heart would not stop pounding. A little tense, he boarded the elevator to the top of the tower.

As the elevator rose, the streets of Osaka sank below him. The winter sun was already close to the horizon, and the roofs he could see were half shadowed in black, creating a beautiful rectangular pattern like the go board.

When he finally arrived at the top and stepped out onto the observation platform, which offered a breathtaking three hundred and sixty degree view, the winter wind he had not noticed so much below whipped sharply past his cheeks. Tsutenkaku was not very popular in the winter, and perhaps because it was already dusk, he could not see any another visitors on the platform.

In the little shop selling snacks and fruit and postcards, a couple sat minding the store, protected from the cold by tarpaulins stretched as windbreaks. There was nobody else. It was desolate, as if he had left the human sphere entirely and ascended to some uninhabited marginal space in the sky.

When he leaned over the railing and looked down, he could see thousands and thousands of people scurrying about like ants, contrasting with the solitude of his perch.

He stood, waiting, the cold wind whipping through, and at last the elevator returned, the steel door rattling open to reveal a kimono-clad woman with gold-rimmed spectacles whose appearance suggested she was someone's wife. Grinning, she approached Iwase.

It struck him as strange that such a genteel women should come by herself to this deserted observation platform at such an hour.

'I guess some women just like the view,' he muttered to himself as he watched.

Suddenly, unexpectedly, she laughed and spoke to him directly.

'Oh, Iwase-san! Have you forgotten me already? It's me, Midorikawa! We shared some pleasant moments together in that Tokyo hotel, remember?'

So this woman was Mme Midorikawa – the Black Lizard! She was a monster, a shape-shifter. Donning a kimono and eyeglasses, and gathering her hair into a *marumage* bun, she presented a wholly different appearance. To think that this refined woman was actually that woman thief, the Black Lizard!

Iwase felt a strong sense of hatred at her oh-so-friendly attitude, and stood silently, just staring at her beautiful visage.

'Please accept my sincere apologies for causing such a commotion,' she said, making an elegant curtsy one would not find out of place among the nobility.

'I have nothing to say to you. I've kept to every one of your conditions. You are going to return my daughter, aren't you?'

He was abrupt, refusing to play her theatrical games and getting to the heart of the matter.

'Yes. Of course… She's doing well, please rest assured on that,' advised Mme Midorikawa. 'You did, naturally, bring the promised item, didn't you?'

'Yes, I have it with me. Here. Check it if you like.'

He extracted a small silver box from an inner pocket, and thrust it out in front of her.

'Oh, my, thank you! I'll just take a little peek inside…' she said calmly, taking the box from his hand. She opened the cover, sneaking a peek in behind her hand, and stared hungrily at the huge gemstone in its white velvet setting.

'…exquisite…'

As he watched, her face gradually flushed with excitement… the rare stone had a mysterious fascination capable of reddening the cheeks of thousands of woman thieves.

'Flames of five colours… it truly does look like it's burning in five colours, doesn't it? How I've longed for this! Compared to this Star of Egypt, even the hundred or so diamonds I've collected through long years of work appear mere stones. Thank you ever so much!'

And she gave a long, eminently polite bow.

Although he had resigned himself to this, the more she enthused over the jewel, the more Iwase felt an indescribable hatred bubbling up inside as he thought of this woman robbing him of what he had treasured as the most important thing after his life. The woman in front of his eyes filled him with loathing and anger. And, as was this elderly merchant's wont, he gave in to the urge to express his feelings in words.

'The payment's done. All I have to do now is wait for you to deliver the goods, and I wonder if I can trust you to keep your half of the bargain. After all, I'm dealing with a thief. And there is certainly nothing more dangerous than dealing with a thief on payment-in-advance terms.'

'Oh, I will certainly keep my promise,' she laughed. 'Please, take the elevator down first. I'll be down in a bit.'

Seemingly not even noticing his insults, she announced an end to the bizarre meeting.

'Hmph. Hand over the goods and I'm no use to you anymore, I see… but wouldn't it be better if you came with me? Are you unwilling to ride the elevator with me?'

'I would so very much like to ride with you, but so many people are searching for me, and I really must watch to see that you return home safely…'

'You mean it's not safe. You think I'd follow you? Hah! That's downright silly. Are you afraid of me? If so you picked a pretty solitary spot to meet with me, alone. I'm a man. If I decided to, *if,* mind you, I decided to sacrifice the life of my daughter and capture this woman thief who befouls God's earth, I certainly could.'

Unable to withstand his hatred for her, he finally spoke his mind.

'Yes, I know. That's why I'm prepared for such a thing.'

Thinking she would take out a pistol, he watched as she strode sharply over to the shop, and brought back a pair of rental binoculars.

'You see that smokestack there for the public bath? Please examine the rooftop just behind it,' she said calmly, holding out the binoculars to Iwase and pointing.

'And there's something on the roof?' asked Iwase, unaccountably captured by his curiosity, putting the binoculars to his eyes.

About three blocks from the tower stood a large building. Just behind the smokestack was a wooden deck, and he could clearly see a man, a labourer by his clothes, huddled on top.

'There is a man in Western-style clothing sitting on the deck, right?'

'Yes, he's there. What of it?'

'Look more closely. What is he doing?'

'Well, how strange! He's got a pair of binoculars, and he's looking this way!'

'And doesn't he have something in his other hand?'

'Yes, he does! It looks like a red cloth. I think he's looking at us!'

'You're quite right. That's one of my men. He watching every move we make, and if anything dangerous should happen to me he will wave that red cloth to signal another of my men... who is watching that rooftop from a different place entirely. When that happens, the second man will telephone the house where your daughter is, and your daughter will die.'

She chuckled.

'You may call me a thief, but even thievery is a profession demanding careful preparation.'

And it was indeed a clever plan. There was a reason why she had chosen this inconvenient tower top for the meeting. On the ground, it would have been impossible to observe the encounter from a safe distance.

'Hah! My sympathy for your troubles.'

While he coldly cut her off, inside he could not but admire the foolproof planning of the Black Lizard.

## CHAPTER 16
## THE SECRET LOVERS

**EVEN THOUGH MR IWASE** finally did ride down by himself before her, and left in a car waiting some distance away, the Black Lizard could not relax.

Behind him stood the detested Akechi Kogorō. She could not imagine what ideas he might come up with, or what plots he might hatch.

She picked up the binoculars again, and carefully examined the throngs of people milling about at the base of the tower. She checked carefully to see if anyone was acting strangely, and while she was observing the dizzying swirls of the crowd below, she gave sway to her own inner fears.

Perhaps that man over there in the suit, looking up at the tower, was a detective? That beggar who had been sleeping there all day looked suspicious, too. Akechi's men could have disguised themselves.

With so many people, it would be easy enough for Akechi himself to adopt a disguise and walk the streets below!

Growing increasingly irritated, she walked the periphery of the observation platform, binoculars to her eyes.

She had no fear of being captured. Her enemy must surely know that the precious Sanae would lose her life if that happened. She was worried about being followed. If she was tailed by a professional, no matter how smartly she rode about, she would be unable to shake him. And Akechi was exactly such a professional at following people. If Akechi Kogorō was hiding in that crowd, and followed her to where Sanae was without being noticed... even the Black Lizard, hardened criminal that she was, shuddered at the thought.

'I guess I'll have to do it after all,' she said to herself. 'It always pays to play it safe.'

She strode back to the shop, and called to the counterwoman.

'I would like to ask a favour of you... would you be willing to help me out a bit?'

The couple, a man and a woman huddled around a charcoal fire warming their hands, lifted their faces in surprise.

'May I help you with something?' asked the gentle-looking woman, smiling pleasantly.

'No, I don't want to buy anything. But I do have a request to make of you, if I may. You saw the gentleman I was speaking to a few minutes ago? He is a devil! I have been blackmailed by that criminal and something terrible could happen! Please, won't you help me? I managed to convince him to leave, but I'm sure he's still waiting for me at the foot of the tower! Please, I beg you! Would you pretend to be me for just a little while, and stand at the railing there? Thanks to that tarpaulin, we can exchange clothing, with you becoming me and me, you. Fortunately we are of the same age and even the same hairstyle, so I'm sure it will all go well.

'And, kind sir, if I may beg your assistance, could you possibly escort me a little distance as though I was your wife? I would be more than happy to repay you for your time, of course! Here, you can have all the money I have! Please, I beg of you!'

She entreated them as she pulled out her wallet, extracted seven one-thousand yen notes, and pressed them into the woman's hand in spite of her protestations.

The couple exchanged a few words with each other, but were astonished by the unexpected profit they had just gained, and readily acceded to her request without doubting her tale.

The canvas windbreaks covered the entire area, so it was a simple matter to exchange clothing in the store, totally hidden from the outside world. The pale-faced shopkeeper donned the soft kimono worn by the Black Lizard, straightened her hair, and put on the gold-rimmed spectacles, metamorphosing into a refined lady of the upper class.

And the transformation of the Black Lizard was a sight to behold. She undid her hair, then smeared dirt over her palms to smudge her entire face, turning into the perfect image of a lower-class shopkeeper's wife. The striped kimono and stained apron went well with the dark blue *tabi* socks, which had been darned.

She gave a delighted laugh.

'Oh, it's wonderful! How do I look?'

'Incredible!' the man praised her. 'The little woman looks like a high-class lady, and yourself, Ma'am, you are all dirty! A wonderful job! Even your own husband wouldn't know you!'

He stood comparing them with each other, flabbergasted.

'Ah, you were wearing a gauze mask, weren't you?' asked the Black Lizard. 'That would be perfect. May I borrow it?'

The white gauze mask, commonly used to prevent colds from spreading, hid her mouth entirely.

'Would you be so kind as to stand at the railing there, and look around through the binoculars, my dear?'

Then the kidnapper, disguised as a lowly shopkeeper, rode the elevator down with her 'husband' to the bustling street.

'Please hurry! It would be terrible if he found me again!'

They pushed their way through the crowd and away from the street of movie theatres, through the clumps of trees in the park toward the quiet, less crowded regions.

'Thank you so much... I think everything's all right now. Oh, my goodness! We're acting like lovers hiding from someone!'

And indeed that is exactly what they appeared to be. The man, perhaps because of a pain in his ear, had a bandage wrapped around his head and jaw, with a deerstalker cap on top, and he was wearing a striped cotton kimono with a black shirt over it. He wore board-soled *zōri*, bound with leather straps to his bare feet. She was dressed as his wife, as mentioned before, and both wore bizarre white masks. The man took the woman's hand and they wove between the trees, trying to keep out of sight as they trotted down the road together.

'Ah! Sorry, forgive me,' apologized the man, suddenly noticing that he had been holding her hand and letting go bashfully.

'Oh, please, don't worry about it… What happened to your head?' asked the Black Lizard, appreciative of his help in escaping her predicament.

'Just an inner ear infection,' he replied. 'It's just about healed now.'

'My goodness! You have to be careful with an ear infection,' she advised him. 'You must be happy to have such a wonderful wife. How enjoyable to be able to work together like that.'

'Her!? Nah, she's not much to talk about,' he shrugged.

*'A bit soft, this chap,'* she chuckled to herself.

'Well, I guess I'll be off now. Please thank your wife for me; I'll not forget your help today! Oh, and please tell your wife it's just an old kimono, and I'd be delighted if she kept it.'

A taxi was waiting on the avenue cutting through the park, just next to the trees. After she left the shopkeeper, she ran for the car.

The driver hurriedly opened the door, as if he had been waiting just for her. She vanished inside and uttered a short signal, and the taxi immediately began to drive on. Surely it was driven by one of her men, who had been waiting for her there by plan.

After the shopkeeper saw the car begin to move, instead of returning to the tower he ran into the street, inexplicably, and spun about searching for something. He shot up a hand to hail a passing taxi and leaped into the empty car. He called to the driver crisply, his voice totally different from the drawl of only moments ago.

'Follow that car! Police! I promise you a healthy tip, just do a good job of it!'

The taxi immediately moved off in pursuit, keeping a healthy distance behind.

'Make sure they don't notice us following them,' the man warned the taxi driver every so often, leaning forward and staring eagerly ahead like a jockey on a racehorse.

He had identified himself as a policeman, but was he really? He certainly did not appear to be an officer of the law. His voice sounded so familiar... no, not just his voice. Those sharp eyes staring forward from under the bandage around his head certainly seemed familiar!

## CHAPTER 17
## THE CHASE

**THROUGH THE GRIM WINTER DUSK,** the two automobiles played their bizarre game of follow-the-leader, threading their way between the host of taxis on Sakai-suji Avenue, a major north-south artery piercing Osaka, with the second car always maintaining a careful distance behind the first vehicle.

In the lead car, a beautiful young woman, dressed in the kimono and apron of a lower-class worker, sat by herself squeezed into the cushions as if hiding.

At first glance, she appeared far too poor to be using a taxi. In fact, though, this was the woman thief, the Black Lizard, in disguise!

But even this thief did not notice that just behind her another car was hot on her trail, chasing her like a wolf. In it sat a strange man dressed like a lower-class worker, head heavily bandaged, gaze locked fiercely on her car as he uttered short commands like 'Speed up!' or 'Slow down a bit!'

Who was this strange man?

Eyes fixed on the lead car, he quickly stripped off his woollen overcoat and striped kimono. From beneath, a lightly soiled khaki uniform appeared, transforming him in an instant from a shopkeeper to a factory worker.

Once he had completed his metamorphosis into a labourer, he began to tear off the bandages which had covered half his face. His face gradually emerged into view. He had not had an ear problem at all! He had merely used that as a convenient excuse to hide his face!

The line of his thick eyebrows above his piercing eyes revealed the identity of the mysterious man: it was Akechi Kogorō.

He had seen through the Black Lizard's scheme, disguising himself as the shopkeeper, waiting with determination to penetrate her secret and finally discover the whereabouts of her headquarters.

She had fallen into his trap unaware, and had even unwittingly asked him to assist in her escape! If he had wanted to apprehend her he could have done so at any time, but until they knew where the kidnapped girl was, until they discovered the Black Lizard's secret base, they could take no overt action. He quieted his racing heart, forced to suffer this prolonged pursuit. His plan was to recover both the girl and the jewel at once, and at the same time hand over the Black Lizard, the infamous woman thief, to the hands of the law.

It was dark outside now, and the cars careened past streetlamp after streetlamp, winding their tortuous way in a bizarre race through the streets of Osaka.

The cabin light was off in her car, so his only glimpse of her was a blurry image of her head through the rear window when a chance light struck. Naturally, Akechi had closed the gap between their cars as much as he thought safe.

The cars turned a corner, and there was one of the famous canals of Osaka. The shutters of a wholesalers district lined one side of the canal, while the other gently sloped upward, scattered with freight-handling machinery. The night was black, and the district surprisingly deserted for a site in huge Osaka.

The lead car slowly nosed into the darkness, and when it reached the foot of a bridge it suddenly halted under a bright streetlamp.

'Stop! Quickly!'

While Akechi was ordering the driver of his own car to stop, the other taxi had already turned around and was coming their way.

The red 'Available' light was on, visible through the windshield.

The rear seat, inexplicably, was suddenly empty. Before he had a chance to even think about what had happened, the suspicious taxi had reached them. Honking rather obviously, it drove slowly past.

Akechi was able to see every part of the other taxi, only a foot away. There was no doubt that it was empty. There was no trace of the woman who had been visible until only moments ago.

Clearly, the driver was one of her men and the taxi belonged to her, but to avoid attracting the attention of the police it was camouflaged as an empty taxi, driven by a blandly smiling driver.

He debated arresting the driver, but quickly abandoned the idea because it would destroy the plan entirely. He had to find the Black Lizard! And he had to discover her hiding place!

But where in the world had that woman hidden herself? No-one had alighted from the taxi when it stopped at the foot of the bridge. Under the bright streetlamp, he could not have missed it. But only moments ago, when the car had turned onto the river-bank, she had clearly been sitting inside.

Could it be that in the half a block or so between the corner and the bridge, the kidnapper had taken advantage of the darkness to leap out of the moving taxi and hide herself? But where? Along one side was a line of commercial buildings, their giant doors shuttered for the night, and on the other side there was only the black water of the canal. Akechi stepped out of his car, and walked down and back along that half-block, checking carefully. There was nobody – not even a dog – anywhere along it.

'Weird, huh?' said the driver jokingly when Akechi returned, 'Surely she didn't jump into the canal…'

'The river. Perhaps she did,' responded Akechi as he looked down from the wharf to see a large, old-style wooden boat.

There was no sign of anyone on deck, but he could see the red glare of a lantern through the oilpaper *shōji* windows in the stern. The family owning and running the boat would be living in the cabin, and when he checked he noted that the gangplank was still in place. Possibly, just possibly, the Black Lizard was hiding in the shadow of that reddish light, quieting her every breath.

It was terribly unlikely, but there was no other place she could have fled to. When it came to the Black Lizard, common sense had to be thrown out the window. Think of the unreasonable, the unlikely, and you stood a better chance of guessing correctly.

'Can you help me out here?' asked Akechi, handing over a bill while whispering into the driver's ear. 'See that window where the light's on there? I want you to turn your lights off for a moment, and move the car so that when you turn them back on you light up that door. First though, and this is a slightly taller order, I want you to scream. Scream out for someone to help you in as loud a voice as you can, then suddenly switch on the lights. Can you do that?'

'A pretty strange request… Right, if that's what you need, I'll do it!'

The cash convinced the driver to play along, and he at once turned out the car's headlights, then quietly moved the vehicle as directed.

Akechi, still in his factory worker's clothes, used both hands to pick up a rock from the roadside, and scrambled down to the riverside.

'Help! Someone, help!'

Suddenly, the driver's scream came, sounding as if he was in deadly fear of his life.

And just at the same time, there was a loud splash as if something heavy had fallen into the canal. Akechi had thrown in the rock, but a listener would surely think that someone had dived in.

As expected, the oilpaper window on the boat opened, and a face peered out. The headlights suddenly went on, catching the person full in the face. The detective got a good look at the face even as it suddenly pulled back – it was the Black Lizard! The Black Lizard, in the form of the shopkeeper!

She could not see Akechi at all, of course. It was clear that she had not noticed them tailing her, or else she would never have stuck her head out the window.

Surprised at the disturbance, the hired labourers rattled open the windows and popped out onto the deck.

'What was that?'

'Probably another fight. Didn't someone fall in?'

'I heard something fall into the canal!'

By then, the taxi driver had already changed direction, and had driven half a block away.

Akechi ran along the riverbank to the public telephone at the foot of the bridge.

The enemy was planning on utilizing the waterway! There was no telling how far the pursuit might continue, and he had to let his comrades know what was up!

## CHAPTER 18
## A GHOST STORY

**BEFORE LIGHT THE NEXT MORNING,** a steamer with a deadweight of less than two hundred tonnes set out from Osaka's Kawaguchi port. Thanks to the absence of any wind-swell, sailing conditions were excellent and the small vessel flew over the sea's mill-pond surface with surprising swiftness, arriving off the southern tip of the Kii Peninsula by the afternoon. However, instead of making for a harbour or toward Kii Bay, she moved straight into the Pacific Ocean bound for the Enshū Sea (off the coast of Shizuoka Prefecture). Despite her diminutive size, the daring vessel was plotting a course more likely to be taken by a large trans-Pacific liner.

From the outside, she seemed to be an ordinary scruffy freighter. Inside, though, there were no cargo holds. Underneath the hatches, the drabness of the exterior gave way to an array of amazingly luxurious cabins. Although made to look like a freighter, she was actually a passenger vessel – or rather a luxury residence.

The spacious and well-appointed cabin located near the aft was particularly impressive. It would surely be the living quarters of the ship's master.

A costly Persian rug covered the floor and hanging from the pure white ceiling was a chandelier so exquisite you would not imagine you were aboard a ship. In addition, there was an ornate wardrobe, a round table with a tablecloth, a sofa, and a few armchairs.

However, the harmony was spoilt by a sofa in the corner whose clashing pattern made it stand out.

But wait! Have we not seen this sofa somewhere before? Aha! See the mark where a rent has been darned? It must be *that* sofa.

The one that was borne off from Iwase's drawing room three days previously after Sanae had been shoved inside. But why would it be on board this ship?

And given that the sofa is on the vessel, could it be that... But there can be no doubt. For so absorbed have we been with the sofa that we have overlooked the person sitting on it. How could we forget this sombre beauty? Lustrous are the black silk Western clothes through which her ample form shows and sparkling the jewels in her ears, at her breast, and on her fingers. The Black Lizard! The lady thief who twenty-four hours ago had hidden behind the oil-paper *shōji* on a large old-style wooden boat, unaware that she was being tailed by Akechi.

Overnight, the wooden vessel concealing the lady thief had rowed down the Edagawa and Ōgawa rivers to Kawaguchi, where the Black Lizard had transferred to the steamer which was moored there for the night.

So what kind of vessel was this small steamer? If it was an ordinary trading ship, a female robber would not be lording it in the best cabin as if it was her own. Could it be, by any chance, that the Black Lizard is the vessel's owner?

If so, that would explain the presence of the 'human chair'. And if this is the 'human chair', then perhaps Sanae, who had been enclosed inside the sofa, is now being held captive somewhere on board.

However that may be, we must now adjust our gaze to take in the doorway of the cabin where another character stands.

If this was a normal trading vessel, the seaman's cap with its gold braid insignia and the black-piped uniform buttoned up to the chin would suggest he might be the ship's purser. But haven't we seen this chap somewhere too? That squashy nose and sturdy frame make him look just like a boxer... Yes, it's him – the criminal pugilist who disguised himself as Dr Yamakawa and kidnapped Sanae in Tokyo's Keiō Hotel, the underling who pledged his life to the Black Lizard – Amamiya Jun'ichi, Jun-chan, in a new guise.

'What? Don't tell me you're worried about it as well. You're a grown man and yet you're afraid of ghosts? Dear oh dear!'

A sardonic smile could be seen on the Black Lizard's beautiful face as she reclined leisurely on the sofa.

'I tell you, I'm getting the creeps. There's something strange going on. And everyone on board, every single one of them, is becoming superstitious. I bet you'd be frightened too if you heard that thing whispering away out of sight.'

There was fear in the 'purser's' eyes as he swayed from side to side with the motion of the ship.

Inside the cabin, the chandelier shone brightly, but beyond the single metal plate forming the wall, night had fallen and all that could be seen was black water. Black sky. Although it was quiet, swells with mountainous peaks came sweeping in at intervals. And when they did, the small frail craft rocked helplessly in the infinite darkness like a fallen leaf.

'What exactly has happened? Tell me the details. Who saw this ghost?'

'Nobody has actually seen it. But Kitamura and Gōda say they definitely heard its voice at different times. So it's not just one person – two people have heard the same voice.'

'Where?'

'In our "guest's" cabin.'

'Sanae's cabin?'

'That's right. Today around lunch time, Kitamura heard some-body whispering in a low voice inside the cabin when he walked past the door. It was when you, me, and the rest were all in the dining room. Sanae was gagged so she couldn't have said anything. Thinking it might be one of the crew playing a prank, he went to open the door but it was still locked on the outside. Kitamura says he thought something wasn't right so he hurried to get the key and tried to open the door.'

'So the little lady had taken off her gag, right? And then I suppose she probably started muttering curses.'

'But the gag was still firmly in place. And the rope binding her hands didn't appear particularly loose. Of course, there was nobody in the cabin apart from her. Kitamura says he shuddered when he realized that.'

'Well, did he ask Sanae?'

'Yes, he took off the gag to ask her, but she was terrified herself and said she didn't know a thing.'

'A peculiar story. I wonder if it's true.'

'I wondered too. Assuming that Kitamura's ears had played a trick on him, I didn't think any more of it. But strangely enough, just an hour ago, again when we were all in the dining room, Gōda heard the voice. He also says he went to get the key and opened the door. Just as in Kitamura's case, there was no sign of anyone else in the room and there was nothing unusual about Sanae's gag. News of this second eerie happening spread among the crew pretty quickly and now it's become one of those ghost stories that teachers are so good at telling.'

'What are they saying?'

'Well you know this lot have all got shady pasts. Two or three of them have even done time for murder. They can sense the spirit world. To tell you the truth, it even gives me the shivers to hear that a vengeful ghost is stalking this ship.'

Another big swell came through and the hull lifted higher and higher making a strange low sound, before finally sinking into the bottomless pit.

At that precise moment, perhaps due to generator trouble, the light in the chandelier turned a brownish red and began blinking dully as if sending some sort of signal.

'What a horrid evening,' Jun'ichi muttered, looking fearfully at the flickering light.

'And you a grown man! What a cry-baby!'

The laughter from the woman in the black dress echoed eerily from the steel-plated hull.

Just then, as if in reply to the woman's laugh, the door slid open and something white came in. It wore a white flat cap, a white button-up jacket, and a white apron. The fat face, which resembled that of a chubby good-luck god, looked anxious. This was the ship's cook.

'Oh, it's you is it? What's wrong with you? You gave me a fright.'

In response to Jun'ichi's scolding, the cook began to quietly report what had happened with the utmost seriousness.

'Something weird's happened again. This ghost thing has been sneaking around in the galley. A whole chicken is missing.'

'A chicken?'

Asked the woman in black dubiously.

'Yeah, but it wasn't alive or anything! There were seven plucked, boiled chickens hanging inside the pantry door. Exactly seven. I saw them there when I was preparing lunch. But when I looked a while ago, one was gone. There were only six birds.'

'We didn't have chicken at dinner did we?'

'No, and that's why it's strange. Nobody on this boat is a big eater. There's nobody who would steal something like that – unless we're talking about a ghost.'

'Are you sure you aren't mistaken?'

'No way! Actually, I've got a very sharp memory.'

*'I tell you, I'm getting the creeps.*
*There's something strange going on.'*

'This is strange now, isn't it Jun-chan? Why don't you all split up and search the ship. Maybe there is something on board.'

After the series of weird events, even the lady thief felt uneasy.

'Yes, I was thinking that too. Whether it's a spirit of the dead or the living, it must be something corporeal if it's speaking and stealing food. If we do a thorough search we might be able to find out the identity of this ghost.'

The 'purser' then left the cabin to give instructions for the search of the vessel.

Suddenly remembering, the cook then said to his lady-chief, 'Oh, and then there was a message from the pretty young miss.'

'From Sanae, you mean?'

'Yes, just a moment ago, when I took her meal in. I untied her hands and took off the gag and I don't know what had changed today but she wolfed the whole lot down as if she was really enjoying it. Then she asked me not to tie her up, promising that she wouldn't make a fuss and scream.'

'She said that she would behave?'

The woman in black asked in surprise.

'That's what she says. According to her, she's completely changed her mind. She's very cheerful. You wouldn't think she was the same young lady as yesterday, she's altered so much.'

'Mmm, how peculiar. Tell Kitamura to bring her here, would you.'

The cook left to do as ordered. A short while later, Sanae was led into the cabin by the crewman called Kitamura, who was holding her unbound hand.

## CHAPTER 19
## THE FRIGHTFUL ENIGMA

SANAE LOOKED TERRIBLY STRAINED. The plain silk clothes she had been wearing when she was kidnapped were now all crumpled and creased. Loose strands from her dishevelled hair covered her pale brow and her cheeks were hollow. The bent temple-pieces of her eyeglasses made them hang awkwardly from her nose, which seemed slightly more prominent.

'How do you feel Sanae? Don't stand over there – come and sit beside me.' The woman in black spoke gently, motioning with her finger to the sofa on which she sat.

'Fine.'

Meekly doing as she was bid, Sanae advanced two or three steps. However, when she recognized the sofa on which the woman in black was sitting a look of fear came into her face and letting out a gasp as if she had seen a ghost she began to back up.

The 'human chair.' The terrifying memory of being stuffed inside that dreadful chair three days ago came vividly into her mind.

'Oh, this thing is it? You're afraid of the sofa? Well, I guess you've got reason to be. Why don't you sit in that armchair over there?'

Sanae sat down in the armchair diffidently.

'I'm sorry for having made such a commotion. From now on, I'll do whatever you say. I apologize.'

Sanae whispered the apology with her head hung low.

'Well, you've finally had a change of heart. That's good. It's to your advantage to quietly go along with things this way. Still, it seems a little strange that you were putting up such resistance until yesterday and suddenly you're all meek and mild. Why? Is there some reason?'

'No, not really...'

Darting a shrewd look at the drooping Sanae, the lady thief shifted to her next question.

'Kitamura and Gōda say that they've heard voices in your cabin. Did somebody enter? Please tell me the truth.'

'No, I haven't noticed anything. I didn't hear anything.'

'Sanae, are you lying?'

'No, I swear..'

The Black Lizard appeared to be considering something as she stared at Sanae. The eerie silence continued for a while.

Then Sanae shyly asked, 'Um, this boat, where is it going?'

'This boat?'

Starting from her meditative pause, the lady thief continued, 'Let me tell you the boat's destination. Presently, we are travelling across the Enshū Sea en route for Tokyo. I have my own private art museum in a secret location in the capital. Hee, hee, hee! And I'd like you to see it. To see what a wonderful museum it is... We're speeding there like this so that I can display you and the Star of Egypt.

'It would be quicker to go by train, but it would be too dangerous to transport live cargo like you over land. A ship might be a little slow, but it's completely safe. And this ship, my dear, is mine. You see, your friendly little old Black Lizard has even got a steam-ship all ready for use. I expect that surprises you. Yes, you see I have the finances to be able to use a vessel like this as I please. When we can't go by land, we use this boat. Without such a splendid tool, I can't think how I could have stayed out of reach of the law for so long.'

'But, I...'

Sanae glanced up at the woman in black stubbornly.

'But what?'

'I don't want to go to such a place.'

'Well I'm not expecting you to want to go there. You might not like it, but I'm going to take you.'

'No, I will not go…'

'Well, you seem to be very sure of yourself. You aren't planning to try and escape from the ship, are you?'

'I have faith. I believe that I will be saved. I'm not afraid in the least.'

The woman in black could not help but be a little startled at the confidence in Sanae's voice.

'Faith in who? Who is going to save you?'

'Don't you know?'

While hinting at some impenetrable enigma, Sanae's voice also contained a conviction of puzzling strength. But whose power had conferred such strength into this fragile young lady?

What if… what if… The Black Lizard's face gradually turned horribly pale.

'Oh. I think I've got an idea. Let's see shall we. Would it happen to be Akechi Kogorō?'

'Well…'

Caught off guard, Sanae seemed a little flustered.

'I've guessed it, haven't I? The person who has been hiding in your room keeping your spirits up. Everyone says it's a ghost, but a ghost wouldn't be talking. It's Akechi Kogorō, isn't it? The private eye has promised to save you, hasn't he?'

'No, of course not.'

'Don't try to deceive me. All right, there's nothing more I want to hear from you.'

Her face as dark as thunder, the woman in black stood straight up.

'Kitamura, tie her up as before, gag her, and lock her in the cabin. I want you to lock the door from the inside and keep guard until I say it's all right. Get yourself a pistol. I don't care what happens – I won't allow her to escape.'

'As you say. I'll obey your instructions.'

Once Kitamura had dragged Sanae off, the Black Lizard rushed out into the corridor where she bumped into the 'purser' who was just then returning after completing the search.

'Oh, Jun-chan. I found out the true identity of the ghost – it's Akechi. It seems that he's lurking on the boat somewhere. I want you to search the ship again. Come on, hop to it!'

So another major search of the vessel took place. With flashlights waving, ten of the crew separately combed the decks, the aft, the engine-room, the ventilation shafts, and even the floor of the coal bunker. But they did not see anybody or find any clue.

## CHAPTER 20
## BURIAL AT SEA

**THE BLACK-GARBED LEADER** returned to her cabin empty-handed, and slumped into the sofa, lost in contemplation as she tried to solve the strange riddle she had been presented.

Oblivious to all these happenings, the ship's engine continued to throb away, pushing the boat through the dark air and sea at full speed, toward the east.

The pulse of the engine vibrating through the boat, the sound of the waves beating incessantly on the gunwales, and the crash of a whitecap hitting the boat when least expected.

The Black Lizard leaned on one arm of the sofa, staring at the rents in its fabric as if looking at something fearsome.

She was unable to shake one particular fear, try as she might. It was the only possibility left, wasn't it? They had searched every other possible nook and cranny. All that was left, a blind spot none of them had thought to search, was inside the sofa...

As she calmed herself, she thought that she felt a tiny beat, quite different from the throb of the engine, against her skin, transmitted through the cushion.

It was a beating human heart: the pulse of whoever was hiding inside the sofa.

She grew pale, and gritted her teeth together, holding in check her instinct to flee.

Even as she sat, though, it seemed that the heartbeat from the sofa was growing steadily louder. She could no longer hear the sound of the waves or the engine – all she could hear was the heartbeat from under her seat, the unknown pulsation echoing eerily, amplified as a drum to her ears.

She could not stand it! But she would never run away, never! Even if that man was hiding inside the sofa, he was just a rat caught in a bag, was he not? Nothing to be scared of, nothing to be frightened of at all.

'Akechi-san, Akechi-san!' she called out in a loud determined voice, as she pounded on the cushions.

And a sombre voice sounded back from within the sofa!

'Like a shadow, I just can't be kept away from you. This trick sofa you built was enormously helpful.'

The melancholy voice, echoing as if from the depths of the earth, or from the wall itself, made the woman in black shiver in spite of herself.

'Aren't you a bit concerned, Akechi-san? These are all my people, here. You are on the open sea, far beyond the reach of the police. Aren't you scared?'

'It looks to me as if you are the one who's frightened,' he chuckled.

What a horrible laugh it was. He made no effort to emerge from the sofa, seemingly perfectly at ease. This man was unfathomable.

'Frightened? No. But I am impressed. How did you know it was this boat?'

'I didn't, but by sticking so close to you, this is where I ended up, quite naturally.'

'So close to me? I don't understand…'

'I'm confident there is only one man who could have followed you here from the top of the Tsutenkaku Tower.'

'Oh, really? How wonderful! I'm so proud of you! So that shop owner was really Akechi Kogorō… How silly I was! It must have been so funny when I believed your story about an inner ear infection and that bandage.'

123

Driven by some strange emotion, she had the weird illusion that the man lying stretched out under her seat was not her enemy, but almost a lover.

'Hmm, rather... I have to admit that it was enjoyable disguising myself to you, as you tried so hard to disguise yourself.'

Suddenly, in the midst of this bizarre conversation, the door abruptly swung open, and Amamiya Jun'ichi the 'purser' stepped in. Apparently he had heard the conversing voices and thought it suspicious.

Before he had a chance to say anything, the Black Lizard put her finger to her lips and commanded silence. She beckoned him closer, then took a pencil and memo pad from her handbag, which lay on the end table nearby. Her hand flew over the page, writing rapidly as she continued her innocuous-seeming conversation with Akechi.

'AKECHI INSIDE SOFA,' she wrote, even as she asked him 'So that strange scream and the splash at the bridge were your doing, then?'

'CALL EVERYONE. HURRY. BRING STRONG ROPE.'

'As you have surmised. If you hadn't looked out the oilpaper window, probably none of this would have happened.'

'Ah, as I feared... And how did you follow us after that?'

As she spoke, Jun'ichi slipped silently out of the room.

'I borrowed a bicycle, and just pedalled along from bank to bank, keeping your vessel in sight from land. I waited for dawn, and then asked a small boat to ferry me out here. In the twilight I managed to crawl up on your deck, although it took some acrobatics to accomplish.'

'But there was a lookout on deck, wasn't there?'

'Yes. That's why it took me so long to get into the cabins. It was quite difficult to discover which room Sanae was being held in.

And, of course, by the time I did find her,' he chuckled, 'The boat had already set sail!'

'Why didn't you flee when you had the chance?,' she asked. 'You must have known you'd be found here.'

'Brr! The water's a bit too chilly for me, I'm afraid, and I can't swim all that well. It was just so much easier to lie down here under these warm cushions!'

What a bizarre conversation! One party was lying inside the sofa in the blackness, while the other was sitting on top of those same cushions – they were almost close enough to feel each other's body heat! And even stranger, they were mortal enemies! They would leap at each other's throats like fierce tigers given the slightest opening. In spite of which, they conversed quietly, gently, almost like the bedtime talk of man and wife.

'You know, I've been hidden away here since dinnertime, and I'm quite bored with it all. And I'd really love to see your beautiful face once again, too. Mind if I come out?' Akechi was bolder than ever, no doubt with some clever plan in mind.

'You mustn't! You must not come out! If my men find you, you're dead. Just be quiet a little longer.'

'Really? So you'll cover up for me, will you?'

Just then young Jun'ichi returned, accompanied by five crewmembers carrying a stout rope. They entered cautiously, silently.

'LEAVE AKECHI IN SOFA, TIE ROPE AROUND OUTSIDE. THROW SOFA AND ALL OFF DECK.'

They followed her directions without making a sound, and began to wind the rope around the sofa starting from one end. Smiling evilly, the Black Lizard stood up to get out of their way.

'Hey, what happened? Has someone come?' asked Akechi, unaware of what was happening but sensing that something had changed in the room outside the sofa.

125

'Yes. We're tying the sofa up with rope.'

The sofa was almost completely bound up.

'Rope!?'

'That's right,' snarled the Black Lizard, revealing her true maliciousness. 'We're tying up the famous private detective right now! Ha, ha, ha!'

She drew herself up, confronting him as if a pitch-black demon, and spat out the words with venom that ill suited a woman.

'Pick up the sofa! To the deck!'

The six men easily lifted the sofa and hurried it through the hallway to the deck. Like a pitiful fish caught in a net, the detective inside struggled to free himself.

Up above the deck, the night was black and starless, both sky and sea a featureless darkness. Stirred up by the ship's screw, a single ribbon of phosphorescence stretched out, a long and eerily pale streamer.

The six stood at the gunwale, carrying the coffin-like sofa.

'One... two... and three!'

With the shout a black shadow fell down over the gunwale, ending in a pale splash of phosphorescence. The famous private detective Akechi Kogorō had finally, without a fight, sunk deep into the waters of the Pacific Ocean.

# CHAPTER 21
## THE UNDERGROUND TREASURE HOUSE

THE SOFA HOLDING AKECHI twirled and jumped like something alive in the phosphorescent wake of the ship, and its black shape sank out of sight under the waves almost immediately.

'I guess that's what they call a burial at sea. And that takes care of the last obstacle in our path! Still, it's sad to think of the spirited Akechi Kogorō becoming mere fish food at the bottom of the sea, isn't it?'

Amamiya Jun'ichi was staring into her eyes as he spoke with sugar-coated grief.

'Who cares? All right, everyone. Back inside!'

She herded all the men back inside the ship, as if scolding them, then turned to lean on the deck railing, alone, gazing fixedly at the sea where the sofa had vanished.

The sound of the ship's screw, the whitecaps marching past with identical shapes, the phosphorescence of the ship's wake... Whether the ship was moving or the water flowing around it, around her was nought but the uncaring and unchanging rhythm.

The Black Lizard stood, immobile, for half an hour in the cold night wind. When she finally went below, her face was a horrible bluish tone in the bright ship's lights. The traces of tears shone on her cheeks.

She went to her own cabin for a moment, and, seemingly unable to bear being there either, soon stepped into the corridor and walked unsteadily toward the room where Sanae was imprisoned.

She knocked, and the crewman named Kitamura opened the door, peering out.

'Go for a little walk, Kitamura... I'll look after Sanae for a bit,' she ordered, and after Kitamura left she stepped inside.

Poor Sanae! Her hands were tied up behind her, and she was gagged, lying on her side in a corner of the room. The Black Lizard removed the gag and spoke to her.

'I have something I must tell you, Sanae. It's very bad news, I'm afraid, and I'm sure you'll burst into tears.'

Sanae sat up, and, silently, stared back at the kidnapper with enmity in her eyes.

'Do you know what I'm about to tell you?'

'...'

'Ha, ha, ha! Akechi Kogorō, your guardian angel, is dead! He was hiding in that sofa, and we tied it up with rope and sank him in the sea! We threw him into a watery grave just now from the deck! Ha, ha, ha!'

Sanae reeled, shocked, and stared up at the face of the Black Lizard, who continued to laugh like a madwoman.

'Is that true?'

'You think I'd be so happy at a mere lie, child? Look at me! I'm so happy I can't bear it! But you must be very disappointed, mustn't you? Your only friend, your only lifeline, has been cut. There is no-one in this whole wide world who can help you now. You'll be locked in my art museum forever, never again to see the light of day!'

Staring at the face of her tormentor, Sanae realized that this dreadful news was not a lie. And she understood just what the death of the detective meant for her.

It was hopeless. The despair of her hopeless situation was as deep as her faith in Akechi had been strong. She was all too well aware that she was entirely by herself, trapped among her enemies.

She bit her lip and tried to be brave, but she was unable to withstand it any more. With her hands tied behind her, she bent over to hide her face against her legs, and began to weep. The hot tears dripped onto her legs.

'Stop crying! How shameful! Have you no manners at all?'

Seeing her begin to cry, the Black Lizard scolded her in a curiously high voice. Suddenly she was kneeling at Sanae's side and tears were streaming down the kidnapper's face as well! Whether it was the loneliness of losing her ultimate enemy, or perhaps for some other reason, she was drowning in a strange, unfathomable sadness.

Somehow, without knowing how, the kidnapper and the kidnapped, the Black Lizard and her prey, these mortal enemies, were sitting, holding each other's hands like close sisters and weeping! The causes of their sadness were different, but there was no difference in the depth and intensity of their sorrow.

The Black Lizard was wailing like a child of five or six years and this led Sanae-san to weep in the same uncontrolled way. What an unexpected and unbelievable scene! They were nothing more than two young girls, or perhaps two innocent barbarians. With no trace of intellect or emotion, they exposed only the sheer passion of their sadness.

This strange paean of grief blended with the monotone of the engine, and continued on and on. They wept and wept until the natural evil awoke in the Black Lizard's breast once again, and Sanae recalled her enmity.

In the evening of the following day the ship entered Tokyo Bay, dropping anchor along the coast of the former landfill known as Tsukishima Island.

They waited for it to grow dark, then lowered the ship's launch, and several people boarded to row to a deserted point on the island.

Leaving the three oarsmen in the launch, the Black Lizard disembarked with Sanae and Amamiya Jun'ichi. With her hands still tied behind her back and her mouth gagged, Sanae also wore a thick blindfold. No doubt these precautions were designed to prevent her from discovering the way to the Black Lizard's hideout. Jun'ichi no longer wore an officer's dress, and he had donned a beard and moustache to hide his face. Wearing a khaki workman's uniform, he looked like a factory machinist.

Tsukishima was a spacious island packed with factories, and had almost no residences. With the recent industrial slump almost none of them were operating at this time of night, and the only sources of light were the scattered white streetlamps. It looked like a deserted ruin.

The three of them crossed a wide grassy area running along the coast, and wove a complicated course amid the buildings, finally entering a ruined factory.

The walls were broken, the gate columns leaned, and the grounds were covered with weeds grown wild in what looked like a haunted factory. There was no light, of course, so the Black Lizard took out her flashlight and lit their steps through the weeds. Behind her came Jun'ichi in his workman's garb, carrying blindfolded Sanae on his back.

Ten or twelve meters from the gate was a large wooden structure, and the light from the flashlight flowed caressingly over its surface. There were many glass windows, but the glass had broken and fallen from every single frame. She rattled the door open, and stepped into the cobweb-choked interior.

The flashlight beam danced over broken machinery, rusty shafts running above their heads, drive wheels and broken drive belts, finally stopping on a little room in one corner, that looked like it could have been the supervisor's office.

The three of them stepped through the broken glass door, and up onto the wooden floor.

'*Tic tac tac... tic tic tac tic... tac.. tac...*'

The Black Lizard kicked the floor sharply with her shoe heel. Surely it could not be Morse code!? But it was a signal of some sort, because before the tapping of her heel had died away, a meter-wide section of the flooring in the circle of light slid open silently, exposing the concrete below. The very ground itself was built as a door, a thick block which dropped down to reveal a black underground passage.

'M'lady?'

A low voice sounded from below.

'Yes. And I've brought an important guest with me today.'

Remaining silent, Amamiya descended the steps to the passage, with Sanae still on his back, treading with care, one step at a time. After the Black Lizard herself followed him down the stairs, the concrete door and wooden floorboards closed up once again, leaving only a dark, ruined factory with no trace that anything out of the ordinary had happened.

*The causes of their sadness were different,*
*but there was no difference in the depth*
*and intensity of their sorrow.*

## CHAPTER 22
## THE ART MUSEUM TERROR

**BECAUSE HER EYES** were tightly bound when she was transferred from the main vessel to the launch, Sanae had no idea where they had landed, where she walked to afterward, or whether the place where she now found herself was above or below ground.

'We've given you rather a hard time, haven't we Sanae-san? Well, it's over now. Jun-chan, set her free.'

After Sanae heard the Black Lizard's kind-sounding voice, she felt the gag being removed and the ropes on both hands being untied. Then her eyes were flooded with light. Because they had been bound tightly by the dark blindfold for so long, the brightness was dazzling.

She was in a long , curved corridor whose ceiling, floor, and walls were made of concrete. A splendid cut-glass chandelier hung from the ceiling and its bright flashing rays illuminated rows of glass display cases arrayed along both walls. Inside the cases, jewels of varying shapes caught the chandelier's beams like countless flickering stars.

In the face of such beauty and magnificence, Sanae forgot she was a prisoner and inadvertently gasped. The daughter of a major jewel trader, she was accustomed to the point of boredom to seeing precious stones each day, but even so she raised her voice in surprise. We shall spare the reader a detailed explanation of the high quality and great number of the jewels gathered there.

'Thank you for being impressed. You see, this is my art museum. Rather, the entrance to it. What do you think? I'm sure you'll agree these display cases would not suffer in comparison with those at your showroom. It has taken me decades of risking my life, racking my wits, and daring all kinds of peril to collect these stones. I'm sure you wouldn't find so many, even in the jewel vaults of the most exalted nobility in the world.'

As she delivered her boastful speech, the woman in black carefully opened the handbag she was carrying and took out a little silver box containing the Star of Egypt.

'I feel a little sorry for your father, but I've desired this for a long time. Today, it has finally come to rest in my art museum.'

She clicked open the lid of the small box to reveal the giant stone, which flamed with colour in the chandelier's rays. The Black Lizard regarded it with delight before pulling out a bunch of keys from her handbag. Unlocking the glass door of a display stand, she placed the massive diamond in the centre, still inside the open silver box.

'Oh my, how beautiful it is! Compared to this, other jewels seem like mere pebbles. Now my art museum has one more treasure. Thank you, Sanae-san.'

There was no irony intended, but it was difficult for Sanae to know how to reply. She remained silent with her eyes cast down.

'All right, let's go further in. I still have many things to show you.'

As they moved along the subterranean passage, they beheld a space lined with famous old paintings, beside that a group of statues of the Buddha, then Western marble sculptures, followed by ancient-looking craftwork. So rich was the display of objects that this indeed seemed to be an art museum.

According to the woman in black, the majority of these art objects had been taken from museums, art galleries, and the treasure vaults of wealthy nobles in every land and replaced with skilfully-made copies.

If this was true, the objects so proudly displayed by museums and passed down through the generations as treasures by wealthy nobles were fakes. The wonder of it was that neither the owners nor the general public had even the slightest suspicion about this.

'Still, this is only an impressive private museum. Any thief with enough wits and financial resources could do the same. I have no intention of boasting about it. What I really want to show you is still further along.'

They rounded a corner in the passage and a peculiar sight completely unlike any they had yet seen came into view.

What! These must be wax mannequins. But how finely they are made.

One of the walls contained a glass display like a show window about six metres wide. Inside were a blonde woman, a black man, as well as a young Japanese man and woman. All four were naked and in various poses, standing, crouching, or lying down.

The black man looked like a boxer, standing straight up with his muscular arms crossed. Squatting with her elbows on her knees, the blonde propped up her chin with her hands. The Japanese girl, who lay stretched out on her stomach with her flowing black hair falling in waves on her shoulders, rested her chin on her folded arms and stared at the onlookers. The young Japanese man was poised like a discus thrower and every muscle in his body stood out in relief. All four were fine-featured, well-proportioned, and beautiful beyond compare.

'Magnificent life-like mannequins, don't you think? But perhaps a little too life-like, no? Move a little closer to the glass. See the fine downy hair on their skin. I bet you've never heard of mannequins having fine body hair.'

Overcome by curiosity, Sanae neared the glass plate. Such was the mysterious attraction of the figures that she forgot about the awfulness of her predicament.

My! They really were covered in downy hair. And the colour of the skin as well as the fine, fine wrinkles! Could something so convincing be a wax model?

'Do you believe these are wax mannequins Sanae-san?'

Smiling oddly, the woman in black seemed to be teasing Sanae. Something in the question frightened the young woman.

'There's something about them that differs from a mannequin, something frightening, don't you think? Have you ever seen a stuffed animal? Didn't you ever think it would be wonderful if a method could be invented for preserving beautiful humans for ever in just that way? Well, that is what has happened. One of my underlings devised a method for stuffing humans. What you see here are prototypes. They're not completely perfect, but they're not lifeless wax dolls. I think you'll agree they seem lifelike. Naturally, the inside is wax, but the skin and hair are truly human. They seem to possess souls. The human scent remains. Isn't it fantastic? To stuff beautiful young people as they are, to preserve for ever the beauty that would surely be lost if they lived – there's not a museum that could do it or would even think of doing it.'

Carried away by her own words, the woman in black had launched into a speech.

'All right, come this way now. There's a much grander exhibit further along. Although these may seem lifelike and appear to possess souls, they cannot move. Deeper in, there's one that is full of movement.'

Sanae was guided around another corner. And there she saw on display an artwork that moved, completely unlike the still scenes they had seen thus far.

There was a cage with thick iron bars like those used for lions or tigers, and shut up inside, along with an electric heater glowing red, was a man.

He was a handsome Japanese youth some twenty-four or twenty-five years old and he bore a striking resemblance to a well-known movie actor.

He had been placed inside the cage like a fine specimen of a wild beast, with his perfectly balanced body exposed to full view.

He was pacing around inside the enclosure pulling at his hair with both hands, but when he saw the woman in black he shook the bars and screamed loudly like a monkey in the zoo.

'Wait, you slut! Are you trying to send me crazy you bitch? Just kill me quickly. I don't want to spend another day alive inside this cage. Open up you! Let me out...'

Slipping his white arm between the bars, he tried to seize the dark garb of the lady thief.

'Well now, I don't think you need to get so angry. What a mess you've made of your pretty face. But I'll soon grant your wish and choke the life out of you. And I'll turn you into an ageless doll, just like Keiko-san who was with you in this cell until a short while ago. Ha, ha, ha!'

The woman in black laughed cruelly.

'What's that you say?! You've made Keiko-san a doll! Oh you bitch, you've gone and killed her and stuffed her... Well, you're not going to make me into any doll! I'm not your toy. You make the slightest move toward me and I'll kill you with my teeth without a trace of mercy. I'll maul your throat and suffocate you to death.'

'Hee, hee, hee. You'd better make as much of a commotion as you can now because once I've turned you into a doll you'll be as motionless as a stone. What's more, there's nothing I enjoy more than seeing a handsome boy kicking up such a ruckus. Ha, ha, ha!'

Relishing the youth's agony, the woman in black progressed to a fresh horror.

'You must be very sad since Keiko-san left. In most zoos, there's usually a male and a female of the species in each cage. Well, I've been thinking for a while now that I should do something about getting you a young lady and I've tried all sorts of things. Today, I've finally brought along a bride for you. What do you think? She's beautiful, isn't she? Do you like her?'

Sanae felt a cold shudder and she could not stop her jaw from trembling.

Now the Black Lizard's evil scheme had become entirely clear. She had gone to such trouble to kidnap the beautiful Sanae in order to strip her naked, thrust her into this cage and then, when the time came, to peel off her living skin and put her on display in this evil art museum as a horrible stuffed doll.

'Sanae-san! What's wrong? You're trembling. Why, you're shaking just like a reed! So you understand your role now, hmmn? But the groom isn't too bad, is he? Or doesn't he appeal? Well, I've decided, so you'll just have to put up with it whether you like him or not.'

Overcome by fear, Sanae had lost the power of speech. It was all she could do to stand. Her mind went blank. Shaking, she looked as if she might fall at any minute.

## CHAPTER 23
## THE BIG TANK

'SANAE-SAN, THERE'S STILL SOMETHING I want to show you. Come this way. This time it's not a zoo, but an aquarium. I'm very proud of it.'

Taking the quivering Sanae by the hand, the Black Lizard pulled her upright and they turned the next corner.

Here the long subterranean passage came to an end and there was a large glass-lined tank beyond. A very bright light had been fixed directly above the tank, making the objects in the water so clear through the thick glass it seemed one could reach out and touch them.

The tank measured about two metres on all sides and on its bottom countless fronds of strange seaweed were waving together like snakes.

But why did she call it an aquarium? There was no sign of any fish.

'You can't see any fish can you? Don't be puzzled. After all, there were no animals in my zoo so why should it seem strange that there aren't any fish in my aquarium?'

The woman in black laughed eerily before launching into another ghastly speech.

'I think it'll be fun to put a human inside. You know how much more interesting they are than fish. That fellow in the cage who got himself into such a tizzy might be handsome, but just think about the magnificent submarine dance a person thrown into this tank would perform...'

Then it was no longer the woman in black's voice – Sanae's field of vision was filled with a vivid monster-movie spectre. Some-

139

thing white was writhing in the gloomy water. Suddenly, from the squirming mass of raised serpentine heads, a large human face appeared at the glass, the mouth hanging open, gasping for breath like a *koi* carp. The eyes were shut and the brows drawn down... the face was not a man's. Nor that of an old person. It was a young woman... but wait, this was definitely no stranger. For writhing there among the snakes was none other than Sanae herself!

'It's wonderful, don't you think? What a superb show! There isn't a classic painting, or a sculpture, or even an inspired performance of Japanese dance that has expressed such beauty. This is art in exchange for life...'

But Sanae was no longer listening to the ghastly declamation. She could not hold her breath that long. In the vision, she had inhaled copious amounts of water. She struggled with all her might until finally all her energy was spent. Then the fear and suffering became too great for her to bear and she fainted.

Realizing what had happened, the woman in black put out both hands to support Sanae but the young woman was now as limp as a jellyfish and she collapsed onto the concrete floor.

## CHAPTER 24
## THE WHITE BEASTS

SANAE HAD NO IDEA how much time had passed, but when she finally awoke and opened her eyes, the first thing she felt was that her body was directly exposed to the air. When she touched herself, her finger slid freely, with nothing to catch on. Her prostrate body had been stripped stark naked!

Next she noticed the countless thick steel bars crossed in front of her like stripes. She knew only too well what they were. She was in a cage. They had put her in a cell while she was unconscious.

It must be the same cage she had seen before she fainted, the one that young man had been imprisoned in. So she was not here alone? That beautiful young man, as naked as she was herself, should be nearby.

When she recalled that much, she totally lost the courage to lift her head and look around. What to do? She had not a stitch on her body! And even worse! She was stretched out in that embarrassing state in front of a young, beautiful and naked man!

But instead of blushing, she turned white as a ghost, sat up abruptly, curled up into a ball, and scuttled backward into the corner. And no matter how she tried to look the other way, in such a cramped cell there was no way to prevent certain sights from entering her field of view quite naturally. And she saw him. The naked man.

In that underground cell together, like Adam and Eve in the garden of Eden, they exchanged glances. What could she say? And what could she do? Ashamed at her nakedness, Sanae's eyes overflowed with tears. Through the dancing lights in her tears she could make out the shining, white body of the man.

'Do you feel all right?'

Suddenly a mellow bass voice echoed – it was the young man!

She started, blinked her eyes to clear away the tears, and looked at his face.

Right in front of her was a white face, as silkily smooth as if oiled. A high, wide brow; soft, curly hair; double eyelids and clear eyes looking into hers; a Grecian nose; and firm red lips... he was truly a beautiful young man, but Sanae was terrified.

Had the Black Lizard given her to this man as his bride? Maybe the young man had that intent! And as that thought occurred to her, she once again had to face the fact that the two of them were trapped in this cage together, naked like beasts of the field... it was enough to freeze the blood in her body!

'Miss, there's nothing to worry about! Despite appearances, I'm not a barbarian, really!'

He spoke hesitantly, bashfully. Sanae's fear dissipated as she heard his words.

As they came to understand each other a little better, they began to discuss their plight, cursing the evil plot of their female kidnapper, huddling closer and closer to each other like white beasts as they whispered together.

At last it seemed that dawn had broken, for they began to feel the people around them stirring in this underground keep, and then the Black Lizard's underlings began to come, one after another, to view their newly-caged guest.

I will leave it to readers to imagine how dreadfully embarrassed Sanae was at their improper attentions; how the young man cursed and shouted at them like a beast; and what lascivious suggestions these criminals offered to her ears. Just as the four or five who had slept there underground were making such a commotion, that Morse-like signal was heard once again. Shortly after, a man who appeared to be a crew member entered the lair in something of a fluster.

## CHAPTER 25
## THE INCIDENT OF THE DOLLS

**THE SEAMAN** was one of the Black Lizard's men who slept in the steamer moored out in the bay. He approached the private chambers of the leader of the gang, deep underground, and knocked on the door with the same code-like tapping.

'Enter!'

Even among such a group of disreputable men, her authority as the boss of the gang freed her of the need to do anything so undignified as locking her door. At any time, even the middle of the night, the door could be opened freely at her simple command.

'My goodness! What in the world is the problem, and so early in the morning? It's still only six, isn't it?'

With no regard for decorum, she lay face-down on the white bed wearing only white silk pyjamas and she lit up a cigar while watching the seaman out of the corner of her eye. Her rich curves were revealed by the sheer white silk. Her men had no difficulties with their boss dressing like that, though...

'Something a little strange has happened. I thought you should know right away.' The man fidgeted, trying to avoid looking at the bed.

'Strange? How?'

'It's Matsu, the stoker. He vanished last night. We searched the whole ship, and he ain't there. He ain't the type to run off, and I thought maybe he'd gotten caught ashore. Little worried 'bout that...'

'Hmm. So you let Matsu go ashore?'

'No, Ma'am! No way! But after Jun'ichi returned to the ship, he came ashore one more time, right? Matsu was one of the rowers,

144

and when the boat got back he weren't in it any more. We figured we must'a made a mistake, and searched the whole ship, then came back here and asked, but the guys said Matsu never showed up. Maybe he was off wandering in town and got picked up by the cops, huh?'

'Not good at all... Matsu is a little slow upstairs, and really can't be depended on to do anything complicated – which is why he's the stoker. But if he's been arrested, he certainly could spill a few secrets...'

She sat up on the bed, her brow furrowed as she thought of what to do, but just then another strange message was delivered.

The door burst open and three of her men looked in, then one explained rapidly.

'M'lady, please come and have a look! Something very strange is going on! The dolls are wearing clothes! And they're covered in jewels, glittering something fierce! We checked around to see who'd play such a bad joke, but nobody knows anything. Surely it wasn't you?'

'You're joking!'

'No. Jun'ichi was so surprised he's still standing there, gawking.'

Strange, indeed unimaginable things were happening. Who knew what connection might exist between Matsu's disappearance and this new event, but it seemed unusual that the two things should happen at the same time! The queen of this underground realm could not remain calm any longer. She evicted them all from her room, changed quickly into her usual black Western-style garb, and hurried to the doll showroom.

It was as if imps had been at work... The upright young black man had donned a khaki uniform that would not look out of place on a beggar, but on his chest the giant 'Star of Egypt' flashed proudly like a medal of honour; the seated blonde girl, elbows propped on her knees, now wore the long-sleeved kimono of a Japanese girl, and bracelets and anklets made of diamond pins and pearl necklaces. The reclining Japanese woman had an old blanket wrapped around her torso, but smiled under a diadem, formed from many jewels, lying on her raven locks; and the discus thrower, the young Japanese man, now had on a grimy knit shirt, with glittering necklaces and bracelets.

Standing there, still looking into Amamiya Jun'ichi's eyes, she was so astonished she could not speak for a moment.

What a joke to play! The long-sleeved kimono was the one that Sanae had been wearing the night before, but the other pieces of clothing were all from her underlings. Someone had taken them from their shelves or wicker baskets in the bedrooms, and dressed the mannequins. The jewellery, of course, was from the Black Lizard's display cases, leaving most of the glass cases empty.

'Who in the world would have done such a silly thing...'

'Nobody knows! There are five men here besides me, and we've all proven ourselves. I've asked them all, and they all swear they had nothing to do with it!'

'What about the watchman at the gate?'

'He says nothing out of the ordinary happened at all. And even if some outsider tried to get in, that trap door can only be opened from the inside... It just isn't possible for a trickster to get in from the outside!'

After their brief and fruitless conversation the pair fell silent again, and looked at each other. As if at a sudden thought, the Black Lizard muttered 'No! Could it be...?' as she ran to the cage where her 'guests' were imprisoned. She examined the lock closely, but there was no sign that it had been broken.

'Has one of you children been playing with this? Tell me the truth! One of you played this trick on me, right?'

She called to them, voice shrill. Inside the cage, Adam and Eve had been whispering together, facing each other, but at her sudden attack each of them braced defensively. Sanae once again curled up into the corner like a monkey, and the young man stood up abruptly and approached the kidnapper, fists ready.

'Why don't you answer? You did it, didn't you? Dressed my dolls!'

'Damn fool! You can see I'm imprisoned in this cage! Are you totally insane?'

His entire body was filled with fury as he shouted his reply.

'Oh, you're still full of pride, I see! Well, as long as it wasn't you who did it, it doesn't really matter, because I have plans of my own. By the way, how do you like our little miss?'

For some reason, the Black Lizard changed the subject. The young man stood silent, and she asked once more 'I asked you if you liked her.'

He exchanged a quick glance with Sanae, huddled in the corner, then he shouted out 'Yes, I like her! I like her, and because I like her, I'll protect her! I won't let you lay one finger on her!'

'Oh, I thought it might be something like that,' she chortled. 'Well, you go right ahead and protect her.'

Still snickering, she turned and saw that Amamiya Jun'ichi, clad in overalls, had just arrived.

'Jun-chan, pull that girl out of there and dump her in the tank,' she commanded sharply, handing Jun'ichi the key.

'Isn't it a bit too soon? She's only been here one night,' commented Jun'ichi, looking to see her reaction as he spoke through his huge false moustache.

'It doesn't matter. This is hardly the first time I've decided things on the spur of the moment. Go ahead and take care of her now... I'll be in my room, eating breakfast. I want you to get everything ready. And make sure they return all those jewels to their display cases. Got it?'

The Black Lizard walked back toward her room, not even turning to face Jun'ichi as she spoke.

She was furious. The bizarre prank with the mannequins had upset her very much, and when she saw her two captives whispering to each other in the cage so harmoniously it had been the final straw, and her fury burst.

She'd had no intention of providing Sanae as a bride-to-be: she only wanted to frighten her, to shame her, to enjoy her terrified and sad state in the cell. But her plans had gone totally awry, with the young man determined to protect Sanae by force, while Sanae had looked up at him with delight and indescribable appreciation in her eyes! It was not hard to understand why the Black Lizard burned with a foul displeasure, much like jealousy.

Faced with a difficult job, Jun'ichi hesitated for a moment, and then, no other choice available, approached the cage door.

'You swine! What do you think you're going to do to this girl?'

Inside the cage, the young man had adopted a fighting stance, with a fearsome expression suggesting he would kill Jun'ichi on the spot if he tried to step inside. However, Jun'ichi had a few fights of his own under his belt and he remained unimpressed as he stood at the door. He inserted the key and rattled it around a little, then suddenly swung the door open and leaped inside.

The two of them – a moustachioed man in factory garb, and a naked youth – grappled each other's arms furiously.

'Not a chance! As long as I'm alive you'll not touch this girl. Go ahead and try! But before you do, you'd better be prepared to be throttled to death!'

His hands, driven by his fury, grew ever closer to Jun'ichi's neck.

And, astonishing as it was, Jun'ichi made no effort to resist them! Still holding the other's arms, he thrust his neck forward, and brought his head close to the young man's ear, whispering something.

At first the youth shook his head, determined not to listen, but then an expression of sheer wonder swept across his face. At the same time, he suddenly grew quiet, dropping his hands from the other's neck to hang at his sides.

# CHAPTER 26
# DOPPELGÄNGER

A SHORT WHILE after having somehow persuaded the young man in the cage to quiet down, Amamiya Jun'ichi took the naked damsel – who seemed numbed out of her wits – under his arm and went to the front of the glass-lined tank. There was an upright ladder on the side of the tank. Holding Sanae, he climbed to the top rung, lifted the steel-plate cover and threw her body in. After closing the cover and descending the ladder, he went to the Black Lizard's private quarters, opened the door slightly and said,

'My Lady, I've carried out your instructions as commanded. Sanae-san is swimming about inside the tank now. Hurry and take a look!'

Next he went to a seat at the side of the tank, took a small folded sheet of newspaper from his overall pocket, opened it, and placed it carefully on the seat. Then, for some reason, he quickly moved off to the other side of the passage.

From the opposite direction, the woman in black opened the door and stalked to the front of the tank.

On the other side of the glass plate, the bluish water swayed violently. The different-sized fronds of seaweed rearing up like serpents from the bottom were also moving wildly to and fro.

And among them, swimming with a flailing action, a naked woman… the phantasm Sanae had seen the night before had become reality.

The woman in black stared at the tank, eyes shining cruelly, pale cheeks twitching strangely with excitement. Both her fists were tightly clenched and she was gritting her teeth. Then she noticed that the naked woman was not moving as vigorously as usual. It was not just a question of degree – the naked woman was not flailing at all. It was the swaying water that made it look that way. She realized that the young woman's white body was simply moving with the water.

Had the frail Sanae fainted before entering the tank, thus avoiding the agony of being under water? It seemed not. As the Black Lizard watched, the body of the woman in the tank gradually revolved and the face, which had been turned away, now appeared at the front glass. Wait a minute! Was this Sanae's face? Yet submersion could not have altered it thus. Oh, but now it became clear. Wasn't this the taxidermist's model of the Japanese girl from the display case? But how on earth could such a slip up have taken place?

'Is there anyone there? Where did Jun-chan go?'

Forgetting herself, the woman in black was shouting at the top of her lungs. Her minions came thronging in from where the stuffed mannequins were exhibited. Their ashen look suggested something had affected them too.

One of the men reported in a panic.

'M'lady, something strange has happened again. One of the dolls is missing. It was there when I took off the clothes and collected the jewels a moment ago, but when I looked just now, the girl, you know the one that's lying down... she's missing.'

But the woman in black was already aware of this.

'Did you look inside the cage? Was Sanae still there?'

'No, there's just the man. Didn't Jun-chan throw Sanae-san into the tank?'

'Well, something was slung in, but not Sanae-san. Here, look closely. It's the stuffed figure you lot are searching for!'

The men peered into the tank. Indeed, the object there in the water was definitely the mannequin that had disappeared.

'That's queer! Who's gone and done that?!'

'Jun-chan. Have you lot seen Jun-chan? He was here just a minute ago.'

'We haven't seen him. He's been very irritable today. It was as though we were hindering him somehow: he kept telling us to get out of the way.'

'Mmn. This is peculiar. But where did he go? He couldn't have gone outside so I want you all to search thoroughly for him. If you find him, tell him to come straight to me.'

After the men had withdrawn, the woman in black seemed somewhat concerned for she stared into space pondering.

What could this all be about? The ship's stoker goes missing. Then something strange happens to the mounted figures. Now the woman that should have been Sanae-san is suddenly transformed into one of the mannequins. Could there be some connection between these uncanny events? It all seemed a little too coincidental.

She felt that an awesome power beyond human abilities was at work. Just what could that be? But wait! What if...? No, that was too silly to fit in. There was absolutely no way it could be that.

The woman in black did her best to repress the overwhelming ghostly presentiment that rose up within her breast. Yet woman thief though she was, so great was her fear that cold clammy sweat drenched her entire body.

After a while, she made to sit down in a nearby chair, when she noticed a sheet of newspaper lying on the seat. This was the sheet that Amamiya Jun'ichi had earlier unfolded and placed there for some reason.

At first, she looked at the newspaper article without much interest, but soon her expression became very intent and her eyes were drawn to it.

'SUPER-SLEUTH AKECHI'S VICTORY — IWASE SANAE RETURNS
HOME SAFE — FAMILY OF JEWEL KING REJOICES'

The lady thief's attention was captured by the unbelievable message splashed out in large headlines across three columns. Hurriedly, she picked up the newspaper, sat down and began to read the article avidly. The outline of the article was as follows.

'On the afternoon of the 7th, Iwase Sanae, beloved daughter of jewel "king" Iwase Shōbei, returned to the family residence after apparently having been abducted by that bizarre villain the Black Lizard. As our enquiries suggested that Mr Iwase had delivered a magnificent gem known as the Star of Egypt to the thief in ransom for his daughter, we believed that the criminal had kept her promise and sent back Miss Iwase. This was your correspondent's understanding when he interviewed Mr Iwase and his daughter. However, both these persons state that it was entirely due to the efforts of private detective Akechi Kogorō and that the criminal had definitely not honoured the agreement. Somewhat unusually, we were asked to refrain from probing too deeply because of certain circumstances that apparently make it impossible to provide details. Where can that villain the Black Lizard be hiding? The detective in question, Mr Akechi, is now in lone pursuit of the Black Lizard and his whereabouts are unknown. Who, we wonder, will emerge victorious from the combat now taking place between the famous detective and the master thief? Will the magnificent Star of Egypt return to the possession of Mr Iwase? We wait with the utmost concern for the next piece of news.'

There was also a large photograph captioned 'Father and Daughter Rejoice', which clearly showed the smiling Iwase and Sanae sitting on a sofa in a drawing room.

After the woman thief had read this newspaper article – as improbable as a ghost story – and looked at the photograph, a rare expression of surprise crossed her beautiful face. More than surprise, it was a look of indefinable fear. This was a major Osaka newspaper marked with yesterday's date. The '7th' mentioned in the article was two days ago, the day when the Black Lizard's steamer travelled across Osaka Bay. On that day, Sanae was in the ship. And yesterday and today – right up to a little while ago – she had been trembling inside the cage.

What was this all about? Surely a leading newspaper like this would not print a mistaken article. And more convincing than anything was the photograph. How could Sanae have been laughing in a seat at the Iwase home in an Osaka suburb when she was supposed to be a captive on the ship?

Not even the wily woman in black could solve this bizarre mystery. For the first time in her life, she found herself crushed by an unnameable fear. Her face was pale as death and her brow sopping with beads of clammy sweat.

For some reason the disquieting word *doppelgänger* floated into her head. The improbable tradition went that one person could become two and the two could act independently. She remembered reading about it somewhere on a candy wrapper. And she had seen it in an overseas magazine on the paranormal. The practical woman in black was definitely not a believer in supernatural phenomena, but now she seemed to have no option but to believe in the unbelievable.

At that moment the men who had been searching for Jun'ichi came thronging back to report that they had not found him.

'Who's on guard duty at the entrance now?'

The woman in black's voice lacked power.

'Kitamura. He says no one has passed him. And he can be trusted.'

'All right. So he's got to be inside then. He can't have just disappeared in a puff of smoke. I want you to search once more very carefully. And for Sanae too. If this thing in the tank isn't her, then she has to be hiding somewhere.'

Although the men stared uneasily at the pale face of their chieftainess, they grumblingly made to withdraw down the passage.

'Hang on! Two of you stay here and get that doll out of the tank. I want you to search it thoroughly just in case.'

The two men who stayed behind climbed the ladder, took the mannequin from the water and lowered it down to the floor where they laid it out at full length. However, although they checked the limp doll very carefully, they could find no clue to the mystery other than that it was not Sanae.

The woman in black strutted about angrily, then sat down on the chair again and started to read the newspaper story once more. As many times as she read it, the result was the same. Sanae had split in two. There was no doubting that it was Sanae's face in the photograph.

Suddenly, from behind her seat, a voice said 'My Lady.'

The woman in black looked back in surprise, but when she saw the man she said, scolding, 'Oh, Jun-chan. Where have you been? And how do you explain this business? Throwing in a doll instead of Sanae-san! I think your prank has gone a little too far, don't you?'

But Jun'ichi just stood there stock-still without saying a word. He looked at the woman in black with a teasing smile on his face.

*But which was the real body and which the reflection?*

## CHAPTER 27
## THE IMPOSTOR

'WHY DON'T YOU SPEAK? Something's happened hasn't it? You seem different. What's wrong? Or are you rebelling against me?'

In response to Jun'ichi's extremely bold manner, the woman in black unconsciously raised her voice. Or perhaps it was because she had finally lost her temper due to the numberless odd things that had happened up to now.

'Where is Sanae-san? Or are you going to tell me that you don't know?'

'That's right. I haven't the slightest idea. I'd guess she'd be in the cage, wouldn't she?'

At last, Jun-chan had answered. But his manner of speaking was very unfriendly.

'In the cage? But you took her out, didn't you?'

'Well, I wouldn't know about that. What say we have a look?'

Having flung out this remark, Jun'ichi nonchalantly strolled off. It seemed as though he really intended to check the cage. Had he taken leave of his senses? Perhaps there was another reason. Very worried now, the woman in black followed Jun-chan, monitoring his behaviour all the while.

When they came before the iron bars of the cage, they saw that the key had been left in the lock.

'You left the key in the lock! There's really something strange going on with you today.'

While muttering this, she peered into the gloomy cage.

'Look! She's not here is she!'

There was just the naked man squatting in the far corner. For some reason, he seemed completely listless today, his head limply drooping. Maybe he was sleeping.

As if talking to himself, Jun-chan said 'Let's ask him,' pulled open the iron-barred gate and walked into the cage. It really seemed that everything he did was out of the ordinary.

'Hey, Kagawa-san, do you know where Sanae-san is?'

The handsome youth in the cage was called Kagawa.

'Hey there, Kagawa-san! Are you asleep? Wake up would you?'

As he made no reply to these questions, Jun'ichi put his hand on the well-formed youth's shoulder and shook him. But Kagawa's body just wobbled back and forth without the least resistance.

'This is very strange my lady. I wonder if he's dead.'

The woman in black was transfixed by an alarming presentiment. What on earth had happened?

'Surely he hasn't killed himself, has he?'

She entered the cage and approached Kagawa.

'Lift up his face and let me see.'

'Like this, you mean?'

Jun-chan put his hand on the handsome youth's jaw and swivelled up the drooping face.

'Aa–! The face!'

Not even the Black Lizard could prevent herself from letting out a scream and stumbling back.

A nightmare. She must be having a nightmare.

The man squatting in the corner was not the handsome young Kagawa. Yet again, a person had been 'replaced' in an inexplicable manner. So, who exactly was this?

The woman in black was beset with a maddening disquiet. If there was some psychological malaise that made one person appear to be two, then perhaps she was affected by this condition.

The face that Jun'ichi had swivelled upward was the face

of – Jun'ichi! Jun-chan had doubled. There was the completely naked Jun-chan and the Jun-chan dressed in a workman's clothes and wearing a beard. There was no other explanation than that a fantastic invisible mirror was reflecting one person as two. But which was the real body and which the reflection?

Sanae-san had 'split' into two earlier with the newspaper photograph. This time it was an actual body. And the faces of the two Jun-chans were right before her.

Such a crazy thing could not really have happened. There must be some prodigious trick lurking here. But who on earth could have conceived of this incredible trick? And to what purpose?

Infuriatingly, the Jun-chan with the bushy beard was smiling derisively at the bewildered woman in black like some apparition. What was he laughing at? Should he not be shocked himself? But he was uncaringly leering away as if he had lost his senses.

Continuing to laugh, this Jun-chan again shook the naked one violently. Finally, the shaken Jun-chan made a strange sound and his eyes suddenly opened.

'Oh so you've finally come to, have you? Come on, get a grip on yourself. What were you doing in this place?'

The Jun-chan in worker's clothes again spoke in a most peculiar way.

For a time, the naked Jun-chan appeared not to know what was going on. He opened and closed his sleepy eyes, but when he saw the woman in black standing before him it was as if he had sniffed smelling salts for he quickly recovered his senses.

'M'lady, I've had a terrible time... Hah! It's him. This blackguard.'

Looking at the overall-clad Jun-chan, the seated Jun-chan jabbered madly. Then the Jun-chans locked together and a fierce struggle ensued.

However, the nightmarish contest did not last long. In an instant, the naked man was thrown onto the concrete floor.

'You bounder! You bounder! How dare you pretend to be me, you swine! M'lady, be careful. He's an impostor! It's Matsu in disguise. It's the stoker Matsu.' The naked Jun-chan yelled out from the floor where he lay flat out after having been thrown.

'Hey, you there. I'll have to ask you to put up your hands and just remain quiet while I listen to what Jun-chan has to say.'

Realizing that the situation would not be resolved simply, the woman in black had quickly grasped her pistol and pointed it at the Jun-chan clad in working clothes. Her voice was kind, but the extent of her determination could be gauged by the hue of her flashing eyes.

The man wearing the overalls obediently raised both hands, but the leer remained on his face. There was something weird about the fellow.

'All right Jun-chan. Tell me your story. What exactly is going on here?'

Suddenly embarrassed by his nudity, Jun-chan coiled himself up and then began to speak.

'You know that after everyone came here last night I went back out to the steamer by myself. It must have been then. Having finished doing what I had to do on the ship, I came back to land on the boat – and who do you think had sneaked along with me in the darkness but this fellow, Matsu, the stoker? I bawled him out in no uncertain terms, but then the bounder suddenly came flying at me.

'I had no idea that the blockhead was so strong. He started really laying in to me. I took some telling blows and finally lost consciousness. I don't know how long after that it was, but when I came to I was lying in one of the storerooms here with my hands and legs tied and without a stitch of clothing on. I tried to shout out but it was no good because I'd been gagged. I was scrabbling to get out when he came into the storeroom. Then I saw he was wearing my working clothes. And he must be an expert in disguise or something because he was also wearing a false beard. His face looked exactly like mine.

'Aha, I thought, he's made himself look like me because he's got some plot in mind. I realized he was a deceptive villain but I couldn't do anything because I was all tied up. Then, the scoundrel says to me "just put up with it a little longer" and lands me another knockout blow. I'm ashamed to say it, but I lost consciousness again. The next thing was when I came to just now.

'You're going to get yours now Matsu! With things this way, looks like you've run out of luck. You can enjoy the wait until I take my full revenge on you.'

After Jun-chan had finished talking, the woman in black suppressed a strong feeling of disquiet and laughed with apparent pleasure.

'You are a deep one aren't you Matsu? I had no idea you were such a villain. I congratulate you. So, you've been behind all these strange goings on from the start, right? You threw the dummy into the tank and dressed up the mannequins with all that strange garb. But what possible purpose could you have for doing that? It doesn't matter now, so you might as well tell me. Hey, stop leering and answer me, would you?'

The man in the work clothes asked teasingly, 'And if I don't answer, what do you intend to do?'

'Kill you. It seems you don't know your boss's character yet. She likes nothing better than the sight of blood.'

'So you mean that you're going to let me have it with that pistol? Ha, ha, ha.'

The insolent fellow laughed loudly.

At some stage he had lowered both his hands, both of which were now thrust nonchalantly in his pockets.

The woman in black gnashed her teeth at such an unthinkable insult from one of her underlings.

She could endure no more.

'Laugh at me, do you? Here, take this!'

No sooner had she shouted this than she levelled the pistol and pulled the trigger.

## CHAPTER 28
## ANOTHER DOLL INCIDENT

DID THE MAN in work clothes lose his life immediately after hearing this trite gibe? Why no, of course not. He stood there with his hands thrust into his pockets laughing with evident pleasure.

The trigger was pulled, but it simply clicked without firing.

'I say, that made an odd sound, don't you think? Perhaps there's something awry with your pistol?'

The derisive laughter infuriated the woman in black. She pulled the trigger again and again in quick succession but there was only the hollow clicking sound.

'You scoundrel! You took the bullets out, didn't you?'

'Oh so you've finally twigged have you? It is indeed as you say. Look here.'

Taking his right hand from the pocket, he opened it to reveal several small bullets snuggled cutely like little marbles in his palm.

Just then, there was a loud sound of footsteps outside the cage and the Black Lizard's rowdy minions came rushing in.

'My lady, we've got a problem. It's Kitamura. He was supposed to be guarding the entrance, but he's been tied up!'

'And he's out like a light!'

Matsu must have done this too. But why tie up just Kitamura and leave the rest alone? Maybe there was a special reason for it.

'Hey, who in the name of creation is he?'

The men's eyes were full of surprise when they realised there were two 'Jun'ichis'.

'It's Matsu the stoker. We've found out that he's the one behind everything. Hurry up and pin him down.'

Heartened by these reinforcements, the woman in black spoke loudly.

'What's that? Matsu? You swine you. How dare you do such a thing!'

The men stampeded into the cage and made to seize the man in the working clothes. But what speed Matsu had! Dodging beneath the clutching hands of the advancing group, he had in an instant dashed outside the cage. Then, while gradually backing away, the grinning figure beckoned with his hand as if saying 'come here.' What unfathomable audacity!

As if hypnotized, the woman in black and her rough henchmen moved out of the cage and edged after him.

What a peculiar procession! The pursued backing off along the concrete-walled subterranean passage, while the pursuers slowly moved directly toward their hated foe with their hairy arms raised in a boxer's pose.

Eventually the strange cavalcade reached the front of the stuffed doll display, where Matsu abruptly stood still.

'Hey you lot! Do you know why Kitamura is tied up?'

Of course, his hands were stuck nonchalantly in his pockets when he launched the odd question.

'Let me through there! I want to ask him some questions.'

It seemed the woman in black had thought of something, for she pushed her way to the head of the group and approached Matsu.

'If you are Matsu, I apologise with all sincerity for having underestimated you. But are you really Matsu? The more I think about it, the less I believe it. You're not Matsu at all, are you? And if that's the case, do me the favour of taking off that damnable false beard, would you? Take of those whiskers please.'

Pitiful though it was, she seemed to be pleading with him.

'Ha, ha, ha. You already know, even without my removing my

beard. You know, but you are scared to say my name, aren't you? Your pale face is proof of what I say – you look as though you've seen a ghost!'

It seemed that the man in working clothes was not Matsu. And he no longer spoke like some lowly thief. What was more, there seemed something familiar about the tone of that articulate voice. Such was the violence of her emotion that the woman in black could not prevent a shudder from coursing through her body.

'All right, then, so you are...'

'Oh there's no need for reserve. Why do you hesitate? Out with it then, what's the rest of the sentence?'

The man in the working clothes was no longer laughing. His overall bearing gave an impression of seriousness. The woman in black felt cold beads of perspiration slowly flowing down under her armpits.

'Akechi Kogorō... you are Akechi Kogorō aren't you?'

She felt better after managing to say it.

'That's right. You realised a long while ago, didn't you? You knew, but you suppressed the thought out of cowardice.'

As he said this, the man in working clothes peeled off his beard. Though made up to look like Jun-chan, the face that emerged was unmistakably that of Akechi Kogorō, the much-missed Akechi Kogorō.

'But why? How can this be?'

'You mean how was I rescued after having been slung into the middle of the Enshū Sea? Ha, ha, ha. You thought you were ditching me into the sea then didn't you? But there was a fundamental misapprehension there. You see, I wasn't trapped inside that sofa – it was poor old Matsu. In order to carry on with my investigations, I decided to disguise myself as the stoker. After tying him up and gagging him I put him in the ideal hiding place – the human chair. Little did I think it would end up like that. I am truly sorry that he met such a tragic fate.'

'Oh. So that was Matsu, you say? And then you disguised yourself as him and stayed in the engine room all the time. Is that correct?'

Somehow the woman thief's words had lost their venom and taken on the dulcet tones of a lady of class.

'Can it really be so, I wonder? But if Matsu had been gagged, how could he have spoken as he did? For after all, the two of us held a long conversation through the sofa's fabric, didn't we?'

'It was me that was speaking.'

'But how could...'

'There's a large closet in that cabin. I hid inside and spoke from there. To you, it sounded as though the voice came from inside the sofa. As there was someone wriggling around within it at the time, your misapprehension was understandable.'

'In that case, then, it was you that hid Sanae-san away somewhere? And put that clipping from the Osaka newspaper on the chair?'

'Indeed it was.'

'Well, very elaborate I must say. So, just to get at me you took the trouble of forging a newspaper?'

'Forging? Don't talk such rot! How could I fake a newspaper at the drop of a hat? The story and the photo are both genuine.'

'Oh really! I mean, it's silly to say that Sanae-san has a double?'

'There's no double. The "Sanae" that you kidnapped and brought here was an impostor. If you only knew the difficulty I had in finding her look-a-like. Of course, I was confident that I could rescue her unharmed, but I was unwilling to expose the only child of a friend to such danger. The girl you took to be Sanae was Sakurayama Yōko, an orphan all alone in the world. What's more, she is a modern girl of somewhat dubious morals. This was precisely why she was able to play her role in this grand drama so well. Even though she found herself in such a pickle, she had the guts to endure it all. Despite all the tears and wailing, she believed in me. She was certain that I would save her.'

Readers will doubtless recall a chapter earlier in our tale entitled 'The Strange Old Man.' It was then that master detective Akechi Kogorō carried out his feat of deception. For the unusual elderly man was none other than Akechi in disguise. From that evening, the real Sanae was concealed in a location known only by the private eye and her place was taken by Sakurayama Yōko, who entered the Iwase household and pretended to be Sanae. Starting the following day, 'Sanae' kept herself to her room, seemingly loath to show her face even to those in the house. Assuming that she had succumbed to some sort of depression as a result of the Black Lizard's barrage of blackmail, her mother and father were not in the slightest bit suspicious that she might be an impostor. Yōko's acting abilities were already outstanding at this stage.

Listening to the super sleuth's tale of how he had countered surprise with surprise, the Black Lizard acknowledged from the core of her being her arch-enemy's superiority. She even felt a deep-seated sense of veneration for this most mysterious great character. However, the veneration was certainly not shared by her ignorant and uncouth underlings. Indeed, they felt an infinite hatred and bitterness toward this rogue and enemy who had completely outdone their leader and sent their comrade Matsu to a watery grave.

They had listened impatiently to the long story, but when they sensed a lull in the to and fro of question and answer they could endure no longer.

'Enough of this! Let's do him in!'

One man's cry sparked the rest and all four burly men leapt toward the lone, unaided detective. Not even the fearsome mastery of the villainess could have prevailed against such force.

One tried to throttle him from behind, another twisted up his arms, and yet another grabbed his legs and sought to topple him. There was no resisting such a deadly, crazed adversary – even for Akechi Kogorō. Things looked bad, very bad. Having struggled so hard to reach this point, was there no way for him to turn the tables at the very last? Or would the greatest detective of the age lose his life to a gang of thugs?

But strangely, in the thick of the uproar, there echoed a surprisingly cheerful laugh. And surely this was the laugh of Akechi Kogorō, who was now being pressed down by the four men. What could it all mean?

'Ha, ha, ha! Don't you lot have eyes? You'd better look closely. Hey, take a good look inside the case.'

This presumably meant the glass case like a show window displaying the stuffed human figures.

Without thinking, they all looked in that direction. They were completely unaware of what had happened inside the glass case – partly due to the tumult of the fight and partly because the display was away at an angle from the fray and thus difficult to see.

But now that they looked inside the case, they saw that an astonishing change had occurred. Every one of the dolls wore a man's coat. All in their original positions, the male and the female figures were now dressed in stiff, serious-looking men's jackets.

Of course, this must be Akechi's handiwork, but how tiresome to carry out such mischief not once but twice! Wait a minute though. Surely Akechi would not play a meaningless prank. Might this weird changing of attires portend something astounding?

Naturally, the woman in black was the first to realize what it was.

'Oh no!'

Amazingly, and before anyone could think of fleeing, the dolls stirred into life and stood up. It was not only the clothes that had changed, the insides had also been replaced with something completely different. These were not stuffed figures but live human beings who had posed like dolls, waiting for the right time to come. And look! Without exception, every one of the jacket-clad men was gripping a pistol and the muzzles were pointed toward the woman thief and her underlings.

At that instant, there came a loud crashing sound and a gaping hole appeared in the show window. Then, from the opening the men in jackets came flying out.

'Black Lizard, you're under arrest! Come quietly!'

The fearsome order used down through the ages rang out. This effective command is used surprisingly frequently by the modern constabulary. Naturally, the men in coats were a taskforce of able police detectives who had infiltrated the underground lair with Akechi's guidance.

When the private-eye asked earlier on why only Kitamura, the man on watch at the entrance, had been tied up, he was hinting at the arrival of the police in support. The signal for them to open the entrance came when Akechi telephoned the police headquarters, enabling the detectives to make their way underground without a hitch. When they came in, they dealt with the watchman. Of course, Akechi was helping from inside. That was when Junchan went missing just a while ago. But why did they not arrest the Black Lizard immediately? This was Akechi's stratagem to heighten the effect of the capture. After all, detectives are not complete bores without a sense of humour.

Naturally, another team had enlisted the co-operation of the harbour police and gone to the pirate vessel out at sea. By now, every one of the Black Lizard's underlings – and the steamer itself – would have been taken into custody.

The pirate crew here underground all quickly lowered their heads before the officers' pistols. Fierce though the rough band was, there was nothing the men could do to oppose this nightmarish surprise attack, and they were all tied up, including the stark naked Jun-chan. However, their leader was more nimble. Having quickly perceived why the dolls were wearing coats, the Black Lizard ran away rapidly, eluding the clutching arms of the detectives and flying like a bird down the passage into her private room where she locked the door shut.

## CHAPTER 29
## THE BLACK LIZARD WRITHES

THE WOMAN IN BLACK could not withstand this ultimate insult to her pride as queen of the underworld. Though her fate was unavoidable, the Black Lizard surely intended to lock herself into her secret chamber and end her life in dignity. When Akechi Kogorō realized that, he slipped away from the commotion of the arrests, and raced alone to her chamber.

'Open up! It's me, Akechi! I have something I must say to you! Please, open the door!'

In response to his shouting came a weak reply: 'Akechi-san. If it's you alone…'

'Yes, just me. Open it, hurry!'

He heard the key turn in the keyhole, and the door opened.

'Ah! I was late! You've already taken poison, haven't you?' he shouted as soon as he stepped inside. The woman in black had collapsed after barely managing to open the door for him.

Akechi dropped to his knees, and cradled the upper half of her body on his lap, hoping to at least soothe some of her dying agonies.

'There's nothing to say now; it's all too late. Sleep in peace. Because of you, I faced mortal danger, but it has been a valuable experience… it is, after all, my profession. I don't hate you. Quite the opposite: I pity you… ah, yes, there was something I had to tell you. The item that you worked so hard to obtain for your collection, Iwase-san's Star of Egypt, I will take home with me. To return it to its rightful owner, of course.'

He withdrew the huge jewel from his pocket, and suspended it in front of the thief's eyes. The Black Lizard forced a weak smile, and nodded two, three times.

*The detectives, finished with their arrests,*
*came charging up the corridor,*
*and stood transfixed in the doorway…*

'What about Sanae-san?' she asked, gently.

'Sanae-san? Oh, you mean Sakurayama Yōko. Rest assured, she has already left this hole together with Kagawa, and is safe in the hands of the police. She had a tough time of it down here. When I get back to Osaka, I plan to make sure that Iwase-san repays her for her trouble.'

'I've lost to you. I've lost completely.'

She had not merely lost at battle. Indicating without words that she also meant her defeat at something totally different, she began to weep, the tears overflowing from her half closed eyes.

'You're holding me in your arms, aren't you... I'm so happy... I had never imagined I could have such a fortunate death.'

Akechi understood what she was saying, and felt his own breast fill with a strange emotion, although it was not one that he could express in words.

The confession of the dying Black Lizard was mysterious indeed. Had she been in love with her mortal enemy Akechi Kogorō without being aware of it? And had that been why she had cried, so full of terrible sadness, when she thought she had buried him in the midnight sea?

'Good-bye, Akechi! Can you grant me a dying wish? Kiss me...'

Her limbs were already shaking. This was the end. And though she may have been a criminal, he could not refuse her this last, dying request.

Silent, Akechi Kogorō softly pressed his lips to her already-cold brow. He kissed the forehead of the murderess who had tried to kill him. She smiled with happiness, from the heart, and with that smile still on her face, she stopped moving.

The detectives, finished with their arrests, came charging up the corridor, and stood transfixed in the doorway when they saw that strange scene. Even these detectives, known as cold-hearted men, had emotions. Stricken to silence by the solemnity they faced, they lost, for a moment, even the power of speech.

The incredible Black Lizard, the woman thief of the age who had shaken society to its roots, was gone. She had passed from this world with a faint smile on her face, lying with her head pillowed on the knees of the famous detective Akechi Kogorō.

But look at the sleeves of her black garb! She must have torn them while fleeing from the police only minutes before. Her beautiful arms were exposed, and the black lizard tattoo that was the source of her nickname seemed to writhe ever so slightly like a living creature desolate at the death of its mistress.

END

# BEAST IN THE SHADOWS

陰
獣

 **CHAPTER 1**

IT SOMETIMES SEEMS TO ME that there are two types of detective novelist. One, you could say, is the criminal sort, whose only interest is in the crime and who cannot be satisfied when writing a detective story of the deductive kind unless depicting the cruel psychology of the criminal. The other is the detective type, an author of very sound character whose only interest is in the intellectual process of detection and who is indifferent to the criminal's psychology.

Now the detective novelist I am going to write about, Ōe Shundei, belongs to the former category, while I fall into the latter.

Accordingly, while my business is concerned with crime, I am in no way a bad person, for my interest is in the scientific deduction of the sleuth. Indeed, it might even be apt to say there are few as virtuous as me.

The real mistake is that such a well-meaning person as me accidentally became involved in this case. Were I somewhat less virtuous, had I within me the slightest trait of evil, I could perhaps have come through without such regrets. I might not have sunk into this fearful pit of suspicion. Rather, I might now be living in the lap of luxury, blessed with a beautiful wife and great wealth.

Quite some time has passed since everything ended and while the awful suspicions may not have disappeared the raw reality is fading into the distance and becoming to some extent a thing of the past. Accordingly, I have decided to set this down as a kind of record and I think it could even be made into a very interesting novel, though even if I completed the work I would not have the courage to release it immediately. You see, the strange death of

Oyamada that forms a crucial part of this record still lingers in people's memories and no matter how names were changed and disguising layers applied nobody would take it as simply a work of fiction.

Thus, there may well be people who could be bothered by this novel and I would be embarrassed and disturbed to discover this. To tell the truth, though, it is more that I am frightened. For not only was the incident itself strangely meaningless and as unfathomable as a dream in broad daylight, the fantasies I built up around it were so terrifying as to discomfort even myself.

Even now, when I think of it this world transforms into something peculiar. Rain clouds fill the blue sky, a sound as of drumming beats within my ear, and all darkens before my eyes.

Anyway, while I am not of a mind to publish this record right away, sometime, just once, I would like to use it to write one of the detective novels in which I specialize. These are simply what you might call the notes for it. Nothing more than a moderately detailed *aide-mémoire*. I intend to write much as if keeping a long diary in an old notebook, blank but for the section around New Year.

Before I describe the case, it would probably be useful to provide a detailed explanation of Ōe Shundei, the detective story author who is the protagonist in this case, of his style, and also of his somewhat unusual manner of life. While I had known him prior to the incident and had even engaged him in discussions in magazines, we had not had any exchanges at a personal level and I knew little of his daily life. I became somewhat more informed about this through a friend called Honda after the events took place. Accordingly, with regard to Shundei I think it most fit that I write about these things in the order in which they occurred and as it was the occasion that led to my becoming caught up in this strange case I will describe the facts I noted when I went to interview Honda.

It was in the autumn of last year, around mid October.

I had a notion to look at some old sculptures of Buddha so I went to the Imperial Museum in Ueno where I walked through the gloomy, cavernous rooms trying to muffle my footsteps. In the large deserted halls, the slightest sound echoed fearfully and I felt like suppressing not only my footsteps but also any impulse to clear my throat.

So deserted was the place, I could not help but ponder why it is that museums are so unpopular. The large glass plates of the display cabinets shone coldly and not a speck of dust had fallen on the linoleum. The building's high ceilings were reminiscent of a temple's main hall and the silence flowed back as if one were deep under water.

I was standing in front of a display case in one of the rooms gazing at an aged wooden bodhisattva that had a dreamlike eroticism. Hearing a muffled footfall behind me, I sensed someone approach with a light sound of swishing silk.

I was startled to see the reflection of a person in the glass in front of me. Projected over the bodhisattva was the image of a woman of class wearing a lined kimono of yellow silk and with her hair done in the *marumage* style denoting a married lady. She drew level with me and stared intently at the Buddhist form. I am embarrassed to admit that while pretending to look at the image I could not prevent myself from snatching occasional glances at her. That was how much she captivated me.

Her face was pale, but I had never seen such an attractive paleness. If mermaids exist, then I believe they must have charming skin like that of this woman. She had the oval face of the beauties of the past and every line, whether of her brows, nose, mouth, neck, or shoulder, had that feminine delicacy described by the writers of old that suggested she might disappear if touched. Even now I cannot forget her dreamlike, long-lashed eyes.

Oddly, I do not now recall which of us spoke first, but perhaps I created some pretext. A brief interchange about the objects in the display case formed a link, and after doing the rounds of the museum together we exited and chatted about many things. Our paths remained the same for a considerable time on the walk from Sannai down toward Yamashita.

As we spoke, the air of beauty she evoked deepened further. When she laughed there was something graceful and shy that produced a strange sensation in me as though I were gazing at an old oil painting of a saint or that reminded me of the mysterious smile of the Mona Lisa. When she laughed, the edges of her lips caught on her large, pure white eye teeth, creating a fascinating curve. A large beauty spot on the pale white skin of her right cheek set off that curve to create an ineffable expression at once gentle and nostalgic.

However, were it not for something odd I discovered on the nape of her neck, my heart would not have been attracted by her so powerfully and she would have seemed but a genteel and tender beauty likely to vanish if touched.

She concealed it with a skilful arrangement of her collar that betrayed no artifice, but as we passed through Sannai I caught a glimpse.

Visible on the nape of her neck was a swollen line like a red weal that looked as though it went deep down her back. While it seemed to be a birthmark, I also wondered whether it might not actually be a recent scar. The dark red weal wormed over the smooth white skin of her soft nape, and strangely the cruelty of it bestowed an erotic impression. When I saw it, the beauty that had seemed to me so dreamlike suddenly pressed in on me with a compelling sense of reality.

I learned that she was a partner in Roku-Roku Trading Company, that her name was Oyamada Shizuko, and that she was the wife of the entrepreneur Oyamada Rokurō. Fortunately, she was a reader of detective fiction and in particular an admirer of my works (I shall never forget how happy I was when I heard this), which meant that ours was the relationship of an author and a fan. As such, we could become better acquainted without a trace of unseemliness and I was spared an unwanted permanent parting of the ways. Following this, we began to exchange letters occasionally.

I was impressed with Shizuko's refined taste, for though a young woman she visited deserted museums. I was also pleased that she was a devotee of my detective fiction, often said to be the most intellectual in the genre. Thus, I fell for her completely, sending her meaningless letters on a frequent basis. For her part, she scrupulously replied to each one in a ladylike style. Imagine how happy it made this lonely bachelor to have made friends with such an admirable woman.

*As the weather was cold, I had placed a rosewood brazier next to my work desk and she now sat down decorously on the other side of the oblong box with the fingers of both hands resting on its edge.*

## CHAPTER 2

**THE EPISTOLARY EXCHANGE** between Oyamada Shizuko and myself continued in this fashion for some months.

As our correspondence grew, I noted with considerable nervousness that my letters were undeniably, if unobtrusively, coming to contain a certain import, but it also seemed to me that the notes from Shizuko, while of the utmost propriety, were becoming infused with a feeling of warmth that went above what you would expect in a conventional exchange, though perhaps this was my imagination.

To speak plainly, I am embarrassed to say that I went to some pains to find out that Shizuko's husband, Oyamada Rokurō, was very much his wife's senior, that he looked older than his actual age, and that he was completely bald.

Then, around February this year, something strange began to surface in Shizuko's letters. I sensed that she was becoming very scared about something.

In one letter she wrote, 'recently something very worrying is happening and I find myself waking up in the night.'

The sentence was simple enough, but behind the words themselves the impression of a woman assailed by fear could be made out all too clearly.

'Sir, I wonder if you happen to be a friend of Ōe Shundei, who is also an author of detective fiction? If you have his address, would you let me know it?'

Of course, I knew Ōe Shundei's works very well, but I had no personal acquaintance with the man because he was extremely anti-social and had never attended any writers' gatherings. I had also heard a rumour that he had suddenly stopped writing around the middle of last year and had perhaps relocated but that his address was unknown. I replied thus to Shizuko, but when I thought that the fear she had recently been experiencing could be connected to Ōe Shundei I had an unpleasant feeling for reasons I shall explain later.

Shortly afterward, I received a postcard from her saying, 'I would like to ask your advice about a matter. Would you permit me to call on you?'

I dimly sensed the nature of this 'matter,' but as I certainly did not imagine it would be particularly frightful I was aflutter with a foolish happiness and gave myself up to all manner of fancies regarding a pleasant second encounter.

On the same day Shizuko obtained my reply that I would be pleased to receive her, she visited my lodgings. So downcast was she when I met her in the entrance hall that all my hopes were dashed, while the 'matter' was extraordinary enough to extinguish the fancies I had entertained shortly before.

'I came here because I am really at a loss as to what to do. I thought that you would be kind enough to listen to me... but I'm not sure if perhaps it would not be too much of an imposition to speak so frankly when you still hardly know me.'

Shizuko laughed tenderly, highlighting her eye teeth and beauty spot, and then glanced up at me.

As the weather was cold, I had placed a rosewood brazier next to my work desk and she now sat down decorously on the other side of the oblong box with the fingers of both hands resting on its edge. Supple, fine, and graceful, but not overly thin, the fingers seemed to symbolize her whole body. Nor did their paleness reflect any ill health, for while their delicacy suggested that they might vanish if pressed they had an uncanny strength. And it was not just her fingers – this was precisely the impression she gave overall.

Perceiving her intensity, I too quickly became serious and replied, 'If there's anything I can do.'

'It really is the most awful thing,' she said, and leaning forward she reported the following strange events, mixed in with anecdotes from her own youth.

To simplify considerably what Shizuko then told me about herself, she came from Shizuoka and she had enjoyed the utmost good fortune up until she was about to graduate from the girls school she attended.

The only thing approaching ill fortune that befell her was in her fourth year at the school when she was beguiled by the artifices of a youth called Hirata Ichirō and fell in love with him very briefly.

'Ill fortune' because this was only an eighteen-year-old girl playing at love as a result of the slightest impulse; she certainly did not love Hirata truly. However, even if she was not really in love, the other party was totally in earnest.

She found herself doing her utmost to avoid the relentless youth, but the more she did the stronger his resolve became. Eventually, a dark figure began to drift around outside the fence beside her home late at night and unpleasant threatening letters appeared in the post. The young girl trembled at the frightful reward for her youthful impulse. Her parents too were upset when they realised that she was not her usual self.

Just at that time her family suffered a serious stroke of bad luck, but it was actually favourable for Shizuko. As a result of the major economic upheavals then taking place, her father closed down his business leaving behind debt so massive that makeshift solutions would not do. Much as if fleeing in the night, he was forced to rely on a slight acquaintance to hide away in Hikone.

Due to this unforeseen change in her circumstances, Shizuko had to withdraw from the girl's school just before she was due to graduate. Nevertheless, she felt relieved that the sudden relocation enabled her to escape from the obsessive attentions of the unpleasant Hirata Ichirō.

As a result of the situation, her father became ill and shortly after passed away, leaving the mother and daughter behind. For a while, they endured a miserable existence, but their misfortune did not continue long. Soon, Oyamada Rokurō, an entrepreneur from the same village where they were lying low, came into their lives. He was their rescuer.

Through glimpses from afar, Oyamada fell deeply in love with Shizuko and sought her hand through a go-between. For her part, Shizuko felt no dislike for Oyamada. Although over ten years older than her, he was smartly turned out in gentleman's attire and had a certain ambitious air about him. The marriage proposal discussions proceeded smoothly. Oyamada returned to his mansion in Tokyo accompanied by his bride Shizuko and her mother.

Seven years passed. Shizuko's mother died of an illness in the third year or so after their marriage and some time after that Oyamada travelled overseas for two years on important business (Shizuko explained that he had returned at the end of the year before last and that she had assuaged the loneliness of her solitary existence each day by attending classes to learn the tea ceremony, flower arrangement, and music). Excluding this, their household was relatively free of incident and the very harmonious relationship between the two was characterized by a succession of happy days.

Oyamada Rokurō was an extremely energetic man and over those seven years he increased his wealth through hard work. He also established a considerable reputation among his peers.

'I am truly ashamed to say that I was not truthful about the situation with Hirata Ichirō when I married Rokurō. Despite myself, I covered it up.'

Shame and sadness made Shizuko lower her long lashed eyes, which filled with tears as she spoke in a pained low voice.

'It seems that he had heard about Ichiro somewhere and that he had some suspicions, but I assured Rokurō that I had not been with anyone but him, taking great pains to hide my relationship with Ichiro. I am still living this lie. The more suspicious my husband has grown, the more I have sought to cover it up. I think that no matter where they may be hidden, our misfortunes are truly fearful. Who would have thought that a lie told seven years ago, and that with not the slightest intention of ill will, should have been the seed for the suffering I now endure. You see, I had forgotten entirely about Hirata Ichirō. So much so that even when a letter from him suddenly arrived and I saw that the sender's name was "Hirata Ichirō", I was at a loss for a while to recall who he was.'

When she had finished, Shizuko showed me several letters from Hirata. She entrusted me with their safekeeping and I have them still. As it may assist in telling the story, let me here include the first of the letters:

*Shizuko. I have found you at last.*

*You did not notice, but I followed you from the place where I encountered you and so learned where you live. I also found out that your surname is now Oyamada.*

*You cannot have forgotten Hirata Ichirō. Surely you remember this miserable wretch.*

*A heartless woman like you cannot understand the agonies I endured after you abandoned me. How many times I wandered around your house late at night in anguish. But as my passion burned ever stronger, you grew cooler and cooler toward me. Evading me, frightened of me, you soon came to hate me.*

*Can you fathom the feelings of a man who is hated after having been adored? Can you understand how my anguish turned to sobs, my sobs to hatred that hardened and took shape as a desire for revenge? When your family's situation so luckily enabled you to disappear from my sight without a word of farewell, as if fleeing, I passed several days sitting in the study without eating or drinking. And I promised to seek revenge.*

*Being young, I did not know how to find out where you had gone. Your father owed money to many people and he slipped out of sight without letting anyone know his whereabouts. I had no idea when I would see you again. But I remembered life is long and I could not believe that mine would end without ever once meeting you again.*

*I was poor and I had to work in order to eat. That was one reason preventing me from asking around about your whereabouts. First one year, then two, the days and months flew past like an arrow, but I had to maintain my struggle against poverty. I was preoccupied with finding my next meal.*

*Then, just three years ago I had a surprising piece of good luck. After failing at various occupations and reaching the depths of despair I decided to write a novel to dispel my gloom. This was a turning point, for I was then able to put food on the table by writing fiction.*

*As you are still a novel reader, I expect you may know a writer of detective fiction called Ōe Shundei. He has not written anything for a year, but I do not think his name will have been forgotten. Well, I am Ōe Shundei.*

*Perhaps you think that I have become preoccupied with my fame as a novelist and forgotten my hatred for you? No, no – it is precisely the deep hatred stored within my heart that has enabled me to write such gory novels. If my readers knew all that suspicion, tenacity, and cruelty were born from my vengeful heart, they would probably be unable to suppress a shudder at the evil presentiment lying within.*

*So Shizuko, having secured a stable life, I sought you out to the extent made possible by time and money. Of course, I held no impossible hopes that I might recover your love. I have a wife, but one whom I wed in form only, to eliminate the inconveniences of life. In my mind, though, a lover and a wife are completely different things. You see I am not someone who forgets his hatred for a lover just because he has taken a wife.*

*Shizuko, now I have found you.*

*I am beside myself with happiness. The time has come for the prayers of many years to be answered. I have put together a means of wreaking my revenge on you with the same pleasure I have enjoyed for a long time in assembling the structure of my novels. I carefully considered the method whereby I might cause you the utmost suffering and fear and at last the moment has arrived to implement it. Just imagine my happiness! You cannot foil my plan by seeking protection from the police or anyone else. I have taken all sorts of precautions.*

*For the past year, the story that I have gone missing has circulated among journalists working for newspapers and magazines. Stemming from my misanthropy and preference for secrecy rather than anything directed at gaining revenge on you, this flight has been useful, unplanned though it was. And with even further subtlety I shall hide myself from the world and step-by-step I will push forward with my plan of revenge.*

*Of course, you must want to know what this plan is, but I cannot let the full outline be known right now because one of its effects is to gradually increase the fear as it unfolds.*

*Still, if you really want to hear, I wouldn't begrudge letting slip just a little piece of my revenge project. For example, I could recount for you in precise detail a variety of trivial little things that took place in your house four days ago, that is, on the night of 31 January.*

*From seven in the evening to half past seven, you were leaning on a small desk in the room you use for sleeping, reading fiction. The book was 'Hemeden,' a collection of short stories by Hirotsu Ryūrō. The only story you read right through was 'Hemeden.'*

*You then asked the maid to serve some tea and from half past seven to seven forty you ate two* monaka *cakes from Fūgetsu and drank three cups of tea.*

*You went to the lavatory at seven forty five and about five minutes later you came back to the room. From then until ten past nine, you were lost in thought as you passed the time knitting.*

*Your husband came home at ten past nine. From around nine twenty until a little after ten you chatted with him, keeping him company while he enjoyed a drink. At your husband's suggestion, you took half a glass of wine. The bottle had just been opened and you used your fingers to pick out a tiny piece of cork that had entered the glass. Soon after finishing your drinks, you asked the maid to prepare your beds and once the pair of you had visited the toilet you got into bed.*

*Neither of you slept until eleven o'clock. When you again lay down in your bed the pendulum clock you had received from your parents struck eleven.*

*I expect you cannot suppress a feeling of fear at reading this faithful record, as precise as a railway timetable.*

> *From the vengeance seeker (this night of 3 February)*
> *to she who stole the love of my life*

'I had heard the name Ōe Shundei before, but had not the slightest inkling it was the pen-name of Hirata Ichirō,' Shizuko explained uneasily.

Indeed, even among authors, very few knew the real identity of Ōe Shundei. Such was Hirata's antipathy to people and his aversion to being seen in society that I would probably never have heard his name had I not heard a rumour about his actual identity from Honda, who often came to my place and who had seen the copyright information.

There were three more threatening letters from Hirata, but the differences between them were slight (each bore the seal of a different post office). They all contained a promise to seek revenge, followed by a meticulous and accurate account of Shizuko's activities on a given night, with the times for these included. In particular, the secrets of her bedroom were outlined with painful frankness, down to the crudest detail. Acts and words that might cause one to blush were recounted with cold cruelty.

I could imagine what embarrassment and suffering she would have felt at showing those letters to another person, but I must say that it was a good thing that she resisted doing so until selecting me as her confidant. On the one hand, this indicated just how frightened she was that her husband should learn the secret of her past, namely that she had not been not a virgin when she married, while on the other hand it underscored the strength of her trust in me.

'Apart from my husband's family, I have no close relations and there is no-one among my friends with whom I am so intimate that I could talk about this, so while I realize it is an imposition I decided to ask you if you would be so kind as to advise me what I should do.'

On hearing this, my heart raced with happiness to think this beautiful woman was relying on me to such an extent. Of course, there were reasons why she would select me as her confidant, for like Ōe Shundei I was an author of detective fiction and I was an accomplished exponent of deductive reasoning, at least in my fiction. Notwithstanding this, she would not have asked me for my advice on such a matter unless she felt considerable trust and affection toward me.

Naturally, I accepted her request and agreed to help her as much as I could.

It seemed to me that for Ōe Shundei to have ascertained Shizuko's movements in such detail, he must have either suborned one of the servants in the Oyamada household, stealthily entered the household and concealed himself close to Shizuko, or carried out some similar nefarious plot. Based on Shundei's style, I deduced that he was just the sort of chap to go to such weird lengths.

I asked Shizuko if she had noticed anything like this, but strangely it seemed there was not the slightest trace. The servants were all trustworthy staff who had lived with the family for many years, while the house's gateway and fences were very secure because her husband was unusually nervous. Accordingly even if someone were able to sneak into the house, it would be almost impossible to approach Shizuko in her room, within the recesses of the building, without catching the eye of one of the servants.

However, the truth is that I was scornful of Ōe Shundei's ability to carry out such an action. What could a mere detective novel writer do? At most, he could use his craft to write letters to frighten Shizuko, but I convinced myself that he would be unable to go beyond that and implement an evil scheme.

While it did seem somewhat strange that he had ascertained Shizuko's movements in detail, this too appeared to be a ploy based on a sleight of hand common to his trade and I simply supposed that he had obtained the information from someone without going to any great trouble himself. To assuage Shizuko's concerns, I gave her my understanding of the situation and as it would also be advantageous to me, before sending her home I assured her that I would determine Ōe Shundei's whereabouts and if possible convince him to put an end to this nonsense.

I focused on calming Shizuko down rather than examining various points in the threatening letters from Shundei. When we parted, I said to her, 'I think it would be best if you didn't say anything about this to your husband. This is not so serious an incident as to require you to expose your secret.'

Fool that I am, I wanted to continue for as long as possible the pleasure of talking alone with her about a secret that not even her husband knew.

Nevertheless, I did indeed intend to establish the whereabouts of Ōe Shundei. He was completely opposite to me in terms of character and I disliked him intensely. I couldn't stand the crone-like stream of suspicion-filled whining or that air of self-importance fed by the clamour of his degenerate readers. So I thought that if things turned out well, I would like to reveal his underhand acts and expose his tear-reddened, humiliated face for all to see. But I did not envisage how difficult it would be to ascertain the whereabouts of Ōe Shundei.

*'It sounds like something out of a dream… I stopped
in surprise and was wondering if I should say something
when he seemed to notice me too.
But the face remained an expressionless blank …'*

 **CHAPTER 3**

AS NOTED IN HIS OWN LETTER, Ōe Shundei was a detective story writer who had emerged quite suddenly some four years ago after having pursued a number of occupations for which he was unsuited.

At that time there was hardly any detective fiction written by a Japanese author and accordingly when he released his first work the reading public greeted the rarity with great acclaim. If you were to couch it in hyperbole, you could say that he instantly became the darling of book-reading society.

Although he was not particularly prolific, a string of new works were released by a variety of newspapers and magazines. Gory, guileful, and evil, every one of these works was full of unpleasant expressions that caused your hair to stand on end, but that actually became a feature that attracted readers and his popularity continued unabated.

At about this time, I changed from writing books aimed at younger readers to detective fiction, and my name became relatively well known in the detective novel market, where there were few practitioners. However, my style was so different from Ōe Shundei's as to be almost entirely opposite.

In contrast to his gloomy, sickly, and grotesque approach, my style was bright and reflected ordinary values. In the natural flow of events, our works often competed and there were even times when we disparaged each other's fiction. Infuriatingly, though, it was usually I who scorned Shundei's writings, for while he occasionally disputed my contentions, for the most part he maintained an aloof silence. And he released his shocking stories one after another.

While I disparaged his works, I could not help but notice in them a certain eeriness. He had a passion that burned like an unquenchable ghostly flame and this unfathomable appeal captured his readers. If this stemmed from his bitterness toward Shizuko, as his letter suggested, then one could half nod in assent.

If the truth be told, I felt unspeakable jealousy each time one of his works received acclaim. I even harboured a childish perception of him as my enemy. Oh, that I could beat him! The desire rankled endlessly within my soul.

But just one year ago, he suddenly stopped writing novels and went to ground. It was not as if his popularity had waned, and the magazine hacks searched high and low for him, but for some reason he was not to be found. While I disliked him, I became a little sad when he suddenly disappeared. I had that lingering, childish feeling of emptiness one has when a 'favourite' enemy has gone.

Now I had heard news of Ōe Shundei from Oyamada Shizuko and what strange news it was. I am ashamed to say that I was secretly happy to have met my old rival again, albeit in such strange circumstances.

But was it not a natural progression, I thought, for Shundei to divert the imagination he had focused on constructing his detective tales into carrying out a plan of action?

I am sure many people are aware of this, but he was the kind of man you would call a 'fantasist about the criminal life.' In the gory pages of his manuscripts, he lived a criminal life with the same passion a brutal killer feels when he commits murder.

I am sure his readers will recall the strange ghastliness pervading his novels. They will remember the uncommon suspicions, secrecy, and cruelty that consistently filled the pages of his works. We can catch a glimpse of this in the following weird lines from one of his novels.

'Perhaps the time would come when he would not be content with just writing novels. Bored with the vanity and monotony of life, he had at least found pleasure in expressing his unusual imagination by putting words on paper. That was the impulse for him to begin writing fiction. But now he had even become bored with the novels. Where would he find the stimulation he craved now? Crime, yes, there was only crime left. Having exhausted so many other avenues, only crime's frisson remained.'

The author was also very eccentric in his ordinary life. Shundei's misanthropy and secrecy became known among other writers and magazine journalists. It was very rare for a visitor to be shown through to his study. His seniors in social standing were turned away at the door with equanimity regardless of their rank. He also moved house often and never attended writers' gatherings on the pretext of illnesses that lasted more or less all year.

Rumour had it that he lay all day and night in a bed that was never made up, doing everything, whether eating or writing, from a recumbent position. Apparently he closed the window shutters in the day, writhing in the candle-lit gloom of his room as he penned those eerie reveries of his.

When I was told that he had stopped writing novels and disappeared, I secretly imagined that he had perhaps set up a base in the jumbled back streets of Asakusa and begun to put his fantasies into action, much as he often described in his fiction. Would he be able to carry it out? Not six months had passed when he appeared before me as someone who did indeed intend to put his fantasies into action.

It seemed to me that the quickest way to ascertain Shundei's whereabouts would be to ask around in the arts sections of the newspapers or to talk to the magazine journalists . Nevertheless, such was the extreme eccentricity of Shundei's daily life that he only received visitors infrequently. In addition, as the magazine houses had already tracked him down before, I needed a journalist who was on very intimate terms with him. Fortunately, a magazine editor with whom I was friendly was just the right person.

A scribe who worked out on the streets, Honda had an outstanding reputation as a specialist in his field. There had been a time when his task was to get Shundei to write fiction, much as if Shundei was Honda's main assignment. In addition, in keeping with his role as a journalist working the front line, Honda had considerable investigative skills.

Accordingly, I telephoned him and invited him over. First I asked him to tell me about Shundei's day-to-day life, of which I knew little.

He replied very informally.

'Shundei, you say? Oh, he's a boor, isn't he?'

He looked like Daikoku, the stout god of wealth, as he smiled sardonically, before answering all my questions earnestly.

According to Honda, Shundei had been living in a rented house in Ikebukuro when he began to write novels, but as his name became better known and his income increased he gradually relocated to more commodious dwellings (albeit mostly rented). Honda named some seven locations that Shundei had lived in over a period of around two years, including Kikui-chō in Ushigome, Negishi, Yanaka-Hatsune, and Nippori Kanasugi.

It was after he had moved into Negishi, that Shundei finally became very popular and the magazine hacks started to arrive in droves. However, from about that time he showed an aversion to people and the front door was always locked, while his wife used the back door to come and go.

Often he would refuse to meet visitors, feigning that he was out, only to send a polite note explaining 'I do not like company; please send a letter stating your business.' Only a few journalists were able to meet and speak to Shundei – most gave up in frustration. While they were used to the strange habits of novelists, Shundei's misanthropy was too much.

As it happens, though, his wife was a woman of considerable sagacity and Honda often went through her when negotiating manuscripts or pressing for something.

That said, it could be quite difficult even to meet the wife because the front door would be closed with strict-sounding notices hanging from it carrying such messages as 'No interviews granted due to illness,' 'Away on a trip,' and 'Journalists: all manuscript commission requests to be sent by letter; no interviews.' On more than one occasion even Honda was discouraged and left in disappointment.

As Shundei did not notify anyone of his new address when he moved, the journalists all had to search for him based on his mail.

'There might be a lot of journalists, but I'm probably the only one to talk with Shundei and joke with his wife,' boasted Honda.

My curiosity was growing steadily and I asked: 'Going by the photographs, Shundei seems quite a handsome chap. Is that how he actually looks?'

'Ha! Those photographs must be fakes. Shundei said they were taken when he was young, but it seems odd to me. He's just not that good looking. You could put it down to extreme puffiness and obesity brought on by lack of exercise. He's always lying down, you know. Although he's overweight, the skin on his face hangs down terribly, giving him the expressionless look of a Chinaman, while his eyes are clouded and turbid. I'd say he looks something like a drowned corpse. What's more, he's terrible at speaking and keeps his mouth shut. It makes you wonder how he could write such marvellous fiction.

'You remember that Uno Kōji novel *Hitodenkan*, right? Well Shundei is exactly like that. He lies down so much he could get bed sores and I'd say it's probably true he eats while in bed.

'Still, there's something peculiar. Even though he is so averse to company and is always in bed, there are rumours that he sometimes disguises himself and wanders around in the Asakusa area. And it's always at night. You'd think he was a robber or a bat. I wonder if he isn't really painfully shy. Perhaps he just doesn't want people to see his bloated body and face. The more famous he becomes, the more ashamed he is of his unsightly body. It could be he wanders secretly around in the thronging quayside at night instead of making friends and meeting visitors. That's the feeling I get based on his character and reading between the lines of what his wife says.'

Honda had created an image of Shundei with considerable eloquence. Finally he told me something very strange.

'You may be interested to know, Mr Samukawa, that I met the elusive Ōe Shundei the other day. He appeared so different that I didn't greet him, but I am sure it was Shundei.'

'Where? Where was this?' I asked instantly.

'In Asakusa Park. Actually, I was making my way home after having been out late and I may still have been a little drunk.'

Honda grinned and scratched his face.

'You know that Chinese restaurant Rai-Rai Ken? Well it was on that corner early in the morning when there are not many people about. I saw a fat person standing there in a clown's costume with a deep-red pointy hat handing out advertising leaflets. It sounds like something out of a dream, but it was Ōe Shundei. I stopped in surprise and was wondering if I should say something when he seemed to notice me too. But the face remained an expressionless blank and he then swivelled away and made off at great speed down the street opposite. I thought about going after him, but then realized that it might actually be out of order to greet him in that get up so I decided against it and just went home.'

Listening to Ōe Shundei's odd way of life, I had felt an unpleasant sensation as if I was having a nightmare. Then when I heard about him standing in Asakusa Park wearing a pointed hat and a clown's costume, for some reason I felt shocked and the hair on the back of my neck stood up.

I could not understand what the connection was between his appearance as a clown and the threatening letters to Shizuko (it seemed that Honda had met Shundei in Asakusa just at the time when the first of these letters arrived), but I knew that I could not just let it slide.

To confirm that the script in the threatening notes I was keeping for Shizuko was indeed Shundei's handwriting, I selected one page only from a section where the meaning was not clear and showed it to Honda.

Honda confirmed that the handwriting was Shundei's and he also said that the flourishes and style could only have been penned by Shundei. Honda knew the features of Shundei's handwriting because he had once tried to write a novel in his style, but he said that he found it impossible to copy that relentless, cloying approach. I knew what he meant. Having read a number of his letters in their entirety, I was even more aware than Honda of the distinctive trace of Shundei contained therein.

Using some flimsy pretext, I asked Honda if he could track down Shundei.

'Sure, leave it to me,' he accepted without fuss. Still, as that was not enough to set my mind at rest I decided to check the area around block 32 of Sakuragi-chō, in Ueno, which Honda had told me was where Shundei had lived.

## CHAPTER 4

**THE NEXT DAY,** I left a manuscript I had started to write where it lay and set out for Sakuragi-chō, where I stopped maids from the neighbourhood and trades people visiting local homes to ask them about the Ōe household. I was able to confirm the veracity of Honda's account, but I could not find out one jot more about Shundei's subsequent whereabouts.

As many of the homes in the area were middle-class establishments with their own gateways, the neighbours did not chat together as they would when living in more tightly packed cheaper dwellings and accordingly the most anybody could say was that the household had relocated without giving a destination. Of course, there was no doorplate bearing the name Ōe Shundei, so nobody knew that the house had been occupied by a famous author. As nobody even knew the name of the movers who had carted the luggage away in a truck, I had to return empty-handed.

With no other alternative available, every day I snatched quick breaks while working urgently on a manuscript and phoned Honda to inquire about the search, but it seemed there were no clues and the days passed by. While we were thus occupied, Shundei steadily pushed forward with his obsessive plot.

One day Oyamada Shizuko telephoned me at my lodgings and after telling me that something very worrying had occurred she asked me to come over. Apparently her husband was away and all of the house staff on whom she could rely were out on errands. It seems she had decided to use a public telephone rather than call from the house, and such was her extreme hesitation that she only had time to make the request before the three minutes elapsed and the line was lost.

I felt a little strange that she had thought to ask me over in this somewhat coquettish fashion with her husband fortuitously away and the servants out about their tasks.

I agreed to her request and went to her house, which was in Yama no Shuku, in Asakusa.

Tucked well down between two merchant buildings, the Oyamada home was an old building that resembled a dormitory from the past. While the Sumida River was not visible from the front, I thought that it probably flowed at the back. The building, which appeared to have been recently extended, differed from a dormitory in that it was surrounded by a very large and tasteless concrete wall (topped with glass shards to ward off thieves), while behind the main building arose a double storey block built in a Western style. The disharmony between the old, very Japanese looking building and these two structures gave an impression of moneyed but unrefined taste.

After presenting my card, I was shown to the parlour of the Western-style building by a young woman who seemed to be from the country. Shizuko was waiting there with a serious expression on her face.

She apologized many times over for her lack of propriety in having called me, and then assuming a low voice for some reason she said, 'First, please take a look at this' as she produced a document in an envelope. Looking behind as if afraid, she edged closer to me. It was of course a letter from Ōe Shundei, but as the content was slightly different from the documents she had received thus far I include it below:

*Shizuko, I can see the anguish you are in.*

*I am also aware that unbeknownst to your husband you are going to great lengths to track me down. However, it is no good so you may as well stop. Even if you had the courage to reveal my threatening letters to him and as a result the matter ended up in the hands of the police, you'll never discover my whereabouts. You only need to look at my novels to understand what a well-prepared fellow I am.*

*Now then, it is about time my prelude came to an end. The moment has arrived for this business of revenge to move to the second stage. First though, I should let you in a little on the background. You can probably broadly surmise how I was able to learn with such accuracy what you were doing each night. Since I found out where you were, I have been following you as closely as a shadow. You cannot see me at all, but I can observe you at every moment, whether you are at home or out about your business. I have become your very shadow. Even now as you read this letter trembling with fear, perhaps this shadow is staring at you from some corner of the room through narrowed eyes.*

*Naturally, as I observed your activities every night I had to see the intimacy between you and your husband and of course I felt extremely jealous.*

*Although this was something I did not allow for when I first brewed up my revenge scheme, it did not hinder my plan in the least. What is more, the jealousy even served as fuel to kindle the flames of my vengeful heart. Then I realized that if I made a slight adjustment to my plan it would better serve my objectives.*

*My original plan called for me to expose you to great torment and fear before eventually taking your life, but since recently having had to witness the intimacy between you and your husband I have come to think that before killing you it would probably be quite effective if I took the life of your beloved right before your eyes and then make it your turn after you have been given sufficient time to savour the tragedy. And that is what I have decided to do.*

*But you do not need to panic. I never rush things because it would be such a waste to move to the next step before you had fully relished the anguish produced by perusing my first letter.*

*Your vengeful devil (this late night of 16 March)*

On reading this horribly cruel letter I could not suppress a shudder. I sensed my hatred toward Ōe Shundei multiply.

But were I to give in to fear, who would comfort poor beleaguered Shizuko? There was nothing for it but to feign complaisance and explain to her repeatedly that the letter's threats were simply a novelist's fantasies.

'I entreat you to speak more softly.'

Shizuko was not heeding my earnest explanations. Her attention was focused elsewhere and from time to time she would stare fixedly at one spot in a way that suggested she was listening intently. Then she lowered her voice much as if someone were eavesdropping on us. Her lips lost so much colour that there was no contrast between them and her pale face.

'I think I could be going a little crazy. But was that real, do you think?'

Mouthing meaningless words in a whisper, it seemed Shizuko could perhaps have lost her mind.

'Did something happen?'

I too had been drawn in and was now talking in a very low voice.

'Hirata Ichirō is in this house.'

'Where?'

I looked at her blankly, unable to grasp her meaning.

Standing up suddenly, Shizuko blanched and beckoned me. I walked after her, becoming nervous myself. Noting my wristwatch, she had me remove it for some reason and then went back to place it on the table. Muffling our footsteps, we next moved down a short corridor to Shizuko's living room, which was in the Japanese style building. As she opened the screen door, Shizuko seemed afraid that there might be some ruffian lurking immediately behind.

'It's a little odd, you know, to think that man would sneak into your house in broad daylight. Are you sure you aren't mistaken?'

After I had spoken, she made to stifle an impulsive gasp with her hand and then taking my hand she went to a corner of the room where she looked up at the ceiling and signalled to me to be quiet and listen.

We stood there for ten minutes our eyes locked together as we listened intently.

Although it was the middle of the day, there was not a sound in the room, which was deep within the large house, and such was the silence you could hear the blood beating in your ears.

After a while, Shizuko asked in a voice so low I could hardly hear her, 'Do you hear the timepiece ticking?'

'A timepiece? No, where is it?'

For a while she remained silent, listening attentively, then apparently reassured she said, 'I can't hear it now.'

Shizuko led me back to the room in the Western style building and with laboured breathing she then began to relate the following unusual events.

She had been doing a little needlework in the parlour, when the maid brought in the letter from Shundei quoted above. By this stage she could recognize his letters from just a glimpse of the envelope and she had an unpleasant feeling when she took the document, but she had to open it. With a heightened sense of uneasiness she fearfully cut the envelope and began to read.

When she realized that her husband was now involved, she could not stay still. For no particular reason, she stood up and walked to the corner of the room. Just as she stopped in front of the wardrobe, she heard a very faint sound above her head that seemed almost like the noise made by a grub.

'I thought it might just be a ringing in my ears, but I stood completely still and listened and heard something that was not my ears ringing. It was a definite ticking like the sound that might be produced by metal touching against metal.'

Somebody must be concealed above the ceiling boards and this was the sound of that person's pocket watch marking out the seconds.

Probably she had been able to detect that ever-so-faint whisper of metal behind the ceiling because she just happened to be standing up, and so her ears were positioned closer to the ceiling, because the room was so quiet, and because nervousness had sharpened her senses. Thinking that perhaps the sound came from a timepiece in a different direction and that, much as with a light beam, reflection made it seem to emanate from behind the ceiling, she searched every nook and cranny but there was no clock or watch anywhere in the area.

Then she recalled a sentence from the letter: 'Even now as you read this letter trembling with fear, perhaps this shadow is staring at you from some corner of the room through narrowed eyes.' Her attention was drawn to a crack just there in the ceiling where the board had pulled back slightly. It seemed to her that she could see Shundei's eyes glinting narrowly in the pitch dark deep inside the crack.

'Hirata Ichirō, it's you in there isn't it?'

Shizuko suddenly felt a strange excitement. As if thrusting herself in front of her enemy, she was speaking to the person in the attic, all the time crying large tears.

'I don't care what happens to me. I'll do whatever you require. Kill me if you must. But please leave my husband alone. I lied to him. It would be too terrible if on top of that he should die for my sake.'

Her voice was weak but she entreated with all her heart.

But there was no reply from above. The excitement faded and she stood there for a long time as if drained. But apart from the tick-tocking there in the attic, not the slightest sound could be heard. Deep within the darkness, the beast in the shadows held its breath as silent as a mute.

In that eerie silence she suddenly felt terribly frightened. Shizuko dashed out of the parlour and, unwilling to stay in the house for some reason, she ran out the front. Remembering me, she rushed to a nearby telephone booth.

As I listened to Shizuko's account, I couldn't help remembering a weird story by Ōe Shundei entitled 'Games in the Attic.' If the ticking sound Shizuko had heard was not a delusion and Shundei was concealed in there, it could mean that he had decided to put into practice the concepts of the story and this would be very typical of Shundei's behaviour.

Because I had read 'Games in the Attic,' I could not laugh off Shizuko's seemingly bizarre story and I too was beset by a great fear. I even seemed to see a bloated Ōe Shundei leering there in the darkness wearing a red pointed hat and a clown's costume.

**CHAPTER 5**

AFTER TALKING IT OVER, I decided that, just like the amateur sleuth in 'Games in the Attic,' I would climb into the attic above Shizuko's parlour and see if I could find any trace of someone having been there, and if there were some trace I would try to determine exactly how the person had entered and exited.

Shizuko tried her best to stop me, saying 'Such an unpleasant thing... you couldn't possibly,' but I would not heed her and, as shown in Shundei's story, I removed the ceiling board inside the cupboard and climbed up inside the hole like an electrician. Apart from the maid who had come out to answer the door, there was no one else in the house, and as the maid appeared to be working in the kitchen I was not concerned about being spied by anybody.

The attic was not as beautiful as the one in Shundei's fiction.

This was an old house, but the attic was not terribly dirty because at the end of the year the cleaners had come in and removed the ceiling boards and washed them thoroughly. Still, the dust had gathered over the past three months, as had the spider webs. First, it was so dark you could not see a thing, so I borrowed a torch that was in Shizuko's house and, carefully navigating along the beams, I approached the spot in question. Gaps had opened up between the ceiling boards, which had perhaps curved back so much due to the cleaning. The light that shone up from below acted as a landmark. I had only gone a meter, but had already discovered something startling.

Although I had climbed thus into the attic, the truth is I thought it could not be as Shizuko said – that she must surely have imagined it. However, the reverse side of the ceiling boards did indeed carry the traces of someone having been there recently.

Suddenly, I felt a cold sensation. An indescribable shudder ran through me when I thought that Ōe Shundei, that poisonous spider of a man whom I knew only through his novels, had crawled through the attic in just the same fashion as I was now doing. I steeled myself and followed the footprints or handprints that had been left in the dust on the beams. At the place from which the ticking sound had supposedly emanated, the dust had indeed been considerably disturbed and there were signs that somebody had been there for a long time.

Preoccupied now, I began to stalk what appeared to be the traces left by Shundei. It seems that he had walked through more or less every part of the attic – the strange footprints were all over. In particular, above Shizuko's parlour and the bedroom she and her husband used some floorboards had gaps between them and the dust was very disturbed.

Just like the character in 'Games in the Attic,' I peeked down into the room below and it seemed entirely possible that Shundei had gazed in ecstasy there. The strange scene in the 'netherworld' visible through the cracks between the boards was truly beyond imagination. In particular, when I looked at Shizuko, who happened to be right below me, I was surprised at how strange a person can appear depending on the angle of vision.

We always look at each other side on and even the most self conscious person does not consider how he or she looks from above. How vulnerable we are! And precisely because of that vulnerability, those who make no effort to adorn themselves are exposed in a somewhat unflattering light. The depression between Shizuko's fringe and glistening chignon (from directly above the *marumage* bob had already lost its symmetry) was thin, but some dust had gathered there and it looked very dirty compared to the other pretty parts. As I was looking from straight above, I could see down past the nape that followed on from her coiffure into the valley formed between the collar of her kimono and her back. I could even see the bumps along her spine and also the poisonous red weal that painfully wound along her moist white skin down into the darkness and out of sight. Regarded from aloft, Shizuko seemed to lose some of her ladylike refinement and instead a certain strange obscenity she possessed loomed larger for me.

To see if any evidence of Ōe Shundei's presence remained, I directed the torch's light onto the ceiling boards and searched around, but the handprints and foot marks were unclear and naturally fingerprints could not be made out. Shundei had probably worn gloves and gone in stockinged feet, as set down in 'Games in the Attic.'

However, a small, mouse-coloured round object had fallen in a hard to see spot at the foot of a strut rising from the ceiling to a beam right above Shizuko's parlour. The faded metal object was hollowed out like a bowl and looked like a button. On its surface, the letters 'R.K. BROS. CO.' stood out in relief.

When I picked it up, I immediately thought of the shirt button in 'Games in the Attic,' but this was a somewhat unusual button. It looked as though it could be some sort of decoration on a hat, but I couldn't be sure. When I showed it to Shizuko later, she could only shake her head.

Naturally, I carefully sought to ascertain how Shundei had managed to sneak into the attic.

Following the traces of disturbance in the dust, I noticed that they stopped above the storeroom beside the entrance hall. The storeroom's rough ceiling boards shifted easily when I tried to lift them. Using a broken chair that had been thrown inside as a platform, I climbed down and made to open the storeroom door from the inside. The door had no lock and opened easily. Immediately outside was a concrete wall just a little higher than a person.

Perhaps Ōe Shundei had waited until no one was about, climbed over the wall (as noted above, the wall was topped by glass shards, but this would be no obstacle to a scheming intruder) and sneaked into the attic through the storeroom's lockless door.

Once I had fully grasped it all, I felt a little disappointed. I wanted to scorn the perpetrator for committing the childish prank of a delinquent. The odd mysterious fear disappeared, leaving only a real feeling of displeasure. (I would only learn later how mistaken I was to scorn the perpetrator.)

Beside herself with fear and anxious that her husband's life should not come into danger, Shizuko suggested going to the police even if it meant revealing her secret. However, I had begun to look down on our opponent and I calmed Shizuko by assuring her the perpetrator would not do anything so silly as to drip poison down from the ceiling, as in 'Games in the Attic,' and that even though he had sneaked into the attic this did not mean he could murder someone. Trying to frighten people like this was just the sort of childish thing Shundei would get up to and it seemed likely that he would make it appear as though he were perpetrating some crime. I consoled her that a mere novelist like him lacked any further ability to put his plans into action. To set her mind at rest, I promised to ask a friend who was keen on such things to watch the area around the wall outside the storeroom every night.

Shizuko said that fortunately there was a guest bedroom on the second floor of the European style section of the building and that she would use some pretext or other to justify using that as their bedroom for the time being. This part of the building did not have any chinks in the ceiling for prying eyes.

These defensive measures were put into action the following day, but Ōe Shundei, the evil beast in the shadows, simply ignored the makeshift ploys. Two days later, on 19 March, the first victim was butchered, exactly as he had forewarned. Oyamada Rokurō drew his last breath.

*The strange scene in the 'netherworld'*
*visible through the cracks between the boards*
*was truly beyond imagination.*

 **CHAPTER 6**

THE LETTER ADVISING of the impending murder of
Oyamada had included the phrase: '*But you do not need to panic. I
never rush things.*' Then why had he perpetrated the crime in such
haste just two days later? Or perhaps that had been a tactic – a
phrase inserted into the letter in order to create a false sense of se-
curity. But it suddenly occurred to me that there could be another
reason.

It was something I feared when I heard Shizuko pleading in tears
for Oyamada's life after she heard the ticking watch and became
convinced Shundei had sneaked into the attic. It seemed certain
that when Shundei became aware of Shizuko's devotion to her
husband his jealously had intensified and at the same time he had
felt threatened. He might have thought: 'Right, if you love your
husband so much, I'll finish him off quick rather than keep you
waiting a long time.' Leaving that aside, in the case of the odd
death of Oyamada Rokurō the body was discovered in extremely
strange circumstances.

I first heard all the details after receiving a message from Shizuko
and hastening to the Oyamada residence on the evening of the
same day. On the previous day, he had returned from the company slightly earlier than normal and there was nothing particularly unusual about his appearance. After finishing his evening
drink, Oyamada said he was going across the river to play go at
his friend Koume's place and as it was a balmy evening he set off
wearing simply a light Ōshima kimono and *haori* rather than a
coat. This was at about seven in the evening.

As he was in no hurry, he strolled as usual by way of Azumabashi

215

bridge and walked along the Mukōjima river bank. He stayed at
his friend's house until around midnight and then left on foot. It
was all clear up to this point, but from there nothing was known.

Although Shizuko was up all night waiting, he did not come
home, and given that she had just received a terrifying threat from
Ōe Shundei she was very worried. As she waited for the dawn, she
tried to contact everyone she could think of using the telephone
and the servants, but there was no indication that he had been
to any of these places. Naturally, she rang me, but I happened to
have been out from the previous evening and as I did not return
until the next night I did not hear anything about these events as
they occurred.

Finally, the moment for Oyamada to show up for work arrived.
As there was no sign of him, the company did its best to find him,
but his whereabouts remained unknown. By this time, it was
nearly noon. Just then, the Kisagata police called to report that
Oyamada Rokurō had died in strange circumstances. A little to
the north of the Kaminarimon gate train stop on the west side of
the Azumabashi bridge, a path descends from the main riverbank
walkway to a landing place for the ferry plying the route between
the Azumabashi and Senju bridges. Recalling the era of the penny
steamers, the ferry service was one of the Sumida River's tourist
attractions. I often boarded the motor launch with no particular
purpose, making the return trip between Kototoi and Shirahige
bridges because I loved the old-time rural atmosphere conjured
up by the traders, who brought picture books and toys on board,
and who described their wares in time to the beat of the screw in
the hoarse voice of a narrator who takes on all the roles in a silent
movie. The landing place was a floating quay on the Sumida River,
and the passenger waiting benches and toilets were all located on
this wallowing boat platform. Having used that toilet myself, I

knew it was just a box-like enclosure with a rectangular opening in the wooden floor that opened directly onto the muddy river, which coiled along thickly about a foot below.

Just as on a steam train or a ship, there was nothing in the toilet to hold up waste matter and accordingly it was indeed clean, but if you stared intently down from the rectangular hole into the eddying fathomless black water, you could occasionally see bits of flotsam appear on one side of the hole and float out of sight on the other side like micro-organisms viewed in a microscope. It gave one a strange feeling.

About eight o'clock in the morning of 20 March, the proprietress of one of the merchant family stalls in Asakusa's Nakamise arcade came to the Azumabashi ferry landing place on her way to Senju on business and while she was waiting for the vessel to arrive she went into the toilet. Immediately after, there was a scream and the woman came flying out.

When the elderly ticket collector asked her what had happened, she told him that she had seen a man's face looking up at her from the blue water directly under the rectangular hole.

At first the ticket collector thought it might be a prank played by one of the crew (there had been some peeping Tom incidents in the water from time to time), but he went into the toilet anyway to investigate, whereupon he indeed saw a human face floating there about a foot directly under the hole. Waving to and fro with the water's motion, half the face would disappear only to pop up again. 'So help me, he looked just like one of them wind-up dolls,' the ticket collector said later.

When he realized it was a corpse, the old man immediately got into a fluster and shouted out to the young fellows among the customers waiting for the ferry at the landing place.

Enlisting the aid of a strapping chap from the fish shop and some other young men, he attempted to lift up the dead body, but they were unable to pull him up through the hole in the toilet. Accordingly, they went outside and used a pole to prod the corpse out into the open water. Strangely, they discovered that the cadaver was stark naked, but for a pair of undershorts.

There was something unusual because this was a man around forty in rude health and it seemed unlikely that he would have been swimming in the Sumida River in this weather. Furthermore, a closer look revealed that his back had what looked to be a wound from a knife and the corpse contained relatively little water for a drowned man.

When it emerged this was a murder case rather than a death by drowning the commotion intensified. Then another queer thing happened when the corpse was lifted out of the water.

Under the instructions of an officer who had rushed from the Hanakawado police station after hearing the news, one of the young fellows at the landing place grasped the sodden hair of the cadaver and made to lift it up, but the hair slid smoothly away from the scalp. It was such an unpleasant feeling that the young man let go with a cry. It seemed odd that the hair should peel away so easily even though the body did not appear to have been in the water all that long, but a closer look revealed that what had appeared to be hair was in fact a wig and the man's head was completely bald.

This was the wretched death of Oyamada Rokurō, Shizuko's husband and director of Roku-Roku Trading Company.

After having been stripped naked, Rokurō's bald head had been covered with a fluffy wig and the corpse dumped into the river beneath Azumabashi. Furthermore, although the corpse had been discovered in the water, there was no sign that water had been ingested. The fatal injury was a wound inflicted by a sharp instrument to the back, in the section near the left lung. Given that there were a number of other shallower stab wounds, it seemed certain that the criminal had stabbed the body multiple times.

According to the police surgeon's examination, the fatal wound had probably been inflicted around one o'clock that morning, but as the corpse was not clothed and there were no belongings, the police were unable to identify it. Luckily, someone who knew Oyamada by sight appeared around noon and the police immediately telephoned the Oyamada residence and the trading company.

When I visited that night, there was considerable confusion at the Oyamada home, which was thronged with relatives from the Oyamada side, employees of Roku-Roku Trading Company, and friends of the deceased. Shizuko said that she had just returned from the police station and she looked around aimlessly amidst a circle of those paying their respects.

Oyamada's corpse had not yet been handed over by the police. Under the circumstances, it had to undergo an autopsy, and accordingly the white cloth on the dais in front of the family Buddhist altar was occupied only by a hastily arranged mortuary tablet on which offerings of incense burned sadly.

From Shizuko and the trading company staff, I gained the full account of the discovery of the corpse as detailed above. When it occurred to me that I had caused this deplorable event, having scorned Shundei two or three days earlier and stopped Shizuko from notifying the police, I felt such shame and regret I wanted to leave.

It seemed to me that Ōe Shundei must be the criminal. When Oyamada was walking past Azumabashi after leaving Koume's house, Shundei must have pushed him down to the dark landing place, struck him with a weapon and thrown the body into the river. Surely there could be no doubt that Shundei was the perpetrator. In terms of timing, Honda had indicated that Shundei was wandering around the Asakusa vicinity, and Shundei had even predicted Oyamada's murder.

Still, it was very strange that Oyamada had been quite naked and wearing an odd wig. If indeed this was the handiwork of Shundei, why had he done such an outlandish thing?

In order to discuss with Shizuko the secret we alone knew, I waited for the right moment then approached her and asked her into another room. Much as if she had been awaiting this, Shizuko bowed to the company and followed me in. Once out of sight of the guests, she cried out my name softly and suddenly clung to me. She looked fixedly at my chest. The long lashes glittered and the swelling in the space between her eyelids turned into large tears that coursed down her pale cheeks. The tears welled up one after another and flowed down ceaselessly.

Shizuko's tears were subsiding, but now I was overcome with emotion and taking her hand in mine I apologized over and over, pressing her hand as if to give her strength.

'I don't know what to say. It's all due to my carelessness. It didn't occur to me that he had the ability to carry this out. It's all my fault. I'm so sorry...'

That was the first time I felt Shizuko's body. I shall never forget that even in that situation it seemed that her core was aflame despite her pale tenderness and I was acutely aware of the wondrous touch of her warm, nimble fingers.

When Shizuko had stopped crying, I asked: 'So did you report that threatening letter to the police?'

'No, I wasn't sure what I should do.'

'So you still haven't said anything then?'

'No, I haven't. I wanted to discuss things with you.'

It seemed strange when I thought about it later, but at that time I was still holding her hand. Shizuko left her hand in mine and remained leaning against me.

'You still think it was his doing, don't you?'

'Yes, I do. And last night something strange happened.'

'Something strange?'

'Well, I shifted our bedroom to the second floor of the European part of the building, as you suggested. It put me at my ease to think that we would no longer be spied upon, but it seems as if he was peeping after all...'

'Where from, may I ask?'

'From outside – through the window.'

Her eyes opening wide as she remembered the fear of the moment, Shizuko haltingly recounted what had happened.

'I went to bed around twelve o'clock last night, but I was very worried because my husband hadn't come home. All alone in that high-ceilinged Western style room I became afraid and it seemed to me I was being watched from every corner. One of the window blinds had not been fully lowered, and the foot or so left open revealed the pitch blackness outside. Even though I was afraid, for some reason my eyes seemed terribly drawn in that direction, when all of a sudden a person's face loomed vaguely into view.'

'Are you sure it wasn't a figment of your imagination?'

'It soon disappeared, but even now I am sure that I was not seeing things. The dishevelled hair was pressed up against the glass and I can still see those eyes staring up at me from the down turned face.'

'Was it Hirata?'

'I don't know... but there couldn't possibly be anyone else who would do such a thing.'

After this exchange, we decided that Oyamada's killer must be

Hirata Ichirō (Ōe Shundei) and we agreed to go to the police together and tell them that he was plotting to murder Shizuko next and ask for their protection.

The detective in charge of this case was a law graduate named Itosaki, and fortunately he was a member of Crime Hounds, a group composed of murder-mystery writers, doctors, and legal professionals. Accordingly, when Shizuko and I went to the investigation headquarters at Kisagata, rather than treating us stiffly – as a detective ordinarily would with the family of the victim – he listened to us kindly as a friend.

It seems that he was very alarmed by the case and that he also felt a considerable interest in it. He said that he would do his best to find Ōe Shundei and promised to protect Shizuko fully by assigning a detective to guard the Oyamada home and increasing the number of patrols. When I told the detective that the photos of Ōe Shundei now in circulation were not good likenesses, he contacted Honda to obtain an expert description of the suspect.

## CHAPTER 7

**FOR ABOUT THE FOLLOWING MONTH**, the constabulary exerted their all in the search for Ōe Shundei and I too did my utmost to establish his whereabouts, asking everyone I met, including Honda and other newspaper journalists and magazine writers, if they had any clue. But it was as if Shundei had woven some kind of spell – there was no trace of him.

It was not as if he were alone; there was his wife to slow him down, so where could the two of them be hiding? Could he, as Inspector Itosaki conjectured, have concocted a plan to smuggle them both on board a vessel and slip off to a distant land?

But the strange thing was that after the bizarre death of Rokurō, the threatening letters suddenly ceased. Perhaps frightened by the police search, Shundei had put off the next step in his scheme – the murder of Shizuko – and was intent only on staying out of sight. Yet, surely a man like him would have expected something like this. If so, then he might be lying low somewhere in Tokyo quietly waiting for a chance to kill Shizuko.

The head of the Kisagata police station ordered his men to search the area near 32 Sakuragi-chō in Ueno, which was Shundei's last known residence. Although I had attempted the same, the experts were able after great effort to discover the transport company that had moved Shundei's belongings (this was a small firm from around Kuromon, far from Ueno), and they then tracked down his next address.

The outcome of the inquiry was that after decamping from Sakuragi-chō, Shundei had gradually relocated to seedier addresses, including Yanagishima-chō in Honjo-ku and Mukōjima

Suzaki-chō. The final residence was a squalid rental house in Su-gisaki-chō that looked just like a barracks and was squeezed be-tween two factories. He had paid several months rent in advance and when the detective went to investigate the landlord thought that Shundei was still living there. However, when they looked inside there were no belongings and the dust-covered interior was in such a state there was no telling when he had left. Noth-ing much could be gained from asking the neighbours because there were no observant housewives around – only the factories on either side.

As a specialist who in his heart enjoyed such things, Honda grew very enthusiastic as he became more aware of the situation. Since he had met Shundei once in Asakusa Park, in between his work gathering articles he began to sedulously emulate the activities of a private eye.

First, given that Shundei had been handing out fliers, Honda visited one or two advertising agencies in the Asakusa area to see if they had employed a man looking like Shundei, but to his chagrin in busy times these firms would hire vagrants from Asakusa Park on a temporary basis, fitting them up with costumes and paying them by the day, and so a description of Shundei did not prompt any recollection of him and the suggestion was that surely he had been one of the vagrants.

Honda next took to wandering around Asakusa Park late at night peering in at each of the benches hidden in the dark shadows under the trees or staying at cheap lodging houses that vagrants might use in the Honjo area, striking up friendly chats with the guests and asking whether they had laid eyes on a man who looked like Shundei. He certainly went to great pains but he was unable to obtain even the smallest clue.

Honda came to my lodgings about once a week to recount his

tales of hardship. Then, one time he assumed the knowing coun-tenance of the beaming god Daikoku and told me the following.

'Samukawa, just recently I learned about this freak show and I came up with a wonderful idea. I expect you know that lately popular attractions at these shows include "the spider woman" and "the woman with only a neck and no body." Well, there's a similar spectacle where conversely the person has only a body and no neck. There's a long box with three compartments, two sections of which generally contain the torso and legs of a sleeping woman. The sec-tion above the torso is empty; although you should be able to see the body from the neck up, it isn't visible at all. What you have then is the neckless corpse of a woman laid out, but every so often the legs and hands twitch to prove that it is alive. It's an eerie and erotic spectacle. The trick is that a mirror is placed at an angle so that the part at the back looks empty. Though it's a bit childish, of course.

'Well, once when I was at Edogawa-bashi in Ushigome, I saw one of these "headless human" freak shows in an empty lot at the corner as I crossed the bridge toward Gokokuji. However, this time the all-body human wasn't a woman, but a very fat man in a clown's costume covered with gleaming black grime.'

At this point, Honda assumed a somewhat tense expression and teasingly fell silent for a while, but after confirming that he had sufficiently piqued my curiosity he resumed his story.

'You know what I thought, don't you? It struck me that to be hired as the "headless man" in such a freak show would be a bril-liant way for someone to completely cover their tracks while at the same time being exposed to the gaze of all and sundry. By hiding the tell-tale section from the neck up, he would be able to sleep all day. Isn't this just the sort of fantastical method Ōe Shundei would dream up? What's more, Shundei has written a lot of freak show stories and he delights in this type of thing.'

'What happened?'

I encouraged Honda to go on, though his calmness made me think that he had not actually found Shundei.

'I immediately went to Edogawa-bashi to have a look, and fortunately the show was still there. After paying the entrance fee, I went inside and stood in front of that fat "headless man," and tried to think of a way to see his face. Then it occurred to me that the man would have to go to the toilet a few times every day. So I waited patiently for him to go to relieve himself. After a while, the few customers drifted out and I was left alone. But I stood there waiting steadfastly. Then the "headless man" clapped his hands together twice.

'That's odd, I thought. Just then one of the barkers came over to tell me there would be a small break and asked me to step outside. Realising this was it, I went out, sneaked round behind the tent and peeped in through a rent in the fabric. Aided by the barker, the "headless man" was getting out of the box and of course he had a head. Running to a corner of the earth floor beyond the spectator seats, he began to relieve himself. So the clap I'd heard earlier was a signal that he needed to pee. Very funny, don't you think? Ha, ha, ha.'

'What is this, a comedy routine? Come on, be serious now.'

Seeing that I was a little angry, Honda's face became serious and he explained,

'Well I was mistaken. It was a completely different person... but it shows you the lengths I went to. It's just one example of the great pains I've taken in the search for Shundei.'

Just as in this humorous digression, no matter how long we searched for Shundei, we were unable to perceive any glimmer of hope.

However, I must note here one unusual fact that came to light that I thought could be a key to solving the case. When I saw the wig worn by Oyamada's corpse, it occurred to me that perhaps it could have come from the Asakusa area. After investigating all the wigmakers in the vicinity, I found an establishment called Matsui in Sensoku-machi that seemed to match. However, although the shop's hair-pieces were exactly like that on the dead man's body, I was surprised – no, completely dumbfounded – when the wig-maker told me that the person who had ordered the wig was not Ōe Shundei but Oyamada Rokurō himself.

The person's description closely resembled Oyamada, and the man gave his name as Oyamada when placing the order, and when the wig was ready (this was near the end of last year) he himself came to collect it. At the time, Oyamada explained that he wished to hide his bald pate, but then why was it that not even his wife had seen him wearing the wig while he was alive? No matter how much I thought about it, I couldn't unravel this odd mystery.

Meanwhile, after Rokurō's bizarre murder, the relationship between Shizuko (now a widow) and myself rapidly became more intimate. Under the circumstances, I stood as both an advisor and a guardian to her. Once the relatives on Oyamada's side had learned of my consideration in searching the attic, they could not turn a cold shoulder to me, while Inspector Itosaki said that it was truly fortunate if it came to that and encouraged me to visit the Oyamada home when I could to comfort the widow with my presence. Accordingly, it became possible for me to come and go in the house without reserve.

I have written above that from the first meeting Shizuko had shown me no little affection as an avid fan of my novels, but a more complex relationship had now developed between us and it seemed entirely natural that she should depend on me more than anyone.

We were meeting frequently now. When it was borne in upon me that she had become a widow, the pale passion – the attraction of a body that looked so delicate it might disappear at any moment, and that yet had a strange strength – no longer seemed something distant, but suddenly pressed in upon me swathed in living colour. In particular, after I happened to find a small foreign-made riding whip in her bedroom, troubling appetites flamed up in me with a frightening force, as if oil had been poured on fire.

Thoughtless though it was, I pointed at the whip and asked: 'Was your husband a horseman?'

She seemed to gasp and blanched immediately. Then her face gradually reddened as if burning. She answered very quietly: 'No.'

It was then that I managed to solve the odd riddle of her livid scar. I recalled that each time I saw the wound its position and shape seemed to differ slightly. I had thought it strange at the time, but it didn't occur to me that her good-natured bald husband might be an awful sex fiend.

Not only that. Today – exactly a month after Rokurō's death – search as I might I could not see that ugly wormlike scar on the nape of Shizuko's neck. Combining this with what I recalled from the past, I was sure that this was not a figment of my imagination without needing to hear a clear confession from her.

But even knowing this, why was it that I was troubled by such unbearable lust? Terribly shameful though it would be, perhaps I was a sexual deviant just like Oyamada…

## CHAPTER 8

AS 20 APRIL WAS THE DAY for commemorating Oyama-da's death, Shizuko went to the temple and then spent the evening at a Buddhist ceremony for the departed accompanied by relatives and friends of the deceased. I was also present. Two new events occurred that evening (even though they were entirely different in nature, as is made clear later, there was a strange and fatalistic link between them) that moved me so much I shall probably remember it all my life.

I was walking beside Shizuko down the dark corridor. I had stayed after all the guests had gone home so that I could talk alone with Shizuko (about the search for Shundei). I thought it would not do to stay too long, what with the servants being there and everything, so I said goodnight at perhaps 11:00 p.m. and returned to my home in a taxi that Shizuko had summoned. She walked alongside me down the corridor toward the hallway to say goodbye. There were a number of glass windows in the corridor that faced on to the garden and as we passed one of them Shizuko suddenly screamed in fear and clung to me.

Surprised, I asked, 'What is it? Did you see something my dear?'

Still grasping me firmly with one hand, she pointed at the window with the other.

I gasped at first, thinking of Shundei, but I soon realized it was nothing. Looking through the glass into the garden, I saw a white dog among the trees. It scratched at the fallen leaves and disappeared into the darkness.

'It's a dog, just a dog. There's nothing to be afraid of.'

I am not sure what it was that possessed me, but I was patting

*'It's a dog, just a dog. There's nothing to be afraid of.'*

Shizuko on the shoulders as I said this, trying to calm her down. Even when she realized there was nothing out of the ordinary, one of Shizuko's arms was embracing my back and when I sensed her warmth spreading inside my body I drew her close and stole a kiss from those Mona Lisa lips, which were lifted slightly by her eye teeth.

Whether it was fortunate or unfortunate for me I do not know, but she did not seek to evade me. Indeed, I even detected a diffident pressure in the hand that embraced me.

The feeling we had of doing something wrong was all the more keen given that this was the day of commemoration for the deceased. We spoke not a word from then until I got into the taxi, and I recall that we even avoided each other's eyes.

We parted and the taxi moved off, but all I could think of was Shizuko. The touch of her mouth lingered on my hot lips and I could still sense the warmth of her body against my pounding chest.

While joy began to soar within me, I also felt a deep sense of remorse. My heart was a tangle of the two, like some complex fabric. I was oblivious of just where the taxi now was, how it was moving, and of the view that lay beyond.

Strangely though, even in that situation I had become intensely aware of a certain small object. Swayed by the vehicle's motion and thinking only of Shizuko, I was staring straight ahead. I could not help but notice a tiny object moving slightly exactly in the centre of my line of sight. At first, I looked without paying attention, but gradually my interest grew.

'Why,' I wondered vaguely, 'why am I staring so much?'

Then, I became aware of what it was.

The all too coincidental matching of two objects was what puzzled me.

Hunched forward in front of me was the driver, a large man wearing an old navy jacket suitable for spring weather. Beyond the fleshy shoulders, the two hands gripping the steering wheel moved jerkily and they were covered by a pair of refined gloves that seemed at odds with the coarse fingers within.

My eye had also been drawn because these were winter gloves and thus out of season, but more than this it was the ornamental button closure on the gloves… finally, the moment of enlightenment came. The round metallic object I had found in the attic of the Oyamada household was the ornamental button from a glove.

I had mentioned the metallic object to Inspector Itosaki, but as I did not happen to have it on me then, and all the signs pointed clearly to Ōe Shundei being the criminal, neither of us had considered this as a material piece of evidence. It should still be in the pocket of my winter waistcoat.

It had not occurred to me that the object could be the ornamental button of a glove. However, thinking about it now, it seemed all too likely that the criminal had worn gloves in order not to leave any fingerprints and that the button had fallen off without the criminal realizing.

The showy button on the driver's glove had thus taught me the provenance of the object I had picked up in the attic, but it held a far more alarming significance. Why was it that the button was so similar in shape and size? Not only that, why had the button on the driver's right hand glove been torn off leaving only the metallic seat of the hook closure? If the metallic object I had picked up in the attic matched this hook closure fitting, what would it mean?

'I say, you there…' I called out to the driver suddenly. 'Would you mind letting me see those gloves please?'

The driver seemed somewhat taken aback by my strange request, but he slowed the taxi, took off both gloves without ado, and passed them to me.

The surface of the button on the complete glove bore the inscription 'R.K. BROS. CO.', the letters I had previously seen, and the dimensions were the same. My alarm grew greater and I began to feel a strange fear.

Having passed me the gloves, the driver focused on the road without looking in any other direction. As I stared at his very stout form from behind, a wild thought came into my head.

'Ōe Shundei…'

I said it as if to myself, but loud enough for the driver to hear. Then I looked intently at the reflection of his face in a small mirror mounted above the driver's seat. But of course it was only my fantasy. The driver's expression showed not the slightest change. What is more, Ōe Shundei was not the type to carry out such a Lupin-like trick. However, when the taxi arrived at my lodging, I had him keep the change and began to ask some questions.

'Do you remember when this button came off?'

The driver replied with an odd look on his face, 'It was torn off from the start. I got it from someone, see. The button had come off, but it was still new, so Mr Oyamada, him that's dead now, he gave it to me.'

'Mr Oyamada did?' I blurted out, considerably surprised. 'The man from the house I've just left, you mean?'

'Yes, that's right. He treated me well when he was alive – it was mostly me that took him to the company and picked him up.'

'When did you start wearing these?'

'Well, they were given to me in winter, but as they were such good quality it seemed a pity to use them and I decided to look after them. Then my old gloves got damaged and today I pulled them down to use for driving for the first time. If I don't wear gloves, the steering wheel slips. But why are you asking?'

'Oh, I've got my own reasons. I wonder if you would sell them to me my good man?'

In the end, I purchased the gloves from him for a hefty consideration. After entering my room, I took out the metallic object I had found in the attic and it was exactly the same size and fitted into the metallic seat of the hook enclosure perfectly.

As noted above, this matching of the two objects seemed all too coincidental.

That Ōe Shundei and Oyamada Rokurō had worn gloves with the same ornamental markings on the hook closure and that the metal button that had fallen off matched exactly the closure's metal seat seemed unthinkable.

I later took the glove to be examined at Izumiya, a premier importer of Western goods located in Tokyo's Ginza. This type of glove was apparently rare within our shores: it might well have been manufactured in England, and R.K. Bros. Co. did not have a single outlet in Japan. Given what the owner of Izumiya had told me and that Oyamada had been overseas until September of last year, it seemed Rokurō was the owner of the glove and that therefore the ornamental button that had fallen off had been dropped by him. It seemed impossible that Ōe Shundei could have obtained such gloves in Japan or that he would just happen to have owned the same gloves as Oyamada.

'So what does that mean?'

Leaning on the desk with my head in my hands I mumbled oddly to myself over and over 'it means that... it means that...', while at the same time massaging my temples in a desperate attempt to focus my concentration to the core of my being and achieve some solution.

Finally, a strange idea came into my head. Yama no Shuku was a long, narrow district and as the Oyamada household was located in the part adjoining the Sumida River it naturally had to touch the river as it flowed past. When I went to the Oyamada household I had from time to time looked at the Sumida River from the window of the Western-style wing without thinking much about it, but now, I was struck by a new significance as if I had discovered the waterway for the first time.

A large letter 'u' appeared in the swirling mist in my head.

The upper left section of the letter contained Yama no Shuku, while Ko-ume machi (where Rokurō's go partner lived) was in the upper right section.

The lower section of the 'u' corresponded exactly to Azuma-bashi. Even now, we were convinced that Rokurō had left the upper right section that evening and travelled to the left part of the u's trough, where he had been killed by Shundei. But we had not taken into account the river's current. The Sumida River flowed from the upper section of the 'u' to its lower section. It seemed more natural to suppose that rather than the corpse being at the site of the murder, it had floated downstream after being thrown in, reached the ferry landing site under Azuma-bashi and come to a halt in the eddying current.

The body had floated down. It had floated down... But where had it floated from? Where had the fatal weapon been used? I found myself sinking further and further into the delusional mire.

*This must have been the moment Shizuko later recounted*
*when she saw a person's face through the window.*

 **CHAPTER 9**

**I KEPT THINKING ABOUT IT** night after night. Even Shizuko's allure seemed less powerful than this monstrous suspicion and as I became more and more obsessed by these bizarre fantasies it was if I had somehow forgotten about Shizuko.

During that time I questioned Shizuko twice in order to confirm something, but she must have thought it strange because after completing this business I told her I had to leave urgently and rushed home. Indeed, her face seemed quite sad and forlorn when she saw me off in the entrance hall.

In just five days, I created an incredible delusion. As I still have the statement I wrote to send to Inspector Itosaki, I shall spare myself the trouble of detailing this delusion by reproducing the statement below and inserting some additional comments. The deductions therein are of a sort that it would probably have been impossible to assemble without the imaginative ability of a crime writer. I later came to realize that it contained something of profound significance.

*...When I realised that the metallic object I picked up in the attic above Shizuko's parlour in the Oyamada household had to have fallen from the closure of Oyamada Rokurō's glove, I recalled a series of disparate facts that had caused me disquiet. These included the fact that Oyamada's corpse wore a wig; that this hairpiece he had adorned himself with had been ordered by Oyamada himself (for reasons I note below, it did not trouble me that the body had been unclothed); that Hirata's threatening letters had stopped at the same time as the bizarre death of Oyamada Rokurō, much as if by arrangement; and*

*that belying appearances Oyamada had been a terrible sadist (though appearances are often deceiving in such cases). It may seem that these facts were a coincidental collection of oddities, but when I thought about it intensely I realized that they each pointed to the one thing.*

*When I became aware what that was, I started to gather together the materials to further confirm my deductions. First, I visited the Oyamada home and after obtaining the permission of Oyamada's wife I searched his study, for nothing tells you so much about a person's traits and secrets than his or her study. Unconcerned about what Mrs Oyamada might be thinking, I spent about half a day looking through book cabinets and drawers. I discovered that one section alone of the book cabinets was locked very securely. I asked for the key and was told that when he was alive Oyamada always carried it about with him on his watch chain and that on the day of his death he left the house with it in his waistband. As there was no other way, I eventually obtained Mrs Oyamada's consent to break open the door to the book cabinet.*

*Inside I found it was full of Oyamada's diaries for the past several years, documents contained in a number of bags, bundles of letters, and books. After searching through them one by one, I discovered three documents connected with this case. The first was the diary for the year in which he had married Shizuko. The following phrases were inscribed in red ink in the margin of the entry three days prior to the wedding ceremony: '...Know about relationship with youth called Hirata Ichirō. But along the way Shizuko came to dislike the boy and no matter what methods he employed she was unresponsive. Next, she used opportunity of father's bankruptcy to hide from Hirata. All well and good. Don't intend to rake up the past.'*

*Thus, by some means Rokurō had known all about his wife's secret from the start of their marriage. In addition, he had not said a single word of this to his wife.*

*The second document was 'Games in the Attic,' the collection of short stories written by Ōe Shundei. I was very surprised to find such a volume in the study of an entrepreneur such as Oyamada Rokurō. In fact, I could not believe my eyes until his wife Shizuko told me that he had been quite a fan of fiction. The frontispiece of the short story collection included a collotype portrait of Shundei and I was very interested to see that the author was credited in the colophon under his real name, Hirata Ichirō.*

*The third document was issue twelve of volume six of* Shin Seinen, *published by Hakubunkan. This magazine for younger readers did not contain a story by Shundei, but it did reproduce a photograph of his manuscript in the frontispiece without any reduction in size. This image commanded half a page and the caption in the margin read 'Ōe Shundei's handwriting.' The strange thing is that when a light was shone on this reproduction, the thick art paper everywhere reflected marks something like those that would be left by a fingernail. It seemed clear that someone had laid a thin sheet of paper on this photograph and traced Shundei's handwriting over and over with a pencil. It frightened me to see that my speculations continued to hit true.*

*The same day I requested Mrs Oyamada to search for the gloves that Rokurō had brought back from overseas. The search took considerable time, but eventually a glove was found that matched exactly the dimensions of the glove that I had purchased from the taxi driver. When she handed the glove to me, Mrs Oyamada said with a troubled look that she was sure there had been another glove exactly the same. If you so desire, I can at any moment produce these pieces of evidence, including the diary, the collection of short stories, the magazine, the glove, and the metallic object I picked up in the attic.*

*There are a number of other facts that I have ascertained, but based only on the key points noted above I think it seems clear that Oyamada Rokurō had a most peculiar character, and that behind his friendly mask he was energetically carrying out a ghoulish plot. Perhaps we were too conscious of the name Ōe Shundei. Being aware of Shundei's blood-thirsty works and his bizarre lifestyle, we may have arbitrarily decided that only he could have committed such a crime. How could he have so completely concealed himself? Does it not seem somewhat strange that he should be the criminal? If he is innocent, it could be that he is so difficult to track down simply because his misanthropy (an aversion that becomes more severe the more his fame grows) led him to cover his trail. It may well be as you once said that he has fled overseas. He could be puffing away on a water pipe in some corner of Shanghai passing himself off as a Chinese. Even if this is not the case and Shundei is the criminal, how could we explain him forgetting the main purpose of a detailed revenge plot put together over months and years with such tenacity and suddenly giving up after killing Oyamada, who was simply a diversion along the way? Anyone who knew his fiction and lifestyle would think this very unnatural and unlikely. Moreover, there is something much clearer. How is it that he could have dropped the button from Oyamada's glove in that attic? Given that this foreign-made glove was unobtainable in Japan and that the ornamental button had been pulled off the glove presented to the taxi driver, it would surely be illogical to think that it was Ōe Shundei rather than Oyamada who had been lurking in the attic (if I say it was Oyamada, you may ask whether he would give such a vital piece of evidence to a taxi driver even unwittingly; but as I note later that is because he was not committing any particular crime from a legal perspective; it was simply a sort of game for someone who enjoyed weird things; thus, even if the glove button was torn off and left behind in the attic, that would be of no consequence to him because he had no need to worry whether the button had fallen off while he was walking in the attic or whether it would serve as evidence).*

*There is still other information that ought to rule out Shundei from the crime. That the evidence mentioned above, including the diary,*

*Shundei's short story collection, and* Shin Seinen, *was in the lockable book cabinet in Oyamada's study and that Oyamada always kept the only key to this lock on his person proves that he was involved in an underhanded piece of mischief. Even if we pause and consider that Shundei could have attempted to cast suspicion on Oyamada by forging these items and placing them in his book cabinet, it seems completely impossible. First, the diary was not something that could be forged and only Oyamada was able to lock and unlock the book cabinet. Although we have thus far believed Ōe Shundei—Hirata Ichirō was the criminal, if we take everything into consideration we must conclude that surprisingly enough he was not a presence in this case from the very start. We could only have come to believe that he was the criminal due to the truly amazing deception of Oyamada Rokurō. It surprises us completely to learn that while this wealthy man had a childishness manifested in the detailed scheme noted above, beneath that mask of benevolence he transformed into a terrible fiend once in the bedroom and lashed the fair Shizuko repeatedly with his foreign-made riding whip. However, there are many instances in which the benevolence of a virtuous man and the guile of a fiend have resided together in one person. Indeed, the more benevolent and appealing to others a person is, the easier it is for the devil within to find disciples.*

*Now then, let me tell you what I think. About four years ago, Oyamada Rokurō travelled to Europe on business, where he lived for about two years. He was chiefly in London, but he also stayed in another two or three cities. I think it may have been in one of these metropolises that his evil habits budded and were fostered (I have heard rumours of his situation in London from an employee of Roku Roku Trading). It seems to me that when he returned from abroad in September of the year before last his stubborn depravity turned on to his beloved bride Shizuko and the savage fury began, for I detected the unpleasant scar on the nape of her neck at our first meeting in October last year.*

*Once one has become accustomed to this type of depravity, the illness progresses with frightening rapidity, just as with morphine addiction.*

*A new, more intense stimulation becomes necessary. What yielded satisfaction yesterday does not serve today and you come to think that today's measures will not be sufficient tomorrow. I think you will agree that it is easy to conceive that in a similar fashion Oyamada found he was no longer able to achieve satisfaction just from whipping his wife Shizuko. In a frenzy, he had to pursue a new stimulus. Right about that time he somehow became aware of a work of fiction called 'Games in the Attic' written by Ōe Shundei, and perhaps after the first reading he decided that he would like to enact the bizarre content. At any rate, he seems to have discovered a strange sense of affinity. He had found someone else who suffered from the same odd malady. The well-worn spine of the book suggests the fervour with which he read Shundei's short story collection. In this fiction, Shundei repeatedly describes the peculiar pleasure of peeping through a crack at someone alone (in particular, a woman) while remaining completely undetected. How easy it is to imagine the sympathy Oyamada must have felt when he discovered this, for him, new pastime. Quickly he copied the hero of Shundei's fiction, becoming himself the one playing in the attic. He dreamed up the scheme of sneaking into the space above the ceiling of his own home to peep at his wife when she was alone.*

*As there is a considerable distance from the gate of the Oyamada house to the entrance hall, it would require no artifice whatsoever when coming home to slip around the side of the entrance hall and into the storeroom unbeknownst to the servants and from there to pass along over the ceiling to the space above Shizuko's parlour. I suspect that Rokurō's frequent evening trips to play go with Koume may have been a way of accounting for the time when he was actually amusing himself in the attic.*

*Meanwhile, this devoted reader of 'Games in the Attic' probably discovered that the real name of the author was Hirata Ichirō, and began to suspect that this was almost certainly the same person who had been jilted by Shizuko and who bore a deep-seated grudge against her for it. He would then have screened all sorts of articles and gossip related to Ōe Shundei to learn that Shundei was the same person who had formerly been Shizuko's lover, that he had a very misanthropic lifestyle, and that by this stage he had already stopped writing and even disappeared leaving no trace. Thus at one and the same time Oyamada had discovered through the one volume of 'Games in the Attic' someone who shared his malady and who was also an arch-rival of his love who ought to be hated. Based on all this knowledge, he came up with a truly alarming piece of mischief.*

*Of course, prying through a chink at Shizuko by herself would certainly have piqued his inordinate curiosity, but it is unlikely that his sadomasochistic character would have been satisfied by such a mild pastime alone. The preternaturally sharp creative abilities of this sick man would have sought for a new, crueller approach to substitute for the crack of the whip. Finally, he hit upon the unprecedented drama of Hirata Ichirō's threatening letters. He had already obtained the photo print at the start of issue twelve of volume six of* Shin Seinen *to use as an example. To increase the interest and plausibility of his drama, he began to carefully practice Shundei's handwriting using this sample. The pencil traces on the original are testimony to this.*

*After Oyamada had created Hirata's hate mail, he sent the envelopes from different post offices one by one, with a suitable number of days intervening between each. It was not for nothing that he would stop at the nearest post box while motoring about on business. As to* the content of the letters, he would have found out about Shundei's past through articles in the newspapers and magazines. The details of Shizuko's activities he could have spied from above the ceiling and what he could not tell from there he would have been able to describe because he was after all her husband. He would have memorized Shizuko's phrasing and gestures from the pillow talk they exchanged when beside each other in bed and put these down on paper to suggest they had been observed by a peeping Shundei. What a fiend! By concealing himself and using someone else's name in the threatening letters, he was able to experience the crime-tinged frisson of sending the documents to his wife and the devilish pleasure of spying on her from the attic with excitement while she read and shuddered in fear. Furthermore, there is cause to believe that during the intervals he continued with the whip lashings because it was after his death that the scar on the nape of Shizuko's neck first disappeared. While he tortured his wife Shizuko thus, he perpetrated such cruelty precisely because of his idolization of her and not from any sense of hatred. You will of course be well aware of the psychology of this type of sexual deviant.

I have completely outlined above the deductive reasoning that leads me to believe Oyamada Rokurō was the one who wrote the threatening letters. Why then did what was only a mischievous prank by a sexual degenerate result in this murder case? Why was it that Oyamada himself was murdered? Not only that, why was he wearing a strange wig and floating naked under Azumabashi bridge? Who was responsible for the stab wounds in his back? If Ōe Shundei was not involved in this case, then a spate of questions arise, including whether there was a different criminal. I must state my observations and deductions concerning this.

To put it simply, he may have been punished by heaven, perhaps because the extreme immorality of his devilry evoked divine wrath.

*There was no crime of any sort, nor any perpetrator – just Oyamada's accidental death. This prompts a question about the fatal wound in his back, but I shall answer that later, for I must follow the course of events in order and explain why I came to think this way.*

*My deductive trail commences with nothing other than his wig. You will perhaps recall that in order to prevent anyone spying on her Shizuko relocated her sleeping quarters to the second floor of the European-style annex on 17 March, the day after I had searched the attic. While it is not clear to what lengths Shizuko went in explaining the need for this to her husband or why her he agreed with her, it would have been from that day that he was no longer able to pry on her from the chink in the ceiling. But if we exert our imagination, we can envisage that peeping through this opening would have started to become somewhat boring around this time. Perhaps the shifting of their bedroom to the European section of the house fortuitously provided the opportunity for another piece of mischief. The wig helps answer why. The fluffy wig that he himself had ordered. As he had ordered the hairpiece at the end of last year, there must initially have been a different use for it but now the wig was just right for the new situation.*

*He had seen Shundei's photograph in the frontispiece to 'Games in the Attic.' As this was apparently a likeness of the young Shundei, naturally enough he was not bald like Oyamada but bore a head of fluffy black hair. If Oyamada had progressed from frightening Shizuko through letters and concealment in the shadowy attic, and now schemed to become Ōe Shundei himself (in order to experience the strange sensation of Shizuko noting his presence and exposing his face to her briefly in the window of the European wing of their home), he would surely have had to hide his bald head, which would be the first thing to give away his identity. This was exactly the right sort of wig. If he wore the hairpiece, there would be no concern of the terrified Shi-*

245

zuko making out who it was when he flashed his face on the far side of the dark glass (and this means would be all the more effective).

That night (19 March), the gate was still open when Oyamada returned from playing go with his friend Koume. Accordingly, unnoticed by the servants he quietly rounded the garden and slipped into the study beneath the stairs in the European annex (Shizuko heard this; he kept that key on the same chain as the key to the book cabinet). There in the darkness he put on the wig, taking care that he did not disturb Shizuko in the bedroom above. He then went out, passed through the trees, climbed on to the eaves moulding and moved around outside the bedroom window where he lifted the blind and peeked in. This must have been the moment Shizuko later recounted when she saw a person's face through the window.

Before explaining how it was that Oyamada came to die, I must relate the observations I made when I peered out from the window in question on my second visit to the Oyamada household after beginning to suspect him. As you yourself will be able to confirm the details if you look, I shall forgo a minute portrayal. The window faces the Sumida River; there is hardly any empty ground underneath the eaves and this is enclosed by the same concrete wall as in front; quite a steep stone cliff follows directly on the other side. To maximize the land area, the wall stands on the edge of the stone cliff.

The upper section of the wall is about four metres above the water's surface and the second-floor window is some two metres from the wall's top. If Oyamada lost his footing on the eaves moulding (which is very narrow) and fell, there is the possibility that he might have the good fortune to fall inside the wall (a cramped space where two people would have difficulty passing each other) but if that was not the case once he hit the wall he would then tumble into the Sumida River. Of course, in Rokurō's case the latter occurred.

As soon as I took note of the Sumida River's current, it seemed more natural to me to think that the corpse had drifted downstream from the spot where it had been thrown in rather than remaining there. I was also aware that the European annex of the Oyamada home was right beside the river and upstream from Inazumabashi bridge. Accordingly, the thought crossed my mind that Oyamada had fallen from near the window, but it puzzled me for a long time that the cause of death was not drowning but the stab wound in his back.

Then one day I remembered a true story resembling this case that I had read about in 'The Latest Crime Investigation Methods,' by Nanba Mokusaburō. I remembered the article because I referred to this book when considering my detective fiction. The story is as follows:

'Around the middle of May in the sixth year of the Taishō period (1917), the body of a dead man washed ashore in the vicinity of the Taikō Steamship K.K. breakwater in Otsu City, Shiga Prefecture. The corpse's head bore a cut that looked very much as though it had been made by a sharp instrument. The investigating physician determined that the wound was received when the man was alive and was the cause of death, while the presence of some water in the abdomen indicated that the body had been thrown into the water at the time of the murder. At this point, we detectives commenced our activities, believing this to be a major case. We exhausted every method we knew to ascertain the victim's identity, but were unable to come up with a lead. The Otsu police station had received a missing persons notification from a Mr Saitō, a goldsmith from Jofukuji-dori, Kamigyō-ku, Kyoto, regarding an employee named Kobayashi Shigezō (23). A few days later, the numerous similarities between the clothing of this subject and the victim in our case led the station to immediately contact Saitō to view the dead body. It became clear that this was indeed the said employee, and also that neither murder nor suicide could be confirmed. It seems that the dead man had used a considerable amount of his employer's money and disappeared leaving a will. The cut to the head resulted when he threw himself into the lake and the revolving screw of a passing steamer left a wound resembling a slash.'

If I had not remembered this true story, I would probably not have come up with such a fantastic-seeming idea. However, in many cases truth is stranger than fiction and that which appears unbelievably outlandish can actually happen with ease. Still, I am not saying that Oyamada was wounded by a ship's propeller. Slightly unlike the story above, in this case no water at all had been swallowed and there are very few steamers plying the Sumida River at one o'clock in the morning.

But what could have caused the wound in Oyamada's back, which was so deep as to reach his lung? What could have made a wound that so resembled that of a blade? Of course, it had to have been the shards of beer bottles embedded on top of the concrete wall around the Oyamada home to ward off thieves. As these are exactly the same as those visible at the building's front gate, you will perhaps have seen them yourself. Some of them are so large they could well cause a wound that would reach the lungs. Given that Oyamada struck these at some speed as he fell from the eaves moulding, it is hardly surprising he sustained such an awful wound. Moreover, this interpretation explains the numerous shallow stab marks around the fatal wound.

Thus, as befit his vice, Oyamada lost his footing on the roof and received a fatal wound when he struck the wall before falling into the upper Sumida River. Flowing with the current, he floated under the toilet at the Azumabashi steamer landing place in an ignominious death he brought on himself. I have stated above most of my new interpretation related to this case. One or two points remain for me to explain. As to why Rokurō's corpse was naked, the extremity of Azumabashi bridge is the haunt of vagrants, beggars, and persons with criminal records and if the drowned man's body wore expensive *garments (that night Rokurō wore an Ōshima kimono, a* haori, *and a platinum pocket watch), I think it is sufficient to point out that there would be numerous villains who would steal these late at night out of sight (*NB: *my speculation proved to be true, for a vagrant was indeed arrested later). Next, reasons you may consider that would explain why Shizuko did not hear Rokurō fall even though she was in the bedroom include that she was out of her wits with fear at that moment; the glass window in the concrete European annex was tightly closed; there is a considerable distance from the window to the water's surface; and even if the splash were audible, it may have been drowned out by the sound of oars and paddles from the mud carriers that sometimes pass along the Sumida River through the night. I think it should be noted that there is not even a hint of foul play in this case and while it led to an unfortunate and bizarre death there was absolutely nothing that went beyond the bounds of a prank. Otherwise, there is no explaining the complete lack of attention to detail by Oyamada, who gave his gloves – a piece of evidence – to the driver, used his real name when ordering the wig, and left crucial pieces of evidence in the book cabinet in his home, albeit under lock and key....*

I have reproduced my statement at great length, but I inserted it here because if I do not make my deductions clear, what I am to write now would be very difficult to understand.

I noted in this statement that Ōe Shundei was not a presence from the very first. But was this actually the case? If so, the extensive details provided about him in the first chapter of my record would have been completely pointless.

## CHAPTER 10

**THE DATE ON THE PERSONAL ACCOUNT** written for submission to Inspector Itosaki is 28 April. First, though, I visited the Oyamada home the day after writing the document to show it to Shizuko and calm her down by informing her that there was now no need to fear the Ōe Shundei phantasm. Since coming to suspect Oyamada, I had visited twice to conduct a sort of house search, but I had not yet told her about this.

At that time, relatives were gathering around Shizuko in connection with the disposal of Oyamada's estate, and it seemed that a number of troublesome issues had arisen, but in her isolated state Shizuko relied on me to a considerable extent, making a great fuss in welcoming me when I visited. After passing through as usual to Shizuko's parlour, I surprised her by very abruptly saying 'Shizuko, you have nothing to worry about now. There was no Ōe Shundei from the first.' Naturally, she did not understand what I meant. I then read aloud a draft of the personal statement that I had brought with me in much the same manner as I always read my detective fiction to friends after completing a story. For one thing, I wanted to allay Shizuko's concerns by informing her of the details; for another I intended to obtain her opinion and discover any shortcomings in order to thoroughly correct the draft.

The section regarding Oyamada's sadistic perversion was very cruel. Shizuko's face reddened and it seemed as though she would like to disappear. In the part touching on the gloves, she commented, 'I thought it strange because I was certain there was one more.'

At the place regarding Rokurō's death by misadventure, she was so shocked that she turned pale and it seemed she was unable to speak.

A little while after I had finished reading she said 'Oh!' remaining blank until eventually a slight expression of relief appeared on her face. When she knew that the threatening letters from Ōe Shundei were not real and that she was no longer in any danger, she must surely have felt a great sense of relief.

If my selfish suspicions may be allowed, I believe that she must certainly have experienced some easing of guilt regarding her illicit relationship with me when she heard about the terrible harvest that Oyamada had reaped.

She would have actually been pleased to have reached a situation in which she could excuse herself, saying 'Oh my, to think that he made me suffer by committing such horrible acts…'

As for myself, I was pleased that she had acknowledged the truth of my statement and I unwittingly drank too much at her bidding. Not being a strong drinker, I soon turned red and then, much unlike my normal self, melancholy. I sat there without saying anything gazing at Shizuko's face.

Shizuko looked quite careworn, but that paleness was her natural colour and that strange attraction reflecting the powerful elasticity of her overall body and the dark flame burning within her core had not only not dwindled in the least, as we were now in the season for woollen garments, the contour of her form appeared more voluptuous than ever dressed in an old-style flannel. Set aquiver by that garment, I gazed at the writhing curves of her limbs and though it troubled me I limned in my heart the parts of her body swathed in some as yet unknown material.

After we had talked together for a while, I came up with a marvellous plan under the influence of the alcohol. I would rent a house in an out of the way spot to be used for assignations between Shizuko and myself and the two of us would enjoy our secret trysts without anyone knowing.

I must make the miserable confession that after making sure that the maid had left I then drew Shizuko suddenly to me and we kissed for the second time. I put both hands behind her back, enjoying the feel of the flannel while I whispered my idea in her ear. She did not rebuff my impolite advances and even accepted my suggestion with a slight nod.

How shall I describe the dreamlike sequence of trysts we enjoyed frequently over the next twenty days or so?

I rented an old house with a mud-walled storehouse on the river-bank near the famous Ogyō-no-Matsu pine tree in Negishi. I asked an old lady from the neighbourhood corner store to look after it and Shizuko usually arranged to meet here during the day.

For the first time in my life, I tasted keenly the intensity and power of a woman's passion. Sometimes, we were like little children, me with my tongue out panting near her shoulder like a hunting hound as we rushed together around the building, which was as big as an old haunted house. As I reached out to catch her, she would twist her body skilfully like a dolphin, evading my grasp and running away. We ran until, almost dead with exhaustion and out of breath, we collapsed together in a tangle.

At other times, we shut ourselves up for one or two hours in the silence of the dark earthen storehouse. Someone listening intently at the entrance would have heard from within the sound of a woman sobbing sadly mixed in, as in a harmony, with the deep sound of a man crying unrestrainedly.

But one day, I became afraid when Shizuko brought the riding whip, used regularly by Oyamada, hidden in a large bunch of peonies. She pressed the whip into my hand and made me lash her naked flesh as Oyamada had.

Having suffered cruelty at Rokurō's hands for such a long time, the perversion had taken root in her and she was now plagued by the irresistible appetite of a masochist. Had my assignations with her continued this way for half a year, I too would surely have been possessed by the same sickness as Oyamada.

For I shuddered to note the odd joy I felt when, unable to refuse Shizuko's request, I applied the whip to her delicate body and saw the poisonous-looking weals rise instantly on the surface of her pale skin.

However, I did not start this record in order to outline the love affair between a man and a woman. As I intend to describe this in more detail another day when I use it to create a piece of fiction, I shall here only note one fact heard from Shizuko during the days of passion we passed together.

This was in connection with Rokurō's wig. Actually, Rokurō had gone to the trouble of ordering this and having it made to hide his unattractive baldness in bedroom romps with Shizuko and although she had laughed about it and sought to stop him, such was his considerable sensitivity on these matters that he went off to place the order as serious as a child. When I asked Shizuko why she had hidden this, she answered 'I couldn't talk about that – it's embarrassing.'

About twenty days had passed by and as I thought it might seem strange if I was not seen at the Oyamada home I pretended nothing untoward had happened and visited the house, meeting with Shizuko and conversing very formally with her for about an hour, after which she saw me to the hallway and I went home by taxi. By coincidence, the driver was Aoki Tamizou, the man from whom I had earlier purchased the gloves, and this proved to be the event that saw me drawn into a bizarre daylight dream.

The gloves were different, but there was no change at all from a about a month ago in the shape of the hands gripping the steering wheel, the old-fashioned dark-blue spring overcoat (which he wore directly over his collared shirt), the appearance of those bulky shoulders, the windscreen, and the mirror above, and that induced in me a sense of uneasiness.

I remembered that I had addressed the driver as Ōe Shundei. Then I found that I was thinking solely of Ōe Shundei – the face in the photograph, the bizarre plots of his stories, recollections of his peculiar daily existence. Finally, I felt his presence so keenly that it seemed as if he were sitting on the cushion right beside me. My mind was a blank and in an instant I blurted out, 'You there, Aoki. You know those gloves: when was it that Mr Oyamada gave them to you?'

'What?' the driver replied turning to me with a bewildered expression, just as he had a month earlier. 'Well, it was last year of course, in November... I'm sure it was on the day I received my monthly salary from accounts because I remember thinking well I'm getting lots of things today. That makes it the 28th of November. I'm certain of it.'

'The 28th of November, you say?'

With my mind still blank, I simply repeated the driver's reply.

'Why are you so preoccupied with the gloves, sir? Was there something special about them?'

The driver was leering, but I said nothing and stared intently at a speck of dust on the windscreen. I remained that way while the car travelled for four or five blocks. Suddenly, I rose up inside the vehicle, grabbed the driver's shoulder, and shouted, 'You're sure it was the 28th of November? Would you be prepared to swear to it in court?'

The taxi had swerved and the driver was adjusting the steering wheel to bring the car under control. 'In a court? Is this some sort of joke? But I'm certain it was the 28th of November. I've even got a witness. My relief driver saw them too.'

Although Aoki was very surprised, he could see how serious I was and he replied earnestly.

'Right then, take me back now.'

Although he was growing more confused and looked a little afraid, the driver turned the taxi around as I had asked and took me to the front gate of the Oyamada home. I leaped out and rushed to the entrance. Taking hold of the maid who happened to be there, I demanded, 'In the major house cleaning at the end of last year the boards of the ceiling in the Japanese section of the house were apparently completely stripped and washed. Is that true?'

I knew this because, as I have indicated above, Shizuko told me when I went up into the attic. The maid must have thought me mad. For a while she looked at me intently before saying, 'Yes, that is true, sir. It wasn't a full scale washing – just cleaning down with water – but the house cleaners were certainly here. It was the 25th of December.'

'The ceilings of all the rooms?'

'Yes, the ceiling of every room.'

Perhaps having heard all this, Shizuko emerged from the house and asked me with a worried look, 'What has happened?'

I repeated my question and after Shizuko had given the same reply as the maid I said a quick goodbye, flew into the taxi, ordered the driver to take me to my lodgings, and sank deep into the cushions and the muddy fantasy that seemed to have taken hold of me.

The boards in the ceiling of the Japanese section of the Oyamada home had been taken up and washed with water last year on the 25th of December. Thus, the ornamental button had to have fallen in the attic after that.

However, the gloves had been given to the taxi driver on the 28th of November. As I have noted above several times, there is no doubting the fact that the ornamental button had fallen from those gloves.

Accordingly, the button from the gloves in question had been lost in a place in which it could not have fallen. I realized what it was this puzzling phenomenon indicated.

In order to be certain, I visited Aoki Tamizou at his garage and met the assistant driver, who confirmed that it had indeed been the 28th of November. I also visited the contractors who had cleaned the ceiling of the Oyamada household and learned that the 25th of December was the correct date. They assured me that nothing, no matter how small the object, could have been left there.

The only explanation that would enable the claim that Oyamada had dropped that button to be maintained is as follows.

The button remained in Oyamada's pocket after it fell from the glove. Unaware of this and not wanting to use a buttonless glove, Oyamada gave them to the driver. In a strange turn of events, the button accidentally fell from Oyamada's pocket when he subsequently climbed into the attic anywhere from a month, at the earliest, to three months later (the threatening letters first began to arrive in February).

It seems strange that the button was in the pocket of Oyamada's waistcoat rather than an overcoat (usually gloves end up in overcoat pockets and it is unthinkable that Oyamada would have worn an overcoat when he climbed up into the attic; indeed, it would even be somewhat unnatural for him to have worn a jacket when he entered the space) and surely a man of means such as Oyamada would not have worn his winter clothes through the spring.

As a result, the pall of darkness cast by Ōe Shundei, the beast in the shadows, spread ever further over my soul.

The news that Oyamada was a sexual fiend such as might be found in a modern detective story had perhaps triggered in me a monumental delusion (though the fact that he had lashed Shizuko with a riding whip was beyond doubt). It might be that he was killed for somebody's purpose.

Ōe Shundei! Ah the image of that beast persists tenaciously within my soul.

Strange, how once the thought begins to bud, everything comes to seem suspicious. That a mere fiction writer like myself should have been able to make the deductions in that personal statement with such ease also seems odd when you think about it. Actually, I had left the draft of the statement uncorrected because I thought an outrageous mistake could be concealed in it somewhere and partly too because I was so absorbed in my affair with Shizuko. The fact is that somehow I did not want to go ahead with it and indeed I had actually come to think that was for the best.

Thinking about it, there is too much evidence on hand in this case. At every turn I made, pieces of evidence rolled about all too conveniently, as if they were lying in wait. Just as Ōe Shundei himself says in his works, detectives must exercise caution when they encounter too much proof.

First, it is hard to believe that Oyamada had forged the genuine-looking lettering of the threatening letters, as I had imagined. As Honda had said, even if it were possible to write characters that resembled Shundei's handwriting, how could anyone copy his unique style, particularly an entrepreneur like Oyamada from a different field?

Only now did I remember a story written by Shundei called 'The Stamp' about a mentally unbalanced medical doctor's wife who hates her husband. She learns how to write like him and forges a document in his hand as part of a scheme to make the doctor appear guilty of murder. Perhaps Shundei had done the same thing to bring about Oyamada's downfall.

Depending on your viewpoint, this case seemed just like a collection of Ōe Shundei's masterpieces. The peeping from behind the ceiling boards was from 'Games in the Attic' and the piece of evidence in the form of a button was also an idea taken from this work. The forging of Shundei's hand came from 'The Stamp', while the raw wound on the nape of Shizuko's neck hinting at a sadist emulated the approach used in 'Murder on "B" Hill.' Indeed the whole case smacked strongly of Ōe Shundei, including the glass shard that had caused the stab wound and the naked body floating under the toilet.

There seemed to be too many odd coincidences. It was as if Shundei had overshadowed the case from start to finish. I felt that I had followed Ōe Shundei's instructions in piecing together deductions exactly as he wished. It even seemed that I had been possessed by Shundei.

Shundei was here somewhere. I was certain that serpent-like eyes glittered at the bottom of this case. It was not my mind theorizing – I sensed it within myself. He had to be here somewhere.

I was thinking about this as I lay on my futon in a room at my lodgings. Strong as my constitution was, even I was now tired of this never-ending fantasy. Thinking it over and over, I finally nodded off with fatigue. I awoke from a strange dream with a start and an odd idea came into my head.

It was late at night, but I called Honda's lodgings and asked for him.

When he answered the telephone, I surprised him by asking without any preliminaries, 'Now, you told me that Ōe Shundei's wife had a round face didn't you?'

After realizing it was me, Honda answered in a sleepy voice.

'Mmn, yes, that's right.'

'She always had her hair done in a European style.'

'Mmn, yes, that's right.'

'She wore spectacles for near sightedness?'

'Yes, that's correct.'

'She had a gold tooth.'

'Yes, that's correct.'

'She had bad teeth, right. And apparently she often applied a poultice to her cheek to kill the tooth pain, didn't she?'

'You are well informed. Have you met Shundei's wife?'

'No. I talked to some of her neighbours in Sakuragi-chō. But she would have been wearing the pain-killing poultice when you met her, right?'

'Yes, she always wore one. I suppose her teeth must have been very bad.'

'Was it the right cheek?'

'I don't remember well, but I have a feeling it was the right.'

'But it seems a little strange that a young woman who wore her hair in the European style would use an old-fashioned poultice for quelling tooth pain. People don't use them nowadays, do they?'

'You're right. But what on earth's this all about? Have you found some clue in the case?'

'I have indeed. I'll tell you all about it later.'

In order to be certain, I thus sought Honda's confirmation of things that I had heard before.

Next, I went to the desk and much as if solving some geometry problem I inscribed on a sheet of paper a variety of shapes and equations, writing and erasing, writing and erasing until it was almost dawn.

*Gradually the redness spread on her pale skin until
a wormlike wound stained with scarlet blood took shape.*

## CHAPTER 11

NOW, IT WAS ALWAYS ME who sent the letters arranging our trysts and after three days had passed without contact from me it seemed that Shizuko could wait no longer, for she sent a message by express mail asking me to come to 'our hiding place' tomorrow around three in the afternoon without fail. She also complained, 'Perhaps you no longer like me now that you have discovered my excessively sensual nature. Could it be that you are afraid of me?'

Even after receiving this letter, I did not feel particularly enthusiastic. I just did not want to see her face. Nevertheless, I went to that ghostly house near the Ogyō-no-Matsu pine tree at the time she set.

It was a maddeningly humid day in June, just ahead of the rainy season, and the sky hung down oppressively overhead as gloomy as a cataract. After getting off the train and walking three or four blocks, my armpits and back were clammy with sweat and when I touched my collared shirt it was soaking wet.

Shizuko had arrived a little earlier and was sitting on the bed in the cool storehouse, waiting. We had laid a carpet on the second floor of this building, decorating the scene of our games as effectively as possible with a bed, a sofa, and some large mirrors. Ignoring my pleas to desist, Shizuko had without reserve purchased ridiculously expensive objects, including the sofa and the bed.

She wore a bright single-layer Yukitsumugi kimono and a black silk sash embroidered with fallen paulownia leaves. As usual, her hair was done in a shiny *marumage* bob and she lounged on the bed's pure white sheets. But the harmony of the European furnishings and her traditional Edo style contrasted bizarrely in the storehouse's dark second storey. Although now a widow, Shizuko continued to wear her hair in a style denoting a married woman, and when I saw that scented, shining *marumage* bob of which she was so fond, I immediately beheld her in a lascivious light, the *marumage* falling apart, the front locks dishevelled, and straggling wisps in a tangle at her neck. For she usually spent as much as thirty minutes in front of the mirror combing her tousled hair before leaving the house we used for our assignations.

As soon as I came in, Shizuko asked me, 'Why did you come back the other day just to ask about the house cleaning? You seemed very agitated. I wondered what it could be, but I couldn't think what it was.'

Taking off my coat I said, 'You couldn't think what it was? Something very important. I made a big mistake. The attic was cleaned at the end of December and the button fell off Oyamada's glove over a month before that. You see, he gave the gloves to the taxi driver on the 28th of November, so the button must have come off before that. The order is all topsy turvy.'

'My!' said Shizuko with a startled look, but it seemed she had not fully grasped the situation for she went on 'But the button fell in the attic after it had come off the glove then.'

'Well, it was after, but the issue here is how long after. It would be strange if the button did not fall when Oyamada climbed into the attic. Precisely speaking, the button fell after, but it fell in the attic at that same time and was left there. You'll agree that it would be beyond the laws of physics to think that the button took more than a month to fall after it had been torn off?'

'I suppose so,' said Shizuko, who had grown somewhat pale and was still thinking.

'If the button was in Oyamada's pocket after dropping off and then accidentally fell in the attic a month later, that would make sense, but do you think Oyamada would have worn the clothes he used in November last year through this spring?'

'No. He was very fastidious about his appearance and at the end of the year he changed over completely to thick, warm clothing.'

'You see. That's why it's strange.'

'Well,' she said, drawing a breath, 'then surely Hirata...'

'Of course. This case smacks too strongly of Ōe Shundei. I have to completely amend that statement I wrote recently.'

I then explained to her in a simple fashion that, as noted in the preceding chapter, this case resembled a collection of Ōe Shundei's masterpieces, that there was too much evidence, and the forging of handwriting seemed all too genuine.

'You won't be well aware of it, but Shundei has a truly strange lifestyle. Why didn't he receive guests? Why did he seek to avoid visitors by shifting house so often, going on trips, and falling ill? Finally, why did he waste money by continuing to pay rent on that empty house in Mukōjima Susaki-chō? Even for a misanthropic novelist, that seems very odd. Too odd, don't you think, unless it was in preparation for murdering someone?'

I was sitting beside Shizuko on the bed as I spoke. When she thought that it could after all be Shundei's handiwork, she quickly became frightened, slid her body right against me, and gripped my left wrist with a clammy hand.

'Now I realize what a fool he made of me, how I did exactly as he wanted. I was put through my paces too with all that false evidence he had set up beforehand, following his deductions directly as a guide. Ha, ha, ha...'

I laughed in self-mockery.

'He's an awful creature. He grasped my way of thinking exactly and set up the evidence accordingly. Why, an ordinary sleuth would have been no good. It had to be a novelist like me with a penchant for deduction because no-one else would have had such a roundabout and bizarre imagination. However, if Shundei is the criminal, a number of illogical points arise. Still, arise though they may, it is because the case is so hard to solve and Shundei such an unfathomable villain.

'When you boil it all down, there are two such points. The first is that the threatening letters suddenly ceased to arrive after Oyamada's death. The second is why the diaries, Shundei's book, and *Shin Seinen* came to be in Oyamada's book cabinet.

'If Shundei really is the criminal, these two points just do not add up. If he copied Oyamada's hand and wrote in the margins of the diaries and made the traces of writing found in the frontispiece of *Shin Seinen* in order to put together "evidence," the thing that is really hard to understand is how Shundei could have obtained the key to the book cabinet because this was carried by Oyamada alone. Next, did he sneak into Oyamada's study?

'I have been thinking about these points so much over the past three days that my head hurts. In the end, I managed to come up with what I think may be the only explanation.

'Given the pervading stench of Shundei's works in this case, I took out his stories and began to read them, thinking that a closer study of his fiction might provide some key to solve this case. Although I have not told you yet, Shundei had apparently been wandering around Asakusa Park in strange garb, including a clown's costume and pointed hat, according to an expert in these matters called Honda. When I inquired about this at some advertising agencies, they could only think that it must have been a vagrant from the park. That Shundei mingled with the homeless in Asakusa Park seems like something right out of Stevenson's *The Strange Case of Dr Jekyll and Mr Hyde*, don't you think? After realizing this, I searched for something similar in Shundei's fiction and discovered two pieces that you will perhaps know: "Panorama Country," a long story published immediately before he went missing, and "One Person, Two Roles," a short story published earlier. When I read these, I understood well how attracted he was by a Dr Jekyll-type approach, in which one person could transform into two.'

'You're scaring me,' said Shizuko, gripping my hand tightly.

'The way you're speaking is strange. Let's not talk about it, shall we. I don't like it, not here in this dark storeroom. We'll talk about it later. Today let's have fun. When I'm here with you like this, I don't even think about Hirata.'

'Now, listen to me. This has to do with your life. If Shundei still has you in his sights...'

I was not in the mood for lovers' games.

'I have still only found two odd correspondences in this case. At the risk of sounding like an academic, one is spatial and the other temporal. Now, here is a map of Tokyo.'

I took out of my pocket a simple map of Tokyo that I had prepared and pointed with my finger as I talked.

'I recall from my conversations with Honda, and the head of the Kisagata police station, the various addresses that Ōe Shundei flitted to one after the other. As I remember, there was Ikebukuro, Kikui, Negishi, Hatsune, Kanasugi, Suehiro, Sakuragi, Yanagishima, and Susaki. Ikebukuro and Kikui are very distant, but if you look at the map you'll see the other seven places are concentrated in a narrow area in the north-east corner. This was a major oversight on Shundei's part. The significance of Ikebukuro and Kikui being so far apart is easy to understand if you consider that it was from the time Shundei lived in Negishi that his literary fame grew and visitors began to throng to his home. Up until the Kikui period, he was able to carry out everything to do with his manuscripts by letter alone. Now, if we trace a line like this from Negishi through the following six places, an irregular circle emerges, and if we were to calculate the centre of that circle we would discover a clue to this case. I will now explain to you exactly what I mean.'

I am not sure what Shizuko was thinking, but letting go of my hand she suddenly put both hands around my neck, smiled that Mona Lisa smile that revealed her eye teeth, and exclaimed 'I'm scared.' Next, she pressed her cheek against my cheek and then her lips against my lips. After a while like that, her lips left mine and next she began to tickle my ear skilfully with her forefinger as she drew closer to my lobe and whispered rhythmically much as if sweetly singing a lullaby.

'I'm so disappointed that we have lost precious time with this frightening talk. My darling, can you not feel the fire burning within my lips? Don't you hear the drumming within my breast? Hold me, my dear. Hold me.'

But I continued speaking regardless, 'Just a little longer. There's not much more. Just bear with me and hear me out. I came here today because I really wanted to discuss things with you. Now, as to the temporal correspondence. I remember well that Shundei's name suddenly disappeared from the magazines at the end of last year. You say that it was also at the end of last year that Oyamada came back from overseas, right? I ask myself why these two things coincide so neatly. Is it just coincidence? What do you think?'

Before I had finished speaking, Shizuko brought the riding whip from the corner of the room, pressed it into my right hand, stripped off her clothes, and fell forward on to the bed. Only her face looked back at me from under the smooth naked shoulder.

'What of it? What of it?' she babbled wildly. 'Now, whip me! Whip me!' she screamed, moving the upper half of her body like a wave.

A mouse-coloured sky showed through the storehouse's small

window. My head thrummed as something like distant thunder, perhaps the sound of a train, mixed in with the ringing in my ears. I grew uneasy when I thought that it also sounded like the drumming of an evil army marching down from the sky. Perhaps it was the weather and the peculiar atmosphere inside the storeroom that made us both mad. Looking back on it, I realize that we were not of sound mind. Gazing down on her pale, sweaty body writhing on its side, I continued tenaciously with my reasoning.

'One the one hand, it is as clear as day that Ōe Shundei is involved in this case. But on the other hand, the might of Japan's constabulary has been unable to ascertain the whereabouts of a famous novelist after two full months and it seems that he has vanished without a trace.

'It terrifies me even to think of it. The strange part is that this is not a nightmare. Why does he not attempt to kill Oyamada Shizuko? He has suddenly stopped writing those threatening letters. What ninja technique did he use to sneak into Oyamada's study? And then he was able to open that locked book cabinet...

'I could not help but recall a certain person – Hirayama Hideko, the female detective fiction author. Everyone thinks the author is a woman, including many writers and journalists. Apparently love letters arrive daily at Hideko's house from admiring readers. But the truth is Hideko is a man. In fact, he is an established government official.

'All writers of detective fiction are peculiar, including Shundei, Hirayama Hideko, and myself. That is what happens when a man pretends to be a woman and bizarre tastes gather force. One author used to dress up as a woman and hang around Asakusa at night. He even played at being in love with another man.'

I continued to babble crazily as if in a trance. My face was covered in sweat that coursed unpleasantly into my mouth.

'Alright Shizuko. Listen closely. Is there some fault in my reasoning? Where is the centre of the circle traced by Shundei's addresses? Please look at the map. It is your house: Yama no Shuku, in Asakusa. All the addresses are within ten minutes of your home.

'Why did Shundei go into hiding at the same time your husband died? It's because you have stopped attending tea-ceremony and music classes. Do you understand? While Oyamada was away, you used to attend tea-ceremony and music classes every day from the afternoon into the evening.

'Who was it that set things up perfectly and led me to make my conclusions? It was you! It was you who lay in wait for me at the museum and thereafter manipulated me at your will.

'You would easily have been able to add the little phrases to the diaries and put the other evidence in Oyamada's book cabinet as well as to drop the button in the attic. This is what I have been able to deduce. Is there any other way to think about it? Now, what do you say? Please answer me.'

Crying out, 'I can't bear this. It's too much!' the naked Shizuko clung to me. She pressed her cheek against my collared shirt and began to cry so hard that I could feel the warm tears on my skin.

'Why do you cry? Why have you been trying to stop me from proceeding with my deductions? Surely you would want to hear me if it were a matter of life or death for you. That alone makes me suspect you. Listen to me. I have not finished yet.

'Why did Ōe Shundei's wife wear glasses? Why the gold teeth and the poultice for tooth pain? And the Western hair style and round face? Is that not exactly the same disguise used in "Panorama Country"? In this story Shundei describes the essentials for disguising a Japanese person's appearance – altering the hairstyle, wearing spectacles, plumping out contours – and in "The Copper

Penny" he writes about covering a healthy tooth with a gold-plated outer bought from a gewgaw stall.

'You have easily recognizable eye teeth. To hide them, you wore gold-plated outer covers. You have a large mole on your right cheek and to disguise that you applied the poultice. And it would be easy to make your oval face look rounder by doing your hair in a Western style. This is how you transformed yourself into Shundei's wife.

'Yesterday I let Honda catch a glimpse of you to confirm with him whether you resembled Shundei's wife. What do you know – he said you would look exactly like her if your *marumage* was changed to a Western hair style and you wore glasses and gold teeth. Come on now, let's have it all out. I have grasped everything completely. Do you intend to keep deceiving me?'

I shook Shizuko off. She fell heavily on the bed, burst into tears, and would not answer no matter how long I waited. I was quite agitated and without thinking I raised the riding whip and lashed her naked back. *Take that, and that*, I thought as, losing control, I lashed and lashed. Gradually the redness spread on her pale skin until a wormlike wound stained with scarlet blood took shape. She lay there at my feet in the same lewd pose as always, with her hands and feet writhing and her body undulating. Then, in the final light breath of one about to faint, she whispered in a small voice 'Hirata, Hirata.'

'Hirata? So you are still trying to deceive me? If you transformed yourself into Shundei's wife, would you have me believe that a separate person called Shundei actually exists? You know he does not. He is a fictional character. To cover that up, you pretended to be his wife and met the magazine journalists and everyone else. And you changed addresses so many times. But as there were some people who would not be convinced by a completely imaginary character, you hired a vagrant from Asakusa Park and had him sleep in that room. It is not that Shundei transformed himself into the man in the clown's outfit – the man in the clown's outfit transformed himself into Shundei.'

Shizuko remained silent as death on the bed. Only the livid wound on her back writhed as if alive as she breathed. She remained quiet and my agitation gradually abated.

'Shizuko, I did not mean to do such a terrible thing to you. I should have spoken more quietly, but you tried so hard to avoid listening to what I had to say and you sought to cover up with such coquettish behaviour that I am afraid I lost control. Please forgive me. Now, it's alright for you not to say anything because I will try to outline everything you did in order. If I make a mistake, be sure to say something and let me know, won't you?'

Then I explained my reasoning in a way that would be easy to understand.

'You are blessed with uncommon sagacity and literary talent for a woman. I saw that very clearly just from reading the letters you wrote. It was entirely plausible that you should have wanted to write detective fiction under a nom de plume, and a man's name at that. However, your stories were exceptionally well received. Then, at exactly the same time as your name started to become famous, Oyamada went overseas for two years. To ease your loneliness and to satisfy your bizarre proclivities you came up with the fearful trick of one person playing three roles. You wrote a novel called 'One Person, Two Roles,' but you went one step further and conceived of one person playing three roles.

'You rented a house in Negishi under the name of Hirata Ichirō. The earlier addresses in Ikebukuro and Kikui were only set up for receiving mail. Inventing "misanthropy" and "trips" to hide Hirata from view, you used disguise to transform yourself into his wife and completely took over as his agent in discussions related to his drafts. Thus, when these were being written, you became Hirata—Ōe Shundei and met the magazine journalists; when renting a house, you became Mrs Hirata; and at the Oyamada household in Yama no Shuku, you were Mrs Oyamada. In this way then, one person played three roles.

'For that reason, you needed to be away from the house and so nearly every day you would go out for the whole afternoon saying that you were off to practise the tea-ceremony or music. The one body was used to play Mrs Oyamada for half the day and Mrs Hirata for the other half. Somewhere far away would not do because you needed time to disguise yourself by arranging your hair and changing your clothes. Accordingly, when you changed addresses you selected a location about ten minutes by car in a radius centred on Yama no Shuku.

'As I am also a student of the bizarre, I understand your feeling well. For while this was a very burdensome labour, there could hardly be another game in this world as amusing as this.

'I recall now that a critic reviewing Shundei's works once said that they are full to an almost unpleasant degree with suspicion that only a woman could possess. As I remember, the critic said it was much as if a beast in the shadows were writhing in the darkness. That critic was telling the truth, don't you think?

'Two years passed quickly and Oyamada came home. You were no longer able to play three roles. Accordingly, Ōe Shundei then disappeared and there were no particular suspicions because everyone knew of Shundei's extreme aversion to the company of other people.

'But why did you decide to commit that awful crime? As a man, I cannot understand well what you felt, but texts on the psychology of perversion indicate that women with a tendency to hysteria

271

often send threatening letters to themselves. There are numerous cases of this both in Japan and overseas.

'There is a desire to attract pity from others even by scaring oneself. I am sure this is your case.

'Receiving threatening letters from a famous male novelist who is actually you – what a wonderful idea!

'At the same time, you began to feel dissatisfied with your aging husband. You clung to the hard to relinquish desires that you had experienced in that life of perverted freedom. Or it might be closer to the mark to say that for a long time crime and murder had held an inexpressible attraction for you, just as in Shundei's stories. And then there is Shundei, the fictional personage who disappears without a trace. By casting suspicion on him you can be safe forever and in addition you rid yourself of an unpleasant husband and inherit a vast legacy that will enable you to live out the rest of your life as you please.

'But that was not enough to satisfy you. To be completely safe, you decided to put in place a double line of defence. And I was the person you chose. I was always criticizing Shundei's works, so you decided to control me like a puppet in order to wreak your revenge. You must have been highly amused when I showed you my personal statement. Deceiving me was no trouble at all, was it? All it took was the ornamental glove button, the diaries, *Shin Seinen*, and "Games in the Attic."

'But as you note in your novels, criminals always make some silly little mistake. You picked up the button from Oyamada's glove and used it as a vital piece of evidence, but you did not find out when it had fallen off. You had no idea that the gloves had been given to the taxi driver a long time before. What a silly little slip. As to Oyamada's fatal wound, I think it was as I earlier reasoned – with one difference. Oyamada was not peeping through the window. You pushed him out of the window, perhaps in the midst of some amorous romp (which is why he was wearing that wig).

'Alright Shizuko, were there any faults in my deduction? Please answer something. See if you can pick a hole in my reasoning. Come on then Shizuko.'

Shizuko was quite inert, so I placed my hand on her shoulder and shook her gently. Whether shame and remorse prevented her from looking up I do not know, but she did not move or say anything.

Having said everything I wanted to say, and stood there in a disappointed daze. The woman who had been my matchless love until yesterday was now collapsed in front of me fully exposed as the pernicious beast in the shadows. Gazing fixedly at her, at some point my eyes began to burn.

'Well I am leaving now,' I said, coming back to my senses. 'Think about it carefully later and please choose the correct course. Thanks to you, I have over the past month been able to glimpse a world of amorous foolishness that I have never experienced before. Even now, I find it hard to leave you when I think of it. But my good conscience will not allow me to continue my relationship with you like this. Goodbye.'

I left a heartfelt kiss on the weal on Shizuko's back and shortly after I left the ghostly house that had been the scene of our passionate romps. It seemed as if the sky was even lower and that the temperature had climbed further. Although my body was drenched in an unpleasant sweat, my teeth chattered as I wandered along as if I had lost my wits.

## CHAPTER 12

**I LEARNED THAT SHIZUKO** had committed suicide in the evening of the following day.

She drowned herself in the Sumida River, perhaps by leaping from the second storey of the Western section of the home, just like Oyamada Rokurō. How awful a thing is fate. A passenger found her body floating by that steamer landing under Azumabashi bridge, presumably because it followed the river's current.

A newspaper journalist who knew nothing about it all added at the end of his article, 'Perhaps Mrs Oyamada came to her awful end at the hands of the same criminal who killed Oyamada Rokurō.'

Reading this article, I felt profoundly sad thinking of the pitiful death of my former lover, but then Shizuko's death seemed to me an entirely natural outcome for it was indeed appropriate that she should confess her terrible crime. I believed this for about a month.

However, finally the intensity of my imaginings began to gradually subside and as it did an awful doubt entered my head.

I had not heard Shizuko herself utter a single word of confession. Even though all the evidence was lined up, the interpretation of this evidence was all of my construction. There was no immovable certainty such as in the equation 'two plus two equals four.' Once I had put together my flimsy deductions based solely on the word of the taxi driver and the evidence from the house cleaner, did I not interpret the evidence in a way that was opposite to the truth? I could not deny that the same things could be accounted for by another piece of deductive reasoning.

274

The truth is that when I challenged Shizuko in the storehouse's second floor, I had at first no intention of going that far. I intended to quietly state my reasons and listen to her defence. But half way through, something in her attitude led me into wicked conjecture and all of a sudden I was making assertions in such an unpleasant way. Finally, even though I tried to make sure several times, she kept her silence and I convinced myself that this proved her guilt. Was this simply me convincing myself?

Certainly, Shizuko committed suicide. (Though was it really suicide? Was she murdered! If so, who was the killer? How terrifying!) But even if she killed herself, does that prove her guilt? There may have been another reason. Perhaps the unforgiving heart of a woman led her to suddenly perceive the vanity of life when I challenged her with my suspicions in that way and she realized there was no means of justifying herself to this person whom she thought she could rely on.

If so, I was clearly her murderer, even if I did not directly lay a hand on her. I mentioned the possibility of murder above, and what else could this be?

Nevertheless, if I am only to be suspected for the death of one woman, I can endure it. But this unfortunate proclivity of mine to fantasy suggests a much more horrifying thought.

Clearly, she loved me. You must consider the feelings of a woman who is doubted by the one she loves and accused of being a fiendish criminal. Did she decide to kill herself precisely because she loved me and was saddened by the persistent suspicions of her lover?

This would apply even if my fearful deductions were correct. Why then did she decide to murder her husband of so many years? Would the thought of liberty or the inheritance have the power to turn a woman into a murderer? Surely it was love. And surely I was the object of her love.

Ah! Such terrifying suspicions. What should I do? Whether she was a murderer or not, I killed this pitiful woman who loved me so much. I could not escape from my accursed petty moralizing. Is there anything in this world as powerful and beautiful as love? Perhaps I had utterly destroyed this clear, beautiful love with the obstinate heart of a moralist.

However, if as I had imagined she was Ōe Shundei and she perpetrated those terrible crimes, I would still have some peace.

Yet how could I be certain now? Oyamada Rokurō was dead. Oyamada Shizuko was dead. And it seemed as if Ōe Shundei had disappeared forever without trace. Honda had said that Shizuko resembled Shundei's wife, but what sort of proof was 'resemblance'?

I have visited Inspector Itosaki several times to find out about subsequent developments, but as he has only made vague replies there would appear to be no resolution in sight in the search for Ōe Shundei. I asked someone to make inquiries about Hirata Ichirō in Shizuko's hometown and the report came back that Hirata Ichirō had gone missing, for my hope that he was merely a fiction proved vain. But even if a person named Hirata did exist, how could one conclude that he was really Shizuko's former lover, that he was also Ōe Shundei, and that he had killed Oyamada? He was nowhere to be found now and it was not possible to deny that Shizuko could have simply used Hirata as the real name for the character of one of the three roles she played. After gaining the permission of Shizuko's relatives, I thoroughly searched her belongings and documents in order to find some sort of evidence either way, but this move did not achieve any results.

I regret my proclivity to reasoning and fantasy, but regret though I might it is not enough. I feel like walking, searching Japan – no, every corner of the earth – in a lifelong pilgrimage to discover the whereabouts of Hirata Ichirō–Ōe Shundei, even though I know it might be pointless.

But even if I found Shundei perhaps my suffering would only grow, though in different ways depending on whether he was or was not the criminal.

Half a year has passed since Shizuko's tragic death, but Hirata Ichirō has still not appeared and my awful doubts about what now cannot be changed deepen every day.

*Originally published as a serial in* Shin Seinen,
*August 1928 special edition–October edition*

 **_PROFILES_**

**Edogawa Rampo** (pseudonym of Hirai Tarō, 1894–1965) is the acknowledged grand master of Japan's golden age of crime and mystery fiction. In the early part of his career, he created the Japanese gothic mystery, developing the work of Edgar Allan Poe and related nineteenth century writers in a distinctly Japanese form. This part of his career coincided with a great flowering in Japanese literature and culture, a relatively free and uninhibited popular press being a defining feature of the times. In this context, Rampo's dark vision and extravagant grotesquery found an avid readership, and had a profound influence on other writers. Public morals tightened in the years leading up to Japan's Asian and Pacific wars, and censorship was tight in the war years. Rampo's early work fell out of favour, and he turned to adventure stories with detective characters in leading roles. After the war, he concentrated on stories for young readers, and on developing the Japan Association of Mystery Writers. The Edogawa Rampo Prize, originally endowed by Rampo himself, is awarded annually to the finest work of the year in the mystery genre. It is the most important prize of its type in Japan. Edogawa Rampo – whose name is meant to be read as a punning reference to 'Edgar Allan Poe' – remains popular and influential in Japan. His work remains in print, in various different editions, and his stories provide the background for a steady stream of film, television, and theatrical adaptations.

Translator **Ian Hughes** went to Japan in his early thirties with the intention of teaching English for six months before traveling further in Asia. Instead, he stayed for eleven years during which time he married, started a family, and moved into translating financial Japanese into English. In late 2003, he and his family moved back to Perth, Western Australia, where he does the same kind of work from home.

**Mark Schreiber** has lived and worked in Asia for the past forty years. Best known perhaps for his summaries from men's tabloid weekly magazines that appeared in the now-defunct *Mainichi Daily News*' 'Waiwai' page (which moved to the *Japan Times* under the name 'Tokyo Confidential' from April 2001), he has authored, co-authored, ghostwritten or translated some dozen books, the most recent of which is *Tabloid Tokyo* (Kodansha International).

Illustrator **Kawajiri Hiroaki** was born in Fukuoka Prefecture, Japan in 1962. He began work in the printing industry in 1985, and has been involved in design for advertising and publishing since 1995. Kawajiri won recognition in the Education/Academic/Teaching category of the Twentieth Annual Independent Publisher Book Awards in 2002 for design of *Getting Ready for Speech* (Language Solutions Inc.). He uses a wide range of techniques and media, from pen and brush to oils, in his illustrations, coupled with digital work. He has handled design and illustrations for a number of books including *Humanity and Technology* and *English–Live!* (Intercom Press Inc.). He can be contacted by e-mail (hirokj@u.email.ne.jp).